THAT THING BETWEEN ELI AND GWEN

THAT THING BETWEEN ELI AND GWEN

J.J. McAvoy

That Thing Between Eli and Gwen
Copyright © 2016 by J.J. McAvoy
Ebook ISBN: 9781943772414
ISBN-13: 9781533120977
ISBN-10: 1533120978

NYLA Publishing
350 7th Avenue, Suite 2003, NY 10001, New York.
http://www.nyliterary.com

Open your heart to a love that makes you feel like you're dreaming, a love that leaves you breathless.

CHAPTER ONE
TELLTALE SIGNS

Guinevere

I should have seen the signs that morning. They weren't massive, but they were there. I had almost slipped and killed myself coming out of the shower—okay, that one was a big, giant sign, but the others were pretty small. I couldn't find the left shoe to my favorite pair of red heels. The pearls *he* had given me slipped off my neck and scattered all across the bedroom floor. And when *he* did show up, twenty minutes late, Taigi would not stop barking at him... like my dog knew March 1st would be a day that would live in infamy for me.

Taking a seat in his brand new midnight blue Mercedes, he didn't say anything as we pulled out of the Hampton beach house. His knuckles were almost white as he gripped the steering wheel. The back of his hand rested just under his lips, something he had done hundreds of times in our three years together, but only when he was either really worried or upset.

"Bash?" I touched his leg and he jumped as if he had forgotten I was sitting next to him.

Turning to me, his light brown eyes met mine. "Yeah?"

"Are you okay? You look like we're going to a funeral, not a wedding," I joked, smiling. He shook his head and took hold of my hand.

"I'm fine." He kissed the back of my hand. "Just work stuff. I'm hoping we can do our rounds and get out of there before it gets too late."

Nodding, I looked back out at the beach as we drove. Sebastian—or Bash as I called him—was the owner and founder of both *Class* and *Rebel* magazines. It was the reason we had met, actually. He had attended one of my gallery openings and loved my photography. I had told myself I would never contract myself with any corporation or brand; I liked being a freelancer. I painted and shot what I wanted, what mattered to me. Yet there was just something about Sebastian Evans. No matter how many times I bluntly denied his request or ignored his emails, he never gave up. After all, no matter what Sebastian Evans wanted, he worked until it was his. Eventually, I agreed to shoot their spring cover. It was only supposed to be that one cover, but three years later I was a contracted photographer and his fiancée.

"Welcome to The Chateau Rouge," the valet said when we pulled up to a gated mansion. As Bash spoke to him, I found myself staring at the decorated landscape; everything was in beautiful greens and blues. Projected on the pure green grass were the initials E & H, and around them was a small orchestra, just for the arriving guests.

Only when I stepped out of the car was I able to see what had to be the icing on the cake: as if these people needed to prove they had money, there were even peacocks walking around.

I looked to Bash.

"What?" He looked at me, confused.

I pointed at everything. "Really?" was all I managed to say.

"You make it seem like you've never seen rich people before. You should have worn the red dress I picked out for you." He frowned and took my hand as we walked toward the seats for guests.

This was another point at which I should have seen the signs, but again, I was blind to it. I can still remember how cold his hand was as I held it. As we mingled with the rest of New York's elite during cocktail hour, I felt as if I were standing in the middle of the Arctic Circle in a bikini.

"Wow, she's beautiful," I whispered as the bride walked up the aisle, her makeup flawless to the point that her skin glowed. Her soft, honey-gold hair shined and her strapless heart-shaped dress clung to her every curve. Her blue eyes filled with unshed tears as she held her roses tightly, walking slow and steady. For a quick second I thought I saw her glance over to us.

I hope I look half as good as her on my wedding day, I thought, my eyes never off her as she made her way to the front.

It passed in a blur. One moment the pastor was saying something, and the next, Bash was no longer holding my hand.

"Hannah," he called out, moving to the center of the aisle.

She looked toward him, looked to her groom, and then back at Bash.

My Bash. *What…*

"Don't, Hannah."

What…is…this…?

"Hannah," Bash called to her.

Stop! My mind screamed.

But, to my horror, she let go of her groom's hands and ran toward Bash.

I couldn't breathe. I was up, knocking over my chair. "BASH!" I yelled.

But they were already running…hand in hand.

3

By this point, every other guest was up. Those around me moved away, allowing everyone to see the girl who'd just gotten dumped. I knew the only person who had it worse than me was the man up front. For the first time since I'd gotten there, I truly looked at him: tall, ivory skin, short dark hair, piercing green eyes watching his bride run from him. He stood there so still, so shocked, I almost forgot my own pain.

Why hadn't I seen the signs?

Eli

Even if I lived to be one hundred and fifty, I would never forget *that* March 1st. It was supposed to be one of the happiest days of my life. After two years of dating, I had finally asked *the* Hannah Michaels to be my wife.

We had met as medical interns at New York Presbyterian, and on the first day she'd had the attention of every straight male at the hospital. What was sexier than beauty and brains? She was dedicated not only to her work, but also to her patients. *The* Hannah Michaels... My Hannah was soft, sweet, focused, and precise. No matter what goal, she worked to achieve it; I liked that about her. Whenever we were around each other, we just clicked. She and I were so alike on so many levels, there were times we would end up finishing each other's sentences. We became close early on, but didn't actually start to date until we both became attendings.

I couldn't imagine dating anyone else.

"You nervous?" My younger brother, Logan, placed his arm around my shoulder as I stood in the dressing room.

I shrugged him off, fixing my cuff links. "Why would I be nervous?"

"Eli Davenport is finally taking the plunge. I just can't believe it. I thought you guys were never going to get married." He pushed me out of the way to fix his tie.

I smacked him over the head.

"Really? Even today you two fight?" My mother sighed, coming into the room. Her gray-auburn hair was cropped at her shoulders, and her soft green gown kissed the ground as she came close and pulled me into a light hug. The tears in her eyes were already starting to build.

"Ma, he's getting married, not dying." Logan chuckled.

She gave him a glare. "Now." She frowned, looking to me. "Are you sure about...this?"

"Mom." I held on to her shoulders; she was being ridiculous. "You like Hannah. I like Hannah. Why wouldn't I be sure? You're finally getting the daughter you always wanted."

"I know." She placed her hand on my chest. Even with heels, she was still a full head shorter than me. "I just can't shake this feeling. Who knew letting you go would be so hard?"

My mother and her dramatics, I'd thought. If only we had listened to her gut.

"You still have me," Logan added, proving he was more like her than our father.

We both looked at him before turning away.

"Wow! Okay, I see how it is," he muttered before walking toward the door, leaving our mother laughing.

"If your father was still with us, I'm sure he would have been proud of the man you've become, Eli. I know I am." She wiped away a few tears.

I wasn't sure what else to do but give her my arm. I was never the affectionate one, but that day I went through so many different emotions.

She held on to me tightly as we entered the grounds. She and Hannah had gone crazy with the decorations, but they really enjoyed it, and I honestly didn't care. I just wanted to skip to the important part.

I stood in front of all our family and friends with Logan to my left. Finally the music started, and my gaze shot toward the doors of the mansion, waiting for them to open. I had known she would be beautiful, but she was absolutely radiant.

God, I'm so lucky.

With every step she took, the grin on my face grew, until her hand was in mine.

"You look beautiful," I whispered.

She smiled, but didn't say anything in return. In that instant, as the pastor began to speak, all the moments we'd ever shared together played in my mind: the very first time we met...our first operation together...first kiss...first night... Everything ran though my mind like a movie, the highlights of our life.

And this is just the beginning of so much more. Today is—

"Hannah," someone called.

Hearing her name pulled me from thoughts. My head snapped to the man standing in the aisle with his hand out-stretched to my soon-to-be-wife.

"Sebastian?" Logan questioned beside me.

Sebastian... The man calling out to my Hannah was Sebastian Evans, one of Logan's closest friends. We weren't close, but I knew of him.

"Hannah," he called again.

Enough! My mind hollered as I took a step forward, but it was too late.

Hannah released my hand. She let go and never looked back as she ran toward him.

I stood there, too shocked to move or speak. That moment was hell on earth.

For hours, I could not speak. My mind was blank. I tried to understand, but my brain, my heart—both were shot. I leaned on the balcony of the dressing room, staring out at the ocean until the sunset. Only then did I regain function of my body, and I ran. Stupidly, I ran out toward the front. All the guests, with the exception of family and the cleaning crew, had left. When I got outside, I saw my brother ripping the "Just Married" sign from the Bentley.

"Eli—"

"Keys." I walked around to the driver's side of the car. As I opened the door, I saw a woman dressed in blue step in front of me. She had long wavy brown hair and warm brown skin. Her brown eyes were now puffy and red, presumably from crying. She stood tall with her head held high.

"This is your number, right?" She pointed to the phone number on the RSVP card before quickly texting something on her phone and adding, "Please kick his ass." She turned toward her taxi without waiting for another word from me.

"Gwen!" Logan called out to her before groaning. "Jesus. He was her fucking fiancé."

Feeling my phone vibrate, I pulled it out of my coat pocket.

He left his email open on my phone. I got a confirmation for a room they just booked.

Prescott Hills

Montauk, NY

Room 1204

"Eli, don't—"

Ignoring him, I got into the car, and without a second thought I drove, the rage in me growing with each passing mile. I gripped the steering wheel, gritting my teeth as

I thought. They were no more than twenty minutes away from the chaos they had unleashed on my life.

When I pulled up at the Prescott Hills, I was prepared to kick the door down. I immediately saw both of them walking toward me, completely oblivious, still holding those godforsaken hands.

"Eli!" Hannah gasped, no longer in her dress, now wearing jeans and a gift shop shirt.

Ignoring her, my fist collided with his jaw and he fell against the wall, but that didn't stop me. Grabbing him by the collar, I kept punching until my knuckles cracked on his face.

"STOP! Eli! Stop or I will call the cops, I swear," she yelled.

I wanted to kill him, but by some miracle, I managed to stop. "Call the cops?" I stood rigid, ignoring the pain in my hand and the fucker at my feet. "What's stopping you, Hannah? Make this day even more special!"

She hung her head, dropping to her knees beside him.

"I understand that you hate—"

"You understand nothing." I cut him off. I couldn't even look at them anymore. I turned to leave but stopped, pulling out my phone to take a picture of his bloody face. It gave me no real satisfaction, but what the hell. Maybe that other woman would get some peace of mind out of seeing it.

All I could wonder as I drove was, how? *How could this happen?*

Chapter Two
Dr. Asshole and the Con Artist

Guinevere

A month had passed since the worst day of my life, and since then I had been able to confirm a universal truth: music was God's gift to the brokenhearted. The first week, I cried to Adele and Mariah Carey. The second week, I was on to Beyoncé and Pink. The third week, Eminem was speaking my language, and the fourth was dedicated to the '90s.

"Gwen? Hello? You still there?"

"Yeah, Dad, I'm here." I adjusted the phone on my shoulder, packing my shoes into the box.

"Are you sure you don't need me to come down there—"

"Daddy, I promise you I'm okay." That was a lie. Yes, it had been a month and I still felt like shit, but I knew I would feel like that for a while.

"When things like this happen, you need family, Gwen. It's the only way to get over this. Besides, New York has nothing on Cypress."

Exhaling deeply, I grabbed another empty box as I headed into the bathroom. "How about I promise to come visit in a few weeks, okay? I still have a lot of work to do in the city. Plus, you know I can't come back home now. People will be staring and judging…"

"Since when has my Gwen ever cared about what others thought of her?" He chuckled into the phone.

Since I was publicly humiliated. "You're right. Screw them all, and tell Mom I want the biggest welcome home party in the state."

"Thatta girl. Chin up."

"Head high. Bye Daddy, love you."

"Love you, too," he replied, hanging up.

Sighing, I threw the box on the ground and Taigi, forgetting he wasn't a puppy any more, tried to use it as a bed but broke through it. Dismayed, he walked away from it and curled up into a ball of white and black fur in the corner. I was about to curl up into a ball next to him when I heard the doorbell ring.

Taigi's head shot up, but he stayed in his corner.

"Don't get up, I'll get it," I said to him when the bell rang again.

"Coming!" I groaned, moving through the maze I had created. I checked to see who it was before opening the door. "Logan?"

Logan Davenport, one of Bash's closest friends, stood at the door with two cups of coffee on a tray in one hand and a bag of groceries in the other. Since the incident, he had taken it upon himself to check up on me every few days.

"You've gotten skinnier." He frowned.

I looked down at my yoga pants and oversized shirt. "Yay?"

"Not yay," he snapped, entering the apartment. "You need to eat, Gwen."

"Logan, I told you, you don't need to do all of this for me." I followed him into the kitchen, where he unpacked some of my pots and pans. "Hey!"

"I'll put them back when I'm done." He flashed me a smile before looking for more utensils.

"Seriously, Logan—"

"Gwen, please let me do this," he muttered over the stove. "You have no idea how guilty I feel. My best friend ran away with my brother's girl while leaving his fiancée alone to pick up the pieces. I introduced them to each other, Gwen. I feel guilty toward you, too. So please, let me do this much… I know we aren't that close, but still."

I stared at him for a moment. It was true, I really didn't know Logan. He and Bash were fraternity brothers. He came over for game nights and dinners we threw, but other than that, Logan and I had never been close. Logan had only just turned twenty-two, five years younger than Bash and two years younger than me; maybe that's why I always saw him as Bash's little brother…and in a way, my younger brother, as well. He and Bash even looked alike. They both had hazel eyes and brown hair, though Bash's was sandier in color. Seeing Logan so serious now was odd.

"Can you even cook?" I grinned, looking through the bag he'd brought.

"Can I cook?" He mocked me as if he was horrified I'd asked the question. "I will have you know I make the best damn omelets in all of New York."

"All of New York?" I crossed my arms.

"You heard me." He winked. "Now, where is the rest of your stuff?"

"It's in those boxes." I pointed to the ones labeled 'KITCHEN' behind him. "Oh how is your music coming along? You're pretty popular, right?"

"Define popular. Besides, I need to focus on school… Jeez, all of these are yours? Did Bash buy anything when you guys lived together?" he muttered, already opening the box. I was not blind to how he tried to change the subject, but I let it go.

"Not really. You know he basically lived at the office…or at least I thought he did. I'm not sure anymore what he did with his time…" My voice drifted off, causing him to pause and look at me. Raising my hands, I shook my head, as if that would stop him from pitying me. "How is your brother?" I tried to change the subject.

"Just like you."

Subject change, failed.

He said nothing else, angrily digging through the box. "Urgh, God, I want to kill him!" he yelled suddenly, punching his hand into the box.

"Logan!" I screamed and Taigi barked, but it was too late. He'd punched right into where the knives were packed.

"Agh, shit!" he shouted, clenching his now-bleeding hand.

Grabbing his hand, I turned on the water and tried to clean it.

"Damn, it's too deep. I'm going to need stitches." He flinched as I grabbed a clean towel and quickly wrapped it around the wound.

"Where are your keys? We have to go the hospital." I looked around the countertop.

"It's okay, I have a med kit in my car. I'm a doctor—"

"Being in medical school does not make you a doctor, Logan…at least, not one good enough to stitch up your own hand in my kitchen." I waited for him to hand me the keys.

Frowning, he grabbed them from his pocket with his good hand and passed them to me before holding his hurt hand, which started to bleed. It was pretty bad, already soaking through the towel.

"Gwen, you're honestly making too much of this—"

"Yep, we're going," I said, seeing the blood run down his arm. I pulled him out of the apartment.

Eli

I had just finished my rounds and was handing a chart to the on-call nurse when she stopped me.

"Dr. Davenport, your brother was just brought in the ER—"

I didn't even let her finish before running down the hall.

"Is everything all right, Dr. Daven—"

I ignored them, following the blue line on the ground toward the double doors leading into the ER. Scanning the beds, I stopped when I saw his black All-Stars shoes.

He sat on the bed, laughing as one of my residents stitched up his right hand.

"What happened?" I asked, already in front of them.

"Eli. I thought you were off—"

"What happened to your hand?"

"He punched my knives."

I turned toward the voice. It took a second to recognize her, and the moment I did, more memories flooded my mind than I could handle.

She stood in the corner, holding Logan's jacket.

"He....punched. Your knives?" I turned to my younger brother.

"It's a long story," he muttered.

"Logan..."

"Honestly, it was an accident. I got him all hyped up, and—"

"Do you still need to be here?" I asked without looking at her.

"Eli." Logan glared.

Out of the corner of my eye, I could see her stiffen.

"Sorry again, Logan. And thank you," she said to him.

Logan grinned and nodded. "No, thank you. Please, use my car to go back home."

"It's fine, I'll call a taxi—"

"How else can I come back and make you my famous omelets?"

"Just work on getting better. See you around." She gathered her things and left.

When she'd gone, he glared at me. "Did you really need to be such an ass?"

"Says the dummy who punched knives," I said in return before following the girl out the front exit. I waited for her to finish giving her location to the taxi company and then stepped up in front of her. "Here." I handed her a fifty. "Thank you for bringing him here."

She looked at the money then back at me. "Do you often reward people with money for doing humane things?"

"Is fifty dollars really a reward?" I countered.

"You're a rich doctor. I'm sorry, I've forgotten my place." She held out her hand and did a small curtsey. "Please, sir, may I have some?"

Biting the inside of my cheek, I gave her the money and turned to leave, but stopped when I noticed she took the bill, walked over to the donation box at the corner entrance of the hospital, and dropped it inside.

She moved back to her corner, looking out onto the street.

Sighing, I went back to her. "Look, I think we got off on the wrong foot."

She scoffed.

"Anyway," I went on. "Thank you for bringing him here, but in the future, if you could just ignore him, I think that would be best for everyone."

"You want me to ignore your brother?" she said slowly.

"You and I both know he is doing this out of some twisted sense of guilt. I can't cut him out of my life, but you being

14

around only makes it twice as bad. I understand you might feel lonely, but please don't abuse my brother's kindness—"

"Excuse me!" She held up her hands to stop me.

"I'm just saying—"

"You're just saying, 'Go away, you bring up painful memories I have yet to deal with, but instead of growing a pair of balls and handling them myself, I've chosen to ignore them altogether and push all of things reminding me I was dumped at my wedding to the corner.'"

"Excuse me!" She was out of her damn mind.

She crossed her arms. "What? Isn't that what you're saying? Your brother isn't a little kid. If he feels guilty and wants to work it out his way, then it is his right to do so. Do you know how many crappy people we meet a day in this city? Of course you do, you are one of them. No way in hell am I ignoring a good person just so you can feel better."

"You don't even know him!" *What hell is this chick's problem?*

"No, I don't know you. There's a difference," she hollered, stepping away from me and toward her arriving cab. "Also, if I feel *lonely,* I wonder how in the hell you must feel, asshole."

The door slammed, and I stared as she was driven away.

"So, you've met Guinevere." Logan chuckled, coming up beside me with his newly bandaged hand.

"Guinevere? I thought her name was Gwen?" Or at least that was what he'd called her on that ugly day.

He nodded. "Her name is Guinevere Poe, she's a pretty famous artist here in the city. You know, that oil painting Mom just bought was done by her."

"What? That thing cost almost two million dollars."

"And you tried to give her a fifty for the cab." He snickered.

Pausing, I looked at him. "You saw that?"

"The moment you followed her, I knew it wouldn't be good." He nodded and forced a smile I knew wasn't sincere. "I know after Dad died you basically raised me alongside Mom, but you need to stop. I'm not a kid. Sometimes I feel like you focus on me just to ignore the shit going on in your own life. Maybe you had to do that before, but not now. You were the one this happened to, and yet here you are trying to look after me again. I'm fine. Honestly, I'm fine."

He waved me off as he headed back toward where he was parked. I watched him go for a moment, realizing once again I was treating him like a child, before heading back into the hospital. I didn't bother making eye contact or conversation. Instead, I headed to the on-call room and rested up on the top bunk of the bed.

Logan and I were nine years apart, making him only two when our father died of a heart attack. It was still ranked first on the list of the worst days of my life, my mother screaming for me to call the ambulance, Logan crying in the living room as the nanny frantically tried to help my mother.

"Urgh, I don't want to think about this," I muttered to myself, pulling out my phone. The screensaver was still of Hannah and me embracing. I'd tried to change it at least a hundred times in the last month, but I couldn't bring myself to do it yet.

If I feel lonely, I wonder how in the hell you must feel, asshole. Her voice replayed in my mind. Who the hell did she think she was? She didn't know me; I was fine.

"What kind of name is Guinevere, anyway?" I whispered to myself.

"God, I've missed you," an intern said as she kissed down a male nurse's jaw.

He began to lift her scrubs.

I sat up. "Does this look like the set of Grey's Anatomy to you?" I yelled.

They jumped and ran so quickly, I was sure one of them fell on their way out.

Picking up my phone, I went to settings, then screen-saver, trying once again to change the damn photo, but once again I couldn't do it.

Damn it!

Just then my phone rang. "Dr. Davenport speaking," I answered.

"So, I figured out how you can make it up to Gwen for being an ass," Logan said. "She's moving into a new place. I was going to help, but—"

"Not interested. Goodbye."

Why the hell did he have to help everyone, for fuck's sake? I was worried that if Logan really did become a doctor, he would become way too attached to his patients.

Buzz. My phone vibrated as he texted me.

Why, God? Why?

Guinevere

Sometimes I hate this damn city. I looked up at the brick build-ing that was to be my new home. A few million dollars for a decent-sized condo on the Upper East Side, and my realtor had even tried to make me raise my budget; it was freaking ridiculous.

"What do you think, Taigi?" I asked as I shifted the box in my hands.

As always, he was less than impressed, but at least this time I couldn't blame him. I looked back in dismay at all the boxes left in the U-Haul. It was going to take a while.

Maybe I should have hired movers? I thought as I entered the building.

Taigi whimpered as his paws slipped and slid on the smooth marble floors.

Laughing, I grabbed his leash as we waited for the elevator. Luckily, the floors on our level weren't as shiny.

34B was at the end of the hall, and just as I gripped the handle, I heard another door open behind me. Turning, I came face to face with Dr. Asshole himself.

His blue-green eyes stared back at me in confusion. He glanced at the box in my hands, then at the door, and finally back to me.

"Please tell me you aren't moving in." He frowned.

"Please tell me you don't live there." I pointed at the door behind him.

His lips formed a straight line, and it looked like he was grinding his jaw.

Taigi, wanting attention as well, ran up to him and started to sniff, rubbing his nose all over his jeans, which only made him sneeze on the fabric.

Good boy.

"Urgh! God damn it! Can you tame your wolf?" he yelled, waving him away.

"He's a Siberian husky, not a wolf, you big baby," I replied, dropping the box in the hall and pulling Taigi, who sneezed on him again.

His eyes widened and one eyebrow twitched as he glared down at me.

"Sorry, he's allergic to jerks." I pushed Taigi behind me.

I swore, if he could have killed me with his gaze, I would have been six feet under at that very moment. Without another word, he turned back to his apartment, most likely to change his clothes.

When the door closed, I cupped the sides of Taigi's face. "Good boy!" I grinned, letting us into our new home.

But really, out of all the condos in the city, why the hell had I ended up next to him? Meeting him at the hospital had left a bad taste in my mouth. I'd had this picture of him in my mind, the heartbroken man who was left by the love of his life at the altar. However, with each meeting, my image of him changed. He was so condescending!

How he and Logan are related is beyond me. I headed back down to get more boxes and got on the elevator.

Sadly, before the elevator door closed he came out again, dressed in track pants and a sleeveless sweatshirt. This time he didn't pay any attention to me, putting his headphones in.

The ride down felt like it took forever, and when the doors opened, I made my escape quickly, heading straight to the back of the U-Haul.

"Can't a con artist like you afford to hire movers?"

He, for some reason, had stopped and stared at the boxes I had to move. *Just go on your damn run already. Wait...* "Con artist?"

He nodded as if he didn't know why I was confused. "I've seen your paintings. There's no way in hell they're worth what you sell them for. You are ripping people off, therefore, you are a con artist."

Speechless, my mouth dropped open.

"That's attractive," he said, acting disgusted before adjusting his ear buds and leaving me as he continued down the street.

"ASS!" I yelled, earning me a few glances from passerby.

My phone buzzed.

Answering it, I snapped, "Hello!"

"Is this a bad time?"

I looked at the caller ID before speaking again. "Katrina. Sorry, yeah, no, we can talk. Is everything okay?"

"Yeah, I'm actually right by your place. Can we meet up for a second?"

"Okay, my place is still a mess, but you can come over," I replied, looking for her on the street. However, she didn't walk up the street. She, like all high-powered lawyers, pulled up right next to me in a sleek town car.

When she stepped out, I saw her short blonde hair was slicked back, and she was dressed in a tailored pantsuit. One word described Katrina Turner: intimidating. Which was why I'd hired her.

"You weren't kidding," she replied when I opened the door to the sea of boxes and canvases lining the walls and appliances.

"Yeah, sorry. It's been a pain moving on such short notice." In fact, it was pretty much unbelievable. Just a few weeks before, I had been searching for wedding dresses and honeymoon destinations. And now...now, this was my life, in boxes.

"I would have stabbed him," she said, moving toward the large window overlooking the city.

"I believe you." I smiled, looking out as well.

She handed me a file. "I submitted this just an hour ago. If he doesn't let you out of the contract, we can always make noise."

She'd never even asked me if I wanted to end my contract with *Class* and *Rebel* magazines. After word had spread, she had drawn up this proposal. I hadn't even known he was back at work; I hadn't dared show my face anywhere near there. Everything was happening too fast, and no matter how hard I tried to stand up, I felt like I was getting beaten into the ground.

"Basically, you would agree to never speak of the incident, and in exchange, they will double your severance. I spoke to your agent; apparently you have more than a dozen offers, not to mention she said you wanted to open a new gallery. No longer being contracted frees up your schedule greatly. You are the winner in all of this."

If I'm the winner, then why do I still feel still like shit? "Let me know what their reply is," I whispered, handing back the file.

"Okay. I'll let myself out. And Gwen." She stopped at the door. "I know it's still too soon to say this, but I know you are much better off without him."

When I was alone again, I glanced back at the window. As I began to tremble, I could feel my body temperature rising. My eyes burned from the tears I fought back.

"No," I said out loud. I was not going to break down, not right then. I was sick and tired of crying, damn it. Moving to the boxes, I searched for my portable speakers, placed my mp3 player in the dock, and, turning up the volume as loud as possible, snatched a blank canvas from the wall.

Eli

I ran for at least two hours, and when I got back, her U-Haul was still open, with three boxes remaining. I wasn't sure if she was stupid or just didn't give a damn. Yeah, this was a nice neighborhood, but you still couldn't just leave things open like that. Stacking them on the corner, I closed the back door of the truck, lifted the boxes, and headed inside.

Why the hell am I doing this? She was most likely going to bark at me anyway. Walking to her door, I could already hear music blaring.

Great, she's this kind of neighbor. Of all the damn places in New York, she had to choose my building.

As I was about to knock, the door creeped open slightly on its own.

"Hello…?" I tried, but my voice was drowned out by music. Her dog glanced up at me but didn't bother getting up. Following his gaze, I saw her. She knelt in the middle of her condo, a canvas lying on plastic over the flooring. She threw paint at it with her bare hands, almost like she was punching it. After a few throws, she would try to wipe her eyes, not seeming to care that the paint rubbed off on her face. She painted and cried, all while on her knees.

Placing the boxes just inside her door, I left quietly, heading back to my place. I took a water bottle from my fridge and tried to not to think about it. This was why having her as a neighbor was a problem! It wasn't her fault, but just looking at her pissed me off. Seeing her cry pissed me off.

"Ah!" I threw my water bottle against the wall.

I needed a stronger drink.

Chapter Three
Science vs. Art

Guinevere

B ang.
"Oh god!"

Bang.

"Yes! Harder."

Bang.

"So good!"

I sat on my bed, staring at the shaking wall with a strange mixture of horror and astonishment. It had been four days since I'd moved in, and it was like this every other freaking night. At first, I'd thought he was shooting a porno.

"Eli...yes!"

The woman screamed in what I could only guess was utter ecstasy. She had a broader vocabulary than the other woman he had brought over; she had just kept singing, "Fuck."

Bang!

I jumped back as, once more, my wall shook.

This is ridiculous! It's two in the morning! I rose to my feet, banging my hand on the wall before jumping off my bed and heading toward the door. Ripping it open, I stomped to his door and raised my fist, ready to slam it down on—

"What!" he yelled, almost pulling the door off its hinges. He stood there in nothing but his pajama bottoms hanging low off his hips, his bare, muscular chest exposed.

"Hi, do you mind screwing at a more reasonable hour? I can't sleep listening to you people moan behind me," I snapped back.

"I'm a doctor, this is a reasonable hour for me," he replied, trying to close the door.

I stuck my hand out to stop it. "Maybe for you, but for normal human beings, not so much."

He shrugged. "And why should I care?"

"Wow, are you really this much of a dick?"

"Baby, is everything all right?" A woman with bottle number nine red hair stepped forward in what looked to be only his shirt. She wrapped her arm around his chest, glaring at me.

"Apparently, you were too loud. My neighbor can't sleep."

Her gaze focused on me, and she looked me up and down. "Sorry."

"Good enough, Con Artist?"

He didn't wait for my reply before closing the door in my face. Once again, I knocked.

"What!"

I looked past him to the woman and smiled. "He has chlamydia."

"What?"

He stared at me, dumbfounded, but the girl seemed clueless. I laughed out loud as I headed back to my apartment. Yes, it was childish, but there was just something about him that got under my freaking skin. I want to punch his face in. *At least they've stopped,* I thought, falling onto my bed. I was there for only a moment before I heard someone knocking.

Please don't be you. I prayed, but it did no good. I opened the door partially and the prick let himself in, now dressed in jeans and a gray shirt. He glanced around my place, which was mostly empty since I didn't have furniture.

"Excuse you! I don't remember inviting you in."

"Chlamydia? Really? What are you, in high school?" He finally spoke, leaning against my kitchen counter.

"Did you come here for an apol—"

"Yes, in fact, I did. My friend left me, and I should sue you for slander."

"Slander? Really? Please, go ahead. As long as I get sleep, I don't care."

"You paint pictures for a living. Sleep in the day."

I wanted to smack him.

"Look, whatever. I'm sorry for what I said, it was rude. Please, for the sake of my sanity, please...I don't know... don't prop up against your bedroom wall at least. If you're civil, I'm civil, Eli." I extended my hand toward him.

"Fine, Guinevere." He shook my hand and frowned.

"Please don't call me that, just Gwen—"

He grinned. "All right, Con Artist, let's be civil." Letting go of my hand, he walked out.

I felt the urge to smack him. There wasn't a civil bone in his body.

Eli

Fixing my tie and grabbing my phone, I tried to ignore the pain in my head. I had the worst hangover. I hadn't planned to get so drunk the night before, but I hadn't been on call and had found myself going to the bar across the street from the hospital. Once there, I met a redhead named... Suzanna...Joanna...I couldn't remember. Anna was in there somewhere. We were getting along fine until that woman came hammering on my door in the middle of the night.

"Good morning," she said cheerfully, stepping out of her apartment at the same time I did, dressed in a white over-sized blazer with paint splatter on it, a tight shirt, shorts, and black military boots. She held on to the bars of her bright yellow bicycle. "You okay? You don't look so well."

"What's with the act?" I walked toward the elevator.

"No act," she said, shifting her helmet under her other arm. "I'm just not going to let you drag me down to your level. From now on, I will reciprocate your rudeness with kindness."

"You were bullied in high school, weren't you?" I questioned as the elevator doors closed.

She opened her mouth to speak, but just mumbled something under breath and tucked a lock of brown hair behind her ear.

"What was that?"

She faced me and shook her head, getting off at the lobby. "Nothing. Have a good day, Dr. As—Dr. Davenport."

My town car was already waiting for me.

She waved to me as she biked down away.

"A friend of yours, sir?" the driver asked.

"Not in the slightest," I said, getting into the car.

"Strange, I swear I've seen her before."

I didn't say anything, going over my notes for the speaking engagement at NYU. Of all the doctors the hospital could have chosen to speak to students, why the hell did it have to be me? I couldn't care less what these kids decided to do with their lives.

"My daughter tells me this event has been sold out for weeks. She's broadcasting it over the campus radio." He glanced at me in the rearview mirror.

"I don't see why." I leaned into the seat, watching as people walked past us. I hated traffic and we were currently moving at a snail's pace. In this city, everyone had some place they needed to go, and quickly.

"Graduation is in two days. I think many of them are hoping all of those speaking will tell them what to do their lives." He laughed as we started to move again.

"Wasn't that the point of college? They had four years to figure that out."

"You know kids, always doubting. I'm sure you had moments where you doubted where your future career would take you."

"Never." I shook my head. "I always knew what I was going to do with my life. It was never a question of if or how, but when. I believe everyone knows what they want to do, but they're just too afraid they won't be able to do it."

"I might just listen in as well," the driver said, pulling up to New York University.

He came around to my door as I fixed my jacket, nodding to him before walking up the steps. He was right; the place was filled with hopeful twenty-something's, all gathered around the large theater.

"Dr. Davenport." The director of the event, Professor Mills, waved as she tried to work her way through the crowd toward me. She was a short, pale woman with big glasses that nearly took over her whole face. In her hands were all kinds of files, which she shifted to one side in order to shake my hand.

"Welcome, sorry for the chaos. After we announced our last guest, we got an influx of students." She smiled, showing her braces as more students passed us.

"I was about to say, I didn't think this many students cared about science so much." Why not was beyond me. "Who is the next guest, a musician or something?"

"No...wait, she was right behind me." She turned, standing on her tiptoes, trying to look over the crowd. "Oh, there she is."

I followed her line of sight. "You've got to be kidding me." There, taking a selfie with two students—one with dreadlocks that almost touched the ground and another with a hot pink mohawk—was the Con Artist herself.

"Ms. Poe!" The director called to her as the campus police helped everyone get in order and move toward the hall.

Finally free of distractions, she focused on us, her brown eyes widening when she saw me. "What are you doing here?" she questioned when she reached us.

Why, God? Why? "I should be asking you that."

"You know each other?" The director clapped in joy. "This is great. I can't wait to get this open debate underway."

"Debate?" the Con Artist and I said at the same time.

"I was under the impression this was question and answer with the students," I stated.

"As was I," she said.

"Really? We let your chair know, Dr. Davenport, and your agent, Ms. Poe. The reason is that the science and art department graduates have basically been having this battle for days now. They hope you both will hammer in their points. Since you two are friends, I'm sure this will be a healthy discussion. Follow me," Director Mills basically proclaimed in one swift breath.

Neither of us understood what she meant until we followed her through a separate door leading to the stage where three red chairs awaited us. The crowd I had just seen blended together outside was now divided between the arts and the professional. The difference was so clear. Even the Con Artist and I were, without realizing it, representing our teams by our outfits. I was dressed in a suit, while she had been more free-spirited in her outfit choice.

"Ladies and gentlemen. It is with great honor that I introduce our first set of speakers for the day," Director Mills said, already sitting in her chair onstage as we waited.

"This is a bad idea," she whispered beside me.

"Our first guest is currently the youngest neurosurgeon at New York Presbyterian Hospital. He graduated from our very own New York University before rising to the top of his class at Yale Medical. Ladies and gentlemen, please welcome Dr. Eli Davenport."

The left side of the room cheered for me, rising to their feet.

"Good luck," I said to her before walking onstage. Waving to the audience, I shook Director Mills's hand once more before taking the first seat.

"Our second guest is also a graduate of New York University. It was at our very own art gala that she debuted her first major work, *Screaming in the City*. Since then, her art and photography have graced almost every corner of the world. *Time Magazine* called her the Anselm Kiefer of this generation. Ladies and gentlemen, please welcome Ms. Guinevere Poe."

I had thought the applause given to me was shocking, but all the art students went completely wild. Stomping their feet and clapping their hands, they cheered as if she had ended world hunger or cured cancer.

She came out, the biggest grin on her face as she waved back with both hands. She even gave a bow.

I rolled my eyes.

"Good luck," she mocked when, finally finished praising herself, she sat in her chair.

I wanted to wipe that look off of her face.

"Thank you for being here," the director said to us as we were handed microphones.

"No problem," she replied gleefully.

"I wouldn't say 'no' problem. I could be saving someone's life right now, but—"

A bunch of ohs and laughter came from my section.

She glared at me, nodding her head as if agreeing to something.

Let the games begin.

Guinevere

That's how he wants to play? I had just made a pact not to allow him to drag me down to his level, and there I was getting into the ring with this...this *thing*...again. I had lived in the city for years, and never had New York felt as small as it had in the last few weeks. I just couldn't get away from him.

"Shall we get started?" the director asked us.

We both nodded, turning to the students.

"Now, please remember to keep all questions respectful. We will go back and forth, starting from the quote, *professionals*."

That got a few soft boos from what I guessed would be called the "creatives."

A female student, her hair pulled into a tight ponytail, dressed in black slacks and a button-down blouse, stood. "My question is for Dr. Davenport." Her gaze focused on him. "Do you not believe that, due to media, this generation is especially deluded about the life of the artist?"

There were a few groans and mutters at her question, but they all waited for him to speak. I watched him relax in his chair as a small grin crept onto his lips.

"Of course," he said.

I was tempted to close my ears to the round of trash he would most likely spit out next.

"I mean, is it really possible for every last one of you in this room to become the next Anselm Kiefer or Lady Gaga? No. The thing about any type of art is: it's not in your control. No matter what, your livelihood depends on whether or not you are, one: noticed, and two: popular. I'm sure there are many artists just as good as Ms. Poe, if not better, but none of them were noticed. Unlike in the professional world, where if you are the best in your field, you will get the recognition you deserve."

How that bullshit answer got any applause worried me for the future of our country. "Am I allowed to respond to this?" I asked the director into the mic.

"Please."

I sighed, rolling up my sleeves. "I told myself I would try to hold back, because often when I lay down the truth, people get hurt." I grinned at the laughter filling the room.

"Anytime, Ms. Poe," he said from beside me, taking a drink of his water.

"Well, Dr. Davenport, your statement highlights the fundamental difference between us. You look for recognition in your work. And don't get me wrong, I'm sure you love what you do, but I'm also sure you don't go into work *every day* hoping to save as many lives as possible. It's about making a name for yourself. For people like me, I couldn't give a damn if someone knows my accomplishments. My art isn't for anyone but myself. When I paint, or take a photo, I'm expressing the innermost parts of myself. That is all the satisfaction I need. It may seem *scary* for all you people who need a path to walk, and the ten steps of becoming whatever, but for us, we artists make our own path, and set our own goals and limits. We are living a technicolor life, my friend."

"Boom!" someone yelled from my side of the hall, and I winked in that direction.

"Next question." The director pointed to someone from the creative side.

He stood. "My question is for Ms. Poe," he said when he was given a mic.

I remembered taking a picture with him; his hot pink mohawk was hard to miss. I nodded, sitting up.

"How do you feel about how the educational system focuses on the sciences while cutting the art budget *once* again?"

"I'm ashamed. I'm living in a culture that has *disillusioned* itself into believing that the focus on arts is no longer needed. An artist designed that NYU shirt you are wearing, and an artist spent time creating the layout of this hall. Art is in everything, and without realizing it, the educational system is chipping away at the core of itself."

"I concur, to a degree." Eli faced the student. "However, a focus on the sciences is in fact more important, not only for our economy, but also our overall status as a society. America is ranked thirty-first in mathematics and twenty-third in the sciences. How can we not place a focus on that? If you want to be an artist, fine, but why does that translate into not understanding chemistry? So many students give up and say, 'I'm more artistic, I don't need to learn this.'"

"Well on that note, when was last time you painted anything or were creative, Dr. Davenport?" I cut in, forcing him to look at me. "What you are saying is that artists should be well-rounded, and I don't find fault in that, but what about professionals? How many students take an art class for an easy A and don't actually learn to draw? When was last time you were an artist, Dr. Davenport?"

He nodded. "Touché."

"Next question."

Another guy stood, dressed in a sweater vest, bow tie, and glasses. "My question is for Dr. Davenport. I also want to become a doctor, though I'm not sure what I want to specialize in. I know the next four years of my life will be medical school, and after that, internships and whatnot. So I was wondering, how do you find time to date? Or is that not even a possibility until after I'm finished with school?"

The moment he asked, my head whipped to Eli. Even though he laughed alongside a few other students, I could tell how uncomfortable he was.

"I'm sorry, dumb question…"

"No, it's fine. It's just…" Eli paused again, going off into his own world.

"Dating is possible," I said for him, looking to the student. "After all, he's managed to still keep me beside him."

The gasps, whistles, and laughter that filled the room were deafening.

Eli's eyes peered into mine as if I had lost my mind.

"You two are dating?" Director Mills leaned in as if I was going to tell her a big secret. I glared at Eli, hoping he would understand what I was trying to say through my eyes.

"Yeah, I don't even know how it happened. One moment we were just neighbors, then the next, we were in a relationship." He laughed, but on the inside, I could tell he was yelling. The sarcasm in his voice was clear only to me.

"There you have it, the left and right brain coming together," Director Mills stated.

"Kiss! Kiss!" they started to chant, to my horror. It was like the hole we were in kept getting bigger and bigger.

When I turned back to Eli, he, in one swift motion, kissed me softly on the lips before sitting again and accepting the applause.

What the hell just happened?

Eli

"What the hell was that?" I hollered at her when we finished, left alone in the backstage area as the students cleared.

"I don't know! You weren't answering, and I felt bad—"

"Who asked you to feel bad for me? Do I look that pitiful to you?"

"Are you saying that dating me is pitiful?" she yelled back.

"Yes! Especially compared to who I actually was dating! Not only was she beautiful and classy, but also extremely intelligent. How do you compare to that?" The words flew out of my mouth before I could stop myself.

She looked away from me, clamping her mouth shut for a moment before lifting her head and facing me. "I get it. I'm not worth a damn, but what about you? You apparently weren't worth her love either. It must have been that extreme intelligence that made her run so quickly without looking back once," she whispered, brushing past me on her way to the exit.

I'm an idiot. I had punched below the belt, and she had punched back.

CHAPTER FOUR
DEFECTIVE TOYS

Guinevere

"**G**wen?"

Fingers snapped in my face. Blinking, I looked up at the small cup of tea in front of me.

"Thank you," I whispered to Katrina's secretary as she left.

Katrina sat at her desk, folding her hands over the papers.

Her office was, in a word, sleek, every surface either white or gray.

"Are you all right?" she asked, drawing my attention back to her.

"I'm fine, I just spent the morning talking to college students about how awesome it is to be me." I forced a laugh, which sounded a lot more pitiful than I'd hoped.

"Maybe this will make your day just a little bit better." She slid the document over to me. "All we need is your signature, and you will be released from your contract. They agreed to all of our terms and even gave you a bigger severance... Why don't you look happy?"

I hadn't realized I'd stopped breathing until she spoke to me directly. Taking a deep breath, I placed the cup on her desk and grabbed a pen. "All I need to do is sign this, right?" I asked, reading it over.

"Yes, they've already signed." When she said they, she meant him.

I stabbed the pen right in the middle of the paper before dragging it down, ripping it until the end.

"What are you doing?"

"Did I do anything wrong?" I asked her.

"What?"

"Did I do anything wrong? I don't think so. So why am I the one running? Why do I feel like the other woman, being paid off, told to keep her mouth shut, to accept the money and disappear?"

"Gwen—"

"How much longer do I have on my contract?"

"Five months, but Gwen—"

"I will work until it's over, and only then will I leave. So call him up and tell him I will be awaiting the next project." I rose, grabbing my things.

"Gwen! Stop for a second." Katrina walked in front of me. "I understand what you are saying, I really do, but you shouldn't let yourself go though that kind of emotional abuse for the sake of your pride. There is nothing wrong with closing the book on him and all of this. It's not running."

"To me it is." I felt like I should be ashamed of something. "I'm closing the book and putting this all behind me, and I need to do that from a position of strength. Five months. I can handle that—it's not like I'm there every day. It could be only three or four shoots. Thank you for your concern, but please just do what I asked and let them know."

"Okay, I'll make the call." She moved out of my way.

"Thank you," I said heading out. I somehow managed to keep my head until I got into the elevator. Alone, I rested my forehead against the wall.

Not only was she beautiful and classy, but also extremely intelligent. How do you compare to that? His voice replayed in my mind, like a knife to my soul. Worse, no matter how deeply I was hurt, I couldn't be angry at him. What did I care if he didn't think I was good enough? I didn't even really know him, and he didn't know me. It was good he thought so highly of her; he had wanted to to marry her, that's how he was supposed to think. Your spouse is the person you are supposed to devote the rest of your life to; shouldn't they be the most perfect person to you? She was his person. If the situation were reversed, I could have said the same thing. What hurt me was the fact that Bash, my person, thought I was no good either. Bash knew me, he had seen me at my best and worst, and in his eyes, I was still not good enough.

Heading toward my bike, I tried to focus on the people passing by instead of my dark thoughts. I reached into my purse, pulled out my camera, and balanced myself on my bike as I took a couple of photos. The world looked so much better through a lens. Maybe it was because I could freeze time for a second and take a good look at the people around me.

New York is so crowded, everyone in a hurry, brushing past people but rarely making connections, rarely truly seeing each other.

Plunging forward, I enjoyed the breeze as I headed back home. It was a short ride back, thankfully. I had the urge to paint again. Making it to my building, I lifted my bike toward the entrance when a little girl ran past me, dropping her teddy bear and almost knocking me over. The bear's arm was torn, one of its button eyes was missing, and the stuffing was falling out of the back.

"I'm so sorry. She's really excited." A dirty blond-haired man whose five o' clock shadow was working on becoming a beard ran up to me, looking me over through the thick-rimmed black glasses perched on his nose. He was cute in a nerdy kind of way.

"It's fine. Here, she dropped this." I handed him the bear.

"You're the new tenant in 34B, right?" He outstretched his hand. "I'm Toby Wesley. I live in 32C, two floors down. Nice to meet you."

"Guinevere Poe, but you can call me Gwen. Nice to meet you." I shook his hand.

"DAD!" the girl yelled from the front door.

"Welcome again," he said before quickly running after his daughter.

I laughed at the sight of the bear hanging helpless under his arm before heading to the elevator. The last thing I'd expected when I got to my floor was to see Eli resting against his door with a bottle of wine in one hand and a gro-cery bag in the other. He had changed out of his tailor-made suit into dark jeans and a button-down shirt.

I said nothing, wheeling my bike to my door. He didn't look at me either, making me wonder again how in the hell I had ended up having him as a neighbor.

"I'm sorry," he said as I put my key in the door.

Turning back, I checked to see if anyone else was in the hall.

"Yes, I'm talking to you." He pushed himself off the floor and faced me. "I'm sorry for what I said, it was… I was an ass. I'm here to call a truce." He lifted the wine for me to see, along with the bag.

Looking away, I opened my door. "I'm fine—"

"I know you aren't."

I felt myself getting irritated again.

"I know you aren't fine because I'm not fine. We say that because we really don't know how we are feeling at any given moment, and that's just too hard to explain to others."

I peeked back at him.

He once again lifted the bottle.

"Aren't you a doctor? Shouldn't you be working or something instead of drinking in the middle of the day?"

"I should be, but I've clocked more hours than our hospital will allow. I was working nonstop for a month when I should have been on my honeymoon," he answered truthfully.

His eyes...his eyes were like mine: broken. The scary thing about reality is all of our monsters are humans... humans who have the ability to make you drink with people you don't even know.

Unlocking the door, I held it open for him to enter, placing my bike by the door.

"You still don't have furniture," he said, looking at the open space.

He was right, my apartment was bare. My living room had nothing but a television mounted on the wall and my large window overlooking the city, with a pillow next to it where I usually sat. "Less furniture, more room to work," I replied, taking off my shoes and heading into the kitchen. "But, I do have wine glasses."

"You don't have a studio or something?" His eyes gaze still wandered.

I wasn't sure what he was looking for. "I do, but a lot of my inspiration happens when I'm home. It's much easier to just grab a canvas here than running to my studio. I save that for bigger, planned projects. Why?" I handed him the glass and bottle opener.

He shrugged. "I'm still figuring out how you make a living off that stuff."

"That *stuff* is my life's work…"

"Not trying to be an ass, just asking." He pulled crackers from the bag and uncorked the wine, then poured a glass for each of us.

So, being an ass is just his default setting. Taking the glass, I walked to the living room and took a seat where the window met the wall.

He followed, walking around Taigi, who lay near the door, foot kicking as he dreamed. Eli sat on the floor in front of me, but neither of us spoke. Then Taigi decided to fart, and the look on Eli's face got me laughing.

"That's one way to break the tension," he muttered, shaking his head at my dog. "I honestly didn't think past the 'I'm sorry' part. Actually, I thought you'd close the door in my face."

"I was tempted to," I said, and drank. *Oh, shit, this is delicious.*

"Good, isn't it?" He grinned.

Frowning, I shrugged. "It's okay."

"Then why are you still licking your lips?"

Damn him. "I should have just closed the door on you." I drank some more.

He leaned against my window before sipping again. "Why didn't you?"

"Honestly?"

He nodded.

"I couldn't after you told me you worked when you were supposed to be on your honeymoon."

"So, pity again." He grimaced, finishing off the glass and pouring himself another.

"I've never pitied you, how can I? You and I are in the same boat. It's more like understanding. Just like how you knew I wasn't fine."

Again, we were silent for a moment.

"You know," I said softly, finishing off my glass before speaking again. "I mean neither of us has actually been properly introduced yet. I know nothing about you."

He filled my glass. "My name is Eli Davenport, I'm 6'1 and a half, 184 pounds, age 31 as of two days ago, born on June 23rd. I'm also a neurosurgeon at New York Presbyterian. I have a younger brother who introduced my fiancée to her lover, and she ran off with him on our wedding day. Nice to meet you."

I laughed, sitting straighter in order to introduce myself. "Guinevere Poe, 5'9 exactly, my weight is not your concern, age 24 since February 13th. I'm also a painter and photographer. My fiancé took me as his date to a wedding only to run off with the bride, leaving me with no way of getting home. Nice to meet you, Eli."

"Cheers." He held up his glass and after clinking them, we drank.

"Okay, this is *really* good." I lifted the bottle to read the name. "Red Savannah Sun? I've never even heard of this."

"That's because it was made by my father and isn't sold in stores." He took the bottle back, once again pouring. "By the way, you are a lot younger than I thought."

I noticed he changed the subject quickly, but I didn't dwell on that. "How old did you think I was?"

He glanced me over. "28 or 29—"

"29!"

"A decent 29?" He tried to save himself. "In my defense, you were giving life advice to college students like you were so much wiser. You probably graduated what, a year ago?"

"Try three." I pouted, drinking. "How old is *she?*" I knew I was walking on thin ice, but for some reason I really wanted to know about her.

"31."

I grumbled, falling back against the wall.

"What?"

"Bash is 27. Don't guys usually want the younger woman? She must be something."

He tensed at Bash's name for a moment before pulling out his phone.

I saw the photo of Hannah and him as his background. They were embracing, laughing. He didn't look half-bad with that smile on his face.

He held it low enough that I watched as he opened the settings menu, trying to change the photo but stopping at the last step.

"Urgh, I am pitiful," he scoffed, slamming down the phone.

"We both are." I lifted my phone to show him the photo that was my background.

"Is that—"

"The photo you sent me after you kicked his ass? Yes, yes it is." I smiled at the image before frowning. "I get a little satisfaction every time I look at it, but doesn't that just mean I'm hanging on? I've moved, cut off all contact, even managed to leave behind some of the gifts he gave me, yet I'm still hanging on."

He took the phone from me and handed over his. "Change the picture, and take satisfaction in the fact that they won't be together for long."

"And how do you know that?"

"Because I've thought about it a million times since they ran off. When could they have been together? Hannah is just as much a workaholic as I am. Between us and the hospital, she didn't have much free time, so how could she have had another relationship? Then I realized it probably wasn't a relationship, just sex. It must have been really exciting, sneaking around, worrying about either of us finding out. But a relationship based on nothing but sex and excitement can't last. Any two people with working organs can have a great screw, but believe me, that doesn't change how empty and meaningless it really is. They may not realize it now, but one day it will hit them." He glanced up at me, showing me the newly changed screensaver of a baby panda. "Or at least, that's what I tell myself."

"Then I'll tell myself that as well," I replied, changing the photo for him.

"Shamelessly promoting your own work, I see," he said when I handed the phone back. I had changed it to one of my oil paintings of a child standing in the rain.

"A girl's got to eat," I joked, accepting my phone.

No matter how badly Bash and I had ended, at least I could never say our relationship had been empty or meaningless.

Eli

Groaning, I rolled over and reached for my phone as it buzzed and vibrated on the floor. My head felt as if it would break open.

Urgh, I drank way too much. "Dr. Davenport," I yawned into the phone.

"Eli, where are you? Are you all right?"

My mother sounded a lot more worried than she should have, seeing as how I was a grown man. "I'm fine, Mom—"

"Then did you just forget about our brunch?"

"No, our brunch, that's not until..." I tilted my wrist to see the time: already quarter to noon. "Shit—"

"Why are you so loud?" said none other than Guinevere, curled up in a ball beside me on her living room floor.

Her dark brown hair covered half of her face, and drool leaked from the corner of her mouth.

That is definitely attractive, I sarcastically thought to myself as I sat up, my back aching from lying flat on the ground.

"Who was that?" My mom was still on the line.

"Mom, where are you now? I'll come meet you in twenty."

"I just got to your apartment—"

"What?" I yelled as I ran toward the door. I had hoped to meet her halfway, but when I opened the door, there she was, dressed in a soft peach suit, her hair tucked behind her ears. With the phone still in one hand and a plate of freshly baked muffins in the other, she turned, staring at me in confusion. "Why are you—"

"What are you yelling about so early in the morning?" Guinevere stumbled out of the living room, coming to stand beside me at the door. She rubbed her eyes and yawned, her dog walking over to rest beside her.

I stared at her, speechless, before glancing back to my mother, whose eyes widened in realization; I did not like whatever she was thinking right then. "Mom, this is Guinevere Poe."

When I said 'Mom', I saw Guinevere's head snap toward my mother.

"Wow, this looks really bad. We were drinking last night—no, I mean—crap, nothing happened." She rambled on, quickly making me want to bang my head against the beam of the door and beg her to shut up.

My mother took a step forward, a grin growing on her face. "Wait, did you say Guinevere Poe? As in the artist?"

"Yes," I answered. "And I'm sure she has a lot of work to get back to."

"Yeah, a lot of work," she repeated.

I stepped out of her apartment. "We should get going ..."

"Wait."

My mother broke away from me as I tried to lead her back to my place.

"We were just going to have brunch at the coffeeshop on 5th. Please, join us. I've been trying to get into your studio for weeks, but it's damn near impossible."

"I'm not really presentable."

I'll say.

My mother laughed. "Presentable? Who are you presenting yourself to? You look lovely."

I coughed at that.

Guinevere glared at me before returning her attention to my mother.

"Don't mind him, he's worried I'll embarrass him. But, I made muffins." She gifted one to Guinevere, whose stare drifted to me as if to scream for help.

I opened my mouth to say something...anything, but nothing came to me. Clasping my hand over my mouth, I shook my head, not really sure what to make of the situation.

Why did we fall asleep? We had drunk and talked all night about our crappy lives... I vaguely remembered going back for more wine before everything became a blur.

"Okay, how about I meet you there in a half hour, if that's all right?"

She'd caved...the weakling.

They chatted for a second longer before my mother let her go, and I opened the door to my apartment. When inside, she hit me on the shoulder.

"Mom!"

"How can you be next-door neighbors to Guinevere Poe, knowing full well I'm in love with her work, and not say a word!"

Rolling my eyes, I walked into my kitchen, grabbing an aspirin and water. "Because she isn't Guinevere Poe to me. She's the fiancée of the man who ran off with Hannah."

"What? That was her?" she whispered slowly, taking a seat on my couch, most likely as the whole scene replayed in her mind.

"You mean the second most-humiliated person on my wedding day? Yeah, that was her. Sebastian Evans was her fiancé."

"This city is too damn small."

It really was.

Chapter Five
Background Noise

Eli

I almost didn't recognize Guinevere when she entered the café. Her hair was styled and curled nicely, and her red cotton shirt hugged every curve of her chest, making her stand out in an odd sort of way. Maybe it was because I had never seen her in heels that her legs looked longer under the white skirt.

"What?" she said, glancing down at herself when she reached our table.

"Nothing, it's just the first time I've ever seen you look nice," I replied, drinking my coffee.

"How is it possible for you to both compliment and insult me at the same time?" She frowned, about to take a seat, when my mother returned. For some reason, she stood back up again.

"Please don't mind my son, I'm not sure where his manners have gone," she said, placing a steaming cup in front of Guinevere. "I wasn't sure what you took, so it's just a cappuccino. I hope you don't mind me ordering, the line was getting long."

"No, it's fine. Thank you so much," she responded politely.

You would have thought she was the one asking for a favor.

"You said you've been trying to get in touch with me?"

My mother smiled sadly, looking between us. "Yes. I never realized we would be connected like this."

"My mother is the chairwoman at the hospital, and was wondering if you could paint a mural," I said, trying to speed things up.

"A mural?"

"I know you're busy, but if you could consider it...you have no idea how much your work means to me. Eli doesn't really understand art, so he thought I was crazy for buying your *Whispers of the East* piece. It brought me to tears."

"That's why he called me Con Artist." She laughed.

My mother shifted her gaze to me. "Con artist?"

She just had to bring that up. Saying nothing, I drank my coffee.

"I can't believe you bought that." She sat up straighter. "I was shocked when it sold, I really didn't think anyone would understand it but me."

"I read that you drew it after the death of your grandparents? You said it hurt to breathe for a while. I saw the date; my husband actually died a week after that, and looking at it, I understood."

For a brief second, I saw an expression on my mother's face I hadn't seen in over two decades...since my father died. She had always done her best to stay upbeat and happy around us. Growing up, I often wondered how she could get on so well with her life, and now it seemed like that was not the case at all.

Guinevere shifted in her seat, gripping the cappuccino. "My grandparents meant more than I could put into words. Painting that was really therapeutic for me. I'm so happy it's found a good home. As for the mural, I will talk to my agent, and I will have to look at the space, but I would be more than happy to do it, Mrs. Davenport."

"Truly?" My mother smiled and took her hand. "Thank you. Eli can show you the space whenever you are free."

"What?"

Guinevere kicked my foot under the table. "Great, I'm sure we will work out a time."

"I have to run to a meeting, but please have your people contact me on the logistics." She stood, as did I, pulling back her chair. "Oh no, please finish your coffee, I will see you all later. Oh, and Eli, call your brother."

"Yes, *Mother*."

She waved, already on her phone. Her driver appeared at the door, holding it open for her and giving me a short nod before leading her out.

When she was gone, Guinevere fell back onto her seat and took a deep breath. Her posture completely changed, and she placed her elbows on the table.

"Why were you so nervous?" I asked.

"I always get nervous around parents, or anyone over the age of 50, really. I don't know, I always want them to like me."

I fought back a laugh. "Why?"

"Do you want to be the person hated by old people?"

I wasn't even sure what to say to that, other than, "You are an odd one, Guinevere Poe."

"Please, just call me Gwen, and do you want this? I'm allergic to coffee."

You're what?

"Why did you take it?"

"Your mother bought it for me, so I didn't want to be rude."

"Guinevere, I'm sure if you told her you couldn't have coffee, she wouldn't have been offended. How bad of an allergy is it?"

"I just can't digest it and drinking it gives me a small headache sometimes or my face swells. But it's no big deal. And just Gwen."

But it's no big deal?

"No," I said, leaving a bill on the table and throwing the coffee in the trash as she followed me onto the street, her heels clicking as she caught up to me.

"Why won't you call me Gwen?"

"Three reasons," I answered as I walked to the corner.

"Which are?"

"One: calling you Guinevere seems to seriously bother you." I smirked.

She smacked my shoulder as we walked across when the light changed.

"Don't you want to know the other two?"

"I already do. You're an ass, and you're an ass."

Ignoring her, I continued. "Second: calling you by a nickname would mean we have a closer relationship than we do. Third: if I did, you might just fall for me, and I wouldn't want to break your heart."

She paused once we reached the opposite sidewalk, looked me up and down, and laughed. "Ha! That would be the day."

"What do you mean, 'ha'?"

"I mean what it sounds like. I mean maybe, from a distance, if I squint and you aren't speaking, you might look attractive. But other than that, I don't see it."

"Yes, because you are definitely a catch, especially with the drool pouring out of your mouth this morning."

Her eyes widened. "I do not drool!"

"I was there, and you do. Even your dog didn't have that much saliva coming out of his mouth." It hadn't been that bad, but seeing the horror creep onto her face was just so amusing. She was really easy to bother.

"You're just a modern day Prince Charming, you know that?" she snapped.

"I get that a lot…" My voice drifted off when I saw her photo hanging in the gallery across the street. *Guinevere Poe: Heroes, Rebels, and Thieves*, read the sign under her name.

"Wow, it's up. With everything else, I almost forgot about this," she whispered, moving to the curb and gazing up at herself in the windows. "Can you believe that? I spent a year working on this, and because of a guy, I almost forgot."

"I'll be sure to check it out when it opens next week."

She turned to me. "Don't be nice, it's weird. It's all right, I know this isn't your thing."

"No, I want to know what my mother is spending her money on, and if it's good enough to be in my hospital."

Her eyebrow twitched.

"What? You told me not to be nice."

"Why don't you see it now? Unless you have someone else's ego to go trample on."

"I can't go back to work until tomorrow, so lead the way." I stepped out onto the street. In all honesty, I wanted to understand why my mother felt so attached to Guinevere's work. Even after finding out who Guinevere really was, she still couldn't stop raving about her art.

That was the only reason I was going.

Guinevere

Even though I knew he knew nothing about art, I was still nervous. I was always nervous when people viewed my work. My art wasn't just for me, but a part of me. Every time I had it on display, I felt like a spotlight was on my soul for everyone to see. If they disliked it, in a way, it was like they disliked me, too.

"Welcome, Lady Guinevere. I was not expecting you." Mr. D'Amour met us at the entrance. He was a short, tan-skinned old man from Le Mans, France, with a hunched back and wrinkles as deep as the Grand Canyon. In his hand was an old wooden cane. He owned the gallery, along with a few others around the world. He had been one of my very first supporters.

He was like a mentor to me, and the only other person who refused to call me Gwen. Hugging him, I said, "I just stopped by to show this place to a critic of mine."

"A critic?" he repeated when I let go.

I moved aside so he could see Eli, who stood with hands behind his back, gazing up at the changing photos on the ceiling of people from all races and walks of life weaving, giving peace signs, or thumbs up.

"Ah," he groaned when I elbowed him in the ribs to get his attention.

"Eli, Mr. D'Amour. Mr. D'Amour, Eli Davenport."

"Only a man with a defective heart would be a critic of Lady Guinevere's art," Mr. D'Amour boasted for me.

I nodded in agreement.

Eli's blue-green eyes seemed to shine as a smirk graced his lips. "*Lady* Guinevere? You two seem quite close, sir. Are you sure you aren't just a tad bit biased?"

"Let's see if you still feel that way once you go through it all," Mr. D'Amour countered as an employee came up to get his attention. "Please feel free to take as long as you like. Keep in mind, they are still putting some pieces up."

"Thank you!" I waved to him as he walked off.

"You have some very passionate fans. Are you sure someone won't stone me if I don't like something?" He had already started walking.

"Just don't dislike anything, then."

"That's a tall order. Well then, *Lady Guinevere,*" he mocked. "Please enlighten me as to what I have apparently been blind to."

Rolling my eyes, I started at the beginning of the gallery. It was the largest space my work had been in to date. The ceilings were low and arched, which worked great for the photos projected on them. All the lights were dimmed slightly, except for the ones on my paintings. The floor was pure black, and so sleek I could see my reflection. Before patrons reached the first piece, they were offered wireless headphones to use as they walked around.

"Hmm…" He took a step back, stroking his chin when we reached my first painting.

I grabbed one of the headsets and placed it over his ears. "Stop trying to understand it and just see it…silently, if you can." *Jeez, he is a pain in my ass.*

Eli

There was a long silence before the music started. For a few moments it was as if I was deaf; I couldn't even hear myself. Slowly, the soft melody drifted into my ears.

She took my hand.

My eyes immediately looked to our joined hands.

Rolling her eyes, she let go, pointing for me to move to the next painting.

When I did, I noticed the volume increased, and the notes changed. Again, I glanced at her.

She just nodded like she could read my mind. The music changed depending on what I was looking at.

This is pretty cool. The thought ran through my head before I could stop myself. From the corner of my eye, I could see her grinning, and I tried to regain my composure, walking slowly to the next piece, stopping and moving backward just to check if the music would change back immediately. To my surprise, it did.

She smacked my arm and, walking behind me, forced my head to face the painting.

Giving in, I focused. I wasn't sure how to describe the music for the next image, other than tragic. The painting was massive, almost taking up the whole wall. It was of red, gold, and orange swirls, with faceless figures dancing around them. Noticing the lighting change, I glanced up to the arched ceiling, upon which was projected a close-up photo of a firefighter battling a burning bus, sweat dripping down his face as he gripped the hose in his hands. I felt like I stared at the photo for hours before my eyes finally fell back to the painting again. I realized those weren't just swirls, but flames, and the faceless figures weren't dancing, they were trapped. My chest felt heavy, and I didn't want to look anymore.

With my next step, the music changed to what seemed like gunshots or firecrackers. This time, the painting was much clearer, depicting a riot in the street between police and civilians. Things were being thrown, and the scene looked like an all-out war was about to take place. When I looked up, this time the photo on the ceiling was of two teens in the midst of the chaos, kissing against a car.

Make love, not war. I smiled, moving on to the next painting.

The music turned to laughter, and the painting was of an old man holding up a bat in front of a toppled ice cream cart, the contents spilling out onto the ground. Above me, the photo showed three young boys, no older than seven, their hands filled with ice cream and the biggest grins on their faces as they ran away.

Taking a few steps back, I tried to view all three paintings at the same time, the music blending the tragedy, gunshots, and laughter together.

"Heroes, Rebels, and Thieves," I said out loud, understanding the transition among them. I realized the whole gallery must have been arranged in sets of threes.

Once I understood how it all worked, I went on. It felt like the space was sucking me in, and I was too curious to stop myself. I wasn't sure how long I spent on each photo or painting. I couldn't deny that each made me feel something, even when I didn't want to. She was able to capture human emotion on extreme levels. One moment you were in pain, and the next you were laughing—all in the span of one footstep.

By the time we reached the end, not only had we spent two hours there, I was emotionally drained…something I hadn't been since my wedding day.

"Well?" she asked me, taking off the headphones. "Am I still a con artist?"

She was something, I just didn't have a name for it yet. "It was…better than I expected, I guess. You're no Jackson Pollock, but it's decent."

I only knew that artist's name because I had seen it in an old textbook. I wasn't sure what else to say though, without giving her a big head. She was hard enough to deal with as it was.

She grinned, giving herself a pat on the back.

I fought the urge to roll my eyes.

"Two compliments in one day from Dr. Davenport. I can die happy—"

"When else did I compliment you?" I tried to remember.

She twirled around, her heels now in her hand. "You said I looked nice."

"Obviously I'm sleep deprived," I muttered under my breath. I didn't like that smile on her face.

"Okay, *sure*... Anyway, thank you for viewing the whole thing."

"He enjoyed it?" the old man asked, his cane clicking against the ground as he approached.

"He did, but his pride won't let him admit I'm amazing," she answered.

Oh god. "Aren't you supposed to be humble?"

"I'll work on it."

"If you don't mind, can I steal her away now?" Mr. D'Amour cut in.

I nodded. "Please do, I need a break. I'll see you." I waved, heading toward the exit. Only when the summer breeze hit my face did I think back on what I'd just done.

I'll see you? Waving? When had we advanced to doing that? I could hardly believe I had spent two hours alone with her, on top of the time we had already spent together.

Apparently we were friends now.

Guinevere

Waving back as Eli left, Mr. D'Amour wrapped his hand around mine, walking slowly with me through the rest of the gallery that had not yet been set up.

"This is your best work yet, Lady Guinevere." He stopped in front of the blank wall, watching as his crew lifted my painting gently, almost like it was a child. He looked grateful for the amount of care they took with it.

"You always say that, Mr. D'Amour." I smiled.

"Of course. If I didn't say it, that would mean you are getting worse. That is one of the goals for an artist, to make each work better than the last."

"I'm not sure if I try to make each work better." Some days it all looked like an absolute mess with no rhyme or reason behind it.

"Are you all right?"

"Huh?" I glanced back down at him. "I'm sorry. What did you say?"

He frowned, stroking his beard. "I said, are you all right? I heard about the end of your engagement, Guinevere, and have not seen you since then. So once again, my dear, are you all right?"

How many people have heard about it? I tried to smile, but for some reason I couldn't fake it with him, and I couldn't handle looking at his face either. I just stared at the wall as I made us keep walking. "I'm sorry for disappearing while you were setting all of this up. I...I forgot. The only reason I came to the city was my art. When I first got here, it was all I cared about, all I wanted. And now I'm opening another gallery, and it's so beautiful. I feel I've come so far, and yet for some reason, I can't feel the way I dreamt I would. I want to be completely over everything that happened and never think about it again. I don't want it to affect me. When do you think that will happen?"

"Your heart broke, Guinevere. There is no way to fast-forward or avoid the pain. You must accept that first before you can heal. You and your art will be better for it. If you don't believe me, there are a billion songs all about it."

I laughed. He was right, because the more I thought about the last few weeks, the more I realized I was able to laugh.

I had forgotten that just because your heart breaks doesn't mean the world comes to an end. I wasn't better. I didn't think I would be better for a while, but I wasn't horrible either, which made me sort of proud.

Chapter Six
Baptism By Fire

Eli

"Look to your right," I told the little girl with a bright pink bow tied in her hair as she sat in front of me. She wasn't sure which way I meant, so I nodded my head to her right.

Grinning, she nodded, her brown eyes shifting.

"Now look to your left. Okay, thank you Molly. You have pretty eyes."

"I get them from my mommy," she replied happily.

I would have called her father a lucky man, but he only seemed more depressed at her words. "My interns here will draw some blood from you while I talk to your dad, okay? If it hurts, tell me, and I'll make sure they go back to school."

"Wait, what?" one of the interns whispered behind me.

I nodded to her father to follow me outside.

"Is she all right?" he asked as soon as I closed the door.

"Mr. Wesley, how long has Molly's eye been twitching like that?"

"I'm not sure. I might have noticed it a week or two ago? It was only after she rubbed it, and not often, so I just thought it was an infection or something."

"Has she been sick? Vomiting at all, or complaining about headaches?"

He nodded. "She just got over the flu last week. Dr. Davenport, what is it? We only came in for her shots."

"I'm not sure, and I don't want to make you panic before I know anything concrete. We will do a full workup, and the second I know for sure what's going on with her, I will let you know. And I'll make sure to rush it—no kid should spend their birthday surrounded by doctors." I tried to smile for his sake.

"Dr. Davenport, we're done," said one of my interns.

Dr…oh whatever, like I was going to remember who the intern was. I just knew him as Four Eyes; the glasses he wore made his eyes look almost cartoonish. "They're done, all right?" I said, walking to where the child waited. "Molly, did it hurt? Point at which one has to go back to school."

She shook her head so hard her bow almost fell off. "Nope, it didn't hurt. They gave me candy."

I glanced up at the three *doctors* who had to bribe a child while taking blood.

They all turned away from me.

"Well, make sure to get more from them; they are going to take you to get your pictures taken," I said, more to them than to her.

"Pictures, then we leave, Daddy? You promised we could go to the aquarium. I wanna see where Ariel lives!" She pointed to her shirt.

"Pictures, then we leave." He laughed, kneeling in front of her.

"Get a full scan for me. If there is a line, tell them Dr. Davenport sent you," I whispered to my interns at the door.

"What if that doesn't do anything?" the intern with a bun on the top of her head said, which got her an elbow from both the tall and skinny Dr. Stretch, as I liked to call him, and Dr. Four Eyes.

"If it doesn't do anything, then you're off my service and in the pit for not thinking of another option," I replied, stepping out toward the nurses' station in the middle of the pale blue and beige hall. Sighing, I dropped my tablet on the counter.

"Was I right?" Dr. Handler, Molly's pediatrician, asked as she came to stand beside me. Her eyes focused on Molly through the panels of the window.

When I didn't respond, I saw her turn to face me, swinging her dark brown curls, cropped right under her chin. Dr. Handler had been at the hospital for more than twenty years. She was one of the best pediatricians, if not the best, we had. She had known the answer before paging me down there.

"Dr. Davenport—"

"I won't know the extent of it until I see her scans, but yes, she has a brain tumor. I don't know what stage yet, but she had trouble following both my finger and the light, not to mention her twitching." She had just turned seven. Sometimes I really hated my job.

"Her mother died last year, Eli. She was six months pregnant. Please, for me, do everything you can for her, all right? She's been a patient of mine since she was three months old."

We weren't supposed to get attached for exactly this reason. I could feel her putting the hope of God on my shoulders. She knew better, and so did I.

"We'll start tomorrow. Let her at least have her birthday," I muttered, walking toward the elevators.

Just as the doors opened, I heard a laugh...*her* laugh, to the right of me. There, walking down the stairs, her blonde ponytail swinging back and forth, was Hannah...my Hannah. She tucked a strand of hair behind her ear as her head turned toward me.

I ran into the elevator, pressing the close button as fast as possible.

Why was she here? Why the hell was she still here?

The only person who could answer that was on the very top floor. With each level I went up, I could feel my blood pressure rising. My fingertips twitched, my vision became tunneled, even the box I was in felt like it was closing in on me.

"Take the next one!" I yelled when the doors opened. I pressed the close button again, shutting out the group of doctors trying to go up as well.

I couldn't deal with them right now. It felt like forever until I finally reached her floor and the offices above. Marching across the carpeted floors, I walked toward the wooden doors.

"Dr. Davenport, she's on a conference —"

I didn't pay any attention to her secretary, letting myself into her office. "Why is she here?" I snapped so loudly she jumped slightly in her chair, the phone almost slipping out of her hands.

"Ben, I'm going to have to call you back. Sorry," my mother said, hanging up with a smile before glaring at me. "Eli Philip Davenport, have you lost your mind?"

"No, but I'm about to. How can she still be employed?"

"Who are you talking about, and stop yelling!" she yelled ironically.

Taking a deep breath, I pinched the bridge of my nose. "Hannah. Hannah Sophia Harper. I hope she is not still working at this hospital."

"Why wouldn't she be?" She calmly placed her hands in the middle of the table. "She's a good doctor."

"Mother!" *Do not yell. Do not yell.* Again, I took a deep breath. "Mother, she can't work here. She—"

"Why, because she left you? She broke your heart? All of those are personal reasons, Eli. I can't have her fired for that, and you know it."

You've got to be kidding me. "Mom."

"Sweetheart, as your mother, every time I see her, I want to wring her skinny little neck 'til her head pops off. But as the chairwoman of this hospital, I can't get involved with personal matters between doctors. That is the risk you took when you chose to see each other. Dr. Harper is a good doctor, and this hospital employs good doctors."

"When did she come back?" I whispered.

"A week ago—"

"A week!"

She folded her arms over her chest.

"A week ago I was here, why didn't I see her?" Not that I wanted to.

"Because she asked to be put on a different floor and a different rotation than you. Why were you on peds anyway?"

"I was called in for a consult by Dr. Handler." Pinching the bridge of my nose again, I tried not to think that her request meant she didn't want to see me, either.

"Sweetheart, just avoid her until...until looking at her doesn't hurt anymore."

I couldn't deal with this. Why had I gotten involved with someone I worked with? Never. Again. With nothing left to say, I just moved to the door.

"Eli," she called.

I had to stop. Not looking back at her, I said, "Yes?"

"Believe me when I say, the moment she slips up in any way, the moment I can say she isn't good enough to be at this hospital, I will have her out of here as quickly as possible."

She was trying to comfort me, but it wouldn't work. I knew Hannah wouldn't screw up, at least not big enough to get her fired...

Well, I thought I knew her.

"Sorry for bothering you, chairwoman. I'll come over for dinner later in the week." I tried to give her a smile before closing the door behind me.

I hated this. I hated how I was torn between never wanting to see her again and hoping to run into her one more time.

Why was I like this?

Guinevere

"You can do this," I said softly to myself, staring at the five-star restaurant in front of me. I gripped the present in one hand, smoothing down my dress with the other before taking a deep breath and stepping into what I knew would be the mouth of hell itself. Reason told me I should avoid this place at all costs, yet I knew I couldn't.

You're going to be fine.

When I walked in, I noticed the place looked like an 18th century palace. Everything was either gold, white, or beige, with the exception of the blue sky painted on the ceiling, where fat angel babies danced on clouds, with harps…yes, the baby angels were playing harps.

This is so like her.

"Gwen!" She stood and waved from the table filled with other women covered in pearls and diamonds on their wrists, necks, and ears.

I almost felt the need to take the cuff earring off the top of my ear before I moved forward.

At the table, she pulled me closer to her, kissing both of my cheeks. "Gwen, you look so artistic! Guys, this is my friend, *Guinevere Poe*, she's a *famous* painter."

Stevie, what happened to you? I smiled at the people she was trying to show off for before sitting down.

"Guinevere Poe?" A woman with long, styled brown hair raised a cosmopolitan to her pink lips. "I've heard of you. Stephanie, I didn't know you were so big into the art scene."

"Oh gosh, I used to love painting, it's such a nice hobby." She laughed loudly, and with such fakeness.

I winced. *Nice hobby?*

Stevie Spencer—or Stephanie as she seemed to go by now—had come with me from our small town of Cypress, Alaska, to study art at NYU. She, however, had dropped out during her third year after meeting Nathaniel Warren Van Allan, son of something something Richie Rich. We had gotten into a big fight about it, too. I thought she had lost her mind; part of me still did. How could she just throw away everything she'd worked so hard for, just for a guy who to me didn't understand a thing about her? He looked like such a tool, and I told her so... We didn't talk to each other for a year after that. Only after I apologized did we try to rebuild our friendship, but it was much harder than even I had thought it would be. She was a whole different person.

Her red hair had always been tied into a braid so she could keep it out of paint. We never spent money on our nails, or even put that much effort into makeup and jewelry...not because there was anything wrong with that, but because it got in the way of our work, and work was everything...or it had been. Now her hair was down and fluffed up, and she wore thick, heavy makeup along with a small fortune's worth of accessories...including her engagement ring. That's why we were all there: for her bridal shower.

"Now that we are all here." The same woman who'd spoken before stood up. "Let's give a toast to the newest member of the Van Allan family. To you, Stephanie, may your life be filled with splendor. I'm so glad you and I are the best of friends, you truly are the sweetest."

"Here, here." We all raised our glasses.

"Aww, thanks you guys! And thank you so much, Josephine, for putting this together. You are amazing." Stevie laughed, giving everyone small, one-arm hugs.

"Of course! Who else would do it?"

For some reason I felt like her words were directed at me, even though I had no idea why.

"Excuse us, ladies." A server came over with three bottles of wine.

"We didn't order this," Josephine said in confusion.

"1920 Blandy's Madeira Bual, sent from Mr. Van Allan. He hopes you ladies have a beautiful evening," the server said, placing the black bottles on the table.

"Oh my gosh," the ladies whispered.

Stevie looked like she was going to cry.

Leaning over, I put my arm around her and whispered, "You'll ruin your makeup if you cry, Stevie. If Nathaniel hears you cried over a glass of wine, he's going to think he did something wrong."

She laughed and nodded. "I know! But he's just so sweet."

The ladies giggled. "Nothing says love like twenty thousand dollar wine."

"Twenty thousand? Dollars?" I gasped, looking at the deep red liquid in my hand. "I feel like it should at least come with a gift or something, for that price."

Stevie let out a small laugh next to me, but she was the only one.

The others just raised their eyebrows at me.

"The gift is the taste." Josephine smiled at me. "Ms. Poe, believe me when I say you will never forget your first glass of Bual."

"With that price, I can't afford to," I whispered to Stevie.

She elbowed me, one hand over her lips to hide a smile. *Maybe she isn't that different.*

"Wait, you're Sebastian Evan's Guinevere!" Josephine gasped, turning toward me, though she didn't seem that shocked.

"No—"

"Isn't your wedding in like, two weeks? Where is your ring?" She leaned closer to look at my fingers.

I slid my hands slowly under the table.

"Josephine, that isn't really..." Stevie tried to figure out what to say.

I put my hands on hers and smiled, looking back to the rest of the waiting women. "Our wedding—"

"Oh my god, did he really leave you for someone else's bride?" One of the women lifted up her cellphone. "I just googled him. He owns *Class* and *Rebel* magazines, right? Is this true?"

There were gasps and a few shocked giggles. Some women covered their mouths as they waited for me to respond.

Reaching into the middle of the table, I grabbed the bottle, poured myself a full glass, and drank. I didn't stop until I'd finished the whole thing.

"Yes..." I paused for a second with my hand on my chest to keep from burping. "Yes, it's all true, and I don't have to give you details about it, nor would any of you find it worth giggling about it if had happened to you. Do you have more questions, Josephine? Or would you like to actually talk about the upcoming wedding of our dear friend here?"

"I'm sorry, I didn't know—"

"Of course you didn't. Let's just not talk about it again so you don't look like a horrible person." I smiled, shifting the bottle back into the middle of the table. "And you were right, I'm sure I'll never forget that glass."

"Well, maybe you've had enough," she announced to the rest of the ladies at the table.

I felt like asking what the hell her problem was. What had I done to her?

Stevie squeezed my arm. "Gwen, that's enough," she whispered.

I didn't know how much longer I could do this. If it hadn't been for Stevie, I would have left a while ago—or probably never come there at all. I could see I didn't fit in with these people, and I couldn't lie, it bothered me how well Stevie did.

"My favorite story of Stephanie is..." Josephine tried to think, and then snapped her polished fingers. "When we were in Brunello Cucinelli, trying to find gifts for Nathaniel and David, but we didn't know their sizes, so we pulled over the clerks and had them wear the clothes—"

"Josephine!" Stevie giggled, smacking her napkin at her.

"I promise you, no clerks were hurt in the process." Josephine went on as the rest joined Stevie in laughing.

I just smiled. It sounded fun...sort of. I guessed it was one of those things where you just had to be there.

When their giggles died down, they looked to me, waiting.

"Oh, it's my turn." I sat up, grinning.

"Oh, good." Stevie put her head in her hands.

"Well, you might not know this, but Stevie and I were the biggest tomboys in Cypress, and we always got in trouble with the boys—"

"No, you got in trouble with the boys. I stood in the background," she replied, pointing at me before drinking.

"Really? Who pushed poor Jeremy in the river with the sockeye salmon and threw fish food at him because he said she looked like a redheaded bear?"

She coughed, almost spitting out her wine.

"She what?" Josephine frowned, confused. "What happened after?"

"Jeremy screamed like a baby and never called me a red-headed bear ever again," Stevie said, proudly nodding her head.

I nodded along with her.

Josephine faked a laugh. "If I was Jeremy's mother, I would have been so angry. He could have gotten hurt."

"Who do you think gave her the fish food?" I muttered, drinking water this time.

"Good ol' Cypress," Stevie whispered.

I wondered if she missed it as much as I did. Our small town had sometimes felt like a prison when I was in it, but now that we had left, I could see all its little charms. By accident, I glanced to my right, and for a second, I thought I saw him.

Bash?

It's just the alcohol.

However, when I saw the blonde woman beside him flip her hair off her shoulder, I stood up.

"Gwen?" Stevie stood up beside me. "Are you okay—"

"I have to go." I gathered up my things as fast as I could, but when I turned to leave, I ran into the server bringing in all of our desserts. The silver platter slipped, pouring all over me before falling to the carpet, and my first instinct was to look up to see if he had seen. I thought he must have moved because I couldn't see him.

"I'm so sorry, I'm so sorry…" I said to her. "I have to go. Sorry, Stevie."

I ran. I ran as fast as I could, my purse and jacket in hand. My ankle twisted once, but, ignoring it, I just threw myself out the door, the cold air blowing across my face.

"Gwen!"

I didn't want to look back.

She caught up to me and placed her hand on my shoulder. "Gwen, what is it?"

"He's in there, Stevie. I saw him, he and she—"

"Gwen." She gripped my sides. "He wasn't there. It looked like him for a second, but when he looked over after the plates shattered…it wasn't him."

"Not him?" I echoed in a whisper.

She shook her head. "No. Come back inside."

I wanted to smack myself. "I'm so sorry, Stevie."

"It's okay, come back inside and let's order dessert."

"Look at me, I'm a mess. I'm just going to sit this one out. I don't want to mess this up any more for you, okay? I'm sorry, please go back in. Your friends are all waiting! This is supposed to be happy, remember? Go be happy. I'm okay, I swear." It was a lie.

She looked me over.

I forced a smile, giving her a little push. "Go, or I promise I will tell even more embarrassing stories at your wedding. I can even gather photos."

"I'm going, I'm going." She lifted her hands and backed up. "Text me later?"

I just nodded and waved, because I knew if I said any more I wouldn't be able to keep it in, and it wasn't fair to take over her day worse than I already had. When she went in, I turned and walked quickly, trying to use my coat to hide the stains on my dress, wiping the tears from my eyes. *God, this sucks. Why am I like this? It wasn't even him.*

Eli

I pressed the close button for the elevator doors when she *limped* in, heels in her hands and a mess of something all over her blue dress. Her mascara was smeared, and she just stood there as the doors closed and we went up.

"Rough day?" she asked me.

It was funny, but I couldn't laugh. "Yes. You all right?"

"Yep," she said when the door opened, and we just went into our separate apartments.

Chapter Seven
We Are Not Okay

Guinevere

I was just deciding whether or not to knock on his door when he opened it wide, a first aid kit in his hands.

"What are you doing?" His eyebrows furrowed together and he took a slight step back.

"I don't have a first aid kit yet, so I was going to ask to borrow yours," I said quickly. "But never mind, I will just buy one tomorrow."

"I figured." He laughed, though he didn't seem to find it funny. He held up the first aid kit. "I was going to give this to you."

"Oh, thanks—" I reached for the kit.

He pulled it back, staring down at my ankle as I balanced on my other leg. "How bad is it?" He knelt in front of me. "Did you feel anything pop?"

"No, it's fine." I put my foot all the way on the ground, only to wince and lift it up again.

"That is not fine. Come in." He took my elbow, helping me inside.

"Eli—"

"Keep walking." He guided me toward his gray sofa.

Everything in his apartment was either navy, gray, or off-white, and annoyingly clean like one of those show homes or...well, like a hospital.

"Sit," he commanded when we reached the sofa.

"I'm not a dog—"

Sighing, he just pushed me back slowly.

When my butt hit the couch, I felt the urge to just lean back into it. The thing was so soft. "This is nice..." I whispered, running my hand over the cushions.

"Isn't it? It's called a couch, a marvelous invention really. With all that empty space in your place, I wasn't sure if you knew about such items." He sat on his wooden coffee table, lifting up my leg.

"You are not funny—ah." I winced as he pressed around my ankle.

"What happened?" He finally looked up.

"Why do you care?"

"Because if people see you coming in like that, the value of this place might go down."

Reaching up, I tried to smack him.

He squeezed my ankle.

"Ouch! What happened to 'do no harm'?"

"Sorry, just checking to see if you tore anything." He shrugged, a small smirk on his lips betraying the lie. "You're going to need to ice this first," he muttered to himself, taking out a large, square instant ice pack. "After the swelling goes down, I'll compress it. Hand me that pillow."

Reaching over, I handed him the navy pillow.

He put it under my leg. "Is there some possible way you could mange to keep still for about twenty minutes? I know it might be hard, but—"

"I don't know, Dr. Davenport. I am five years old." I rolled my eyes, shifting my foot again when he left it on the pillow and walked around the couch. "Thank you," I muttered.

"What was that?" he pressed, even though I was sure he had heard me.

This man is trying to annoy me to death. "I said thank you!" I shouted.

"Okay, jeez, no need to yell."

Shifting, I turned to look back at him.

He gave me a blank look, holding up a bottle of beer and waving it. "Want some? I also have Coke, and—"

"Do you have vanilla ice cream?" I sounded so excited, I could tell he was fighting back a comment.

"Sadly, I hate vanilla, so that would be a no."

"How do you hate vanilla? It's the cornerstone of ice cream."

"No, that would be chocolate. So, are you saying no to the beer then?"

He was being too nice. "Does it come with a catch?"

"Tell me what happened?"

"No, thank you, I'm fine." I faced front again, where he, like all guys I knew, had a massive television hanging on the wall.

"Suit yourself." He took a seat beside me, popping off the cap and flicking on the TV to a man trying to walk across a tightrope between two mountains.

I turned, not looking at the screen.

"What?"

"Nothing?"

"Why are you looking at me, then?"

"Sorry." I shifted, staring up at the clock.

"Are you afraid of heights? It's so bad you can't even look at it?"

"No."

"All right. Right now, he's about 180 feet off the ground—"

"I have a fear of heights."

"Seriously?"

I glared at him.

He changed the channel to Animal Planet.

"Better?" he asked, nodding to the sea turtles.

"Much."

"So demanding," he muttered, drinking his beer.

We were silent for a while, watching the turtles swim slowly across the bottom of the sea. The silence, and him comfortably drinking without me, made me sing like a canary.

"I hurt my ankle running away from a restaurant. I thought I saw Bash—Sebastian and Hannah together, so I tried to leave, but knocked over a waiter who spilled ice cream on me." I sighed.

He didn't say anything, just rested back against the couch and handed me his beer. "But it wasn't them, right? He and Hann—they weren't on a date?" he asked softly, watching the sea turtles on the screen.

"No, I was wrong, which made me feel like even more of an idiot, so I just limped my pitiful self back home and took a shower. That's my story." I handed the bottle back to him.

He took a long sip, and then stared at the bottle. "I actually saw her today. It wasn't a mistake; she was really there. She's been at the hospital for a week, and I didn't know. When I saw her, I almost had a panic attack in the elevator. So, which one of us is actually more pitiful?"

"What would you say to her if you came face to face with her? I've thought about it so many times, that big confrontation. That moment where I could just walk up to him and tell him how badly he hurt me, how...how I felt."

He drank again. "Hi."

"What? You'd just say hi?"

"Yes." He nodded. "Telling her I was hurt or showing anger just means I still care. It means in some way, I'm still connected to her. That's why I want to just say hi, not like nothing happened, but like it is so far removed from my current reality that it no longer matters." He looked proud of that thought, but the pride faded from his eyes. "I don't think I will be able to do that, though, which is why I'm pitiful."

"I still have you beat today, though," I said.

He finally looked at me. "Why?"

"Because I embarrassed myself in front of the future true housewives of New York. What's worse is, in three weeks I have to go to a wedding with all of them there. You would not believe how out of place I looked—"

"Oh, I can, believe me." He laughed, finishing the rest of the beer.

"Hey! We are supposed to be helping each other here."

"I thought we were just sulking."

He had a point. "Can't we do both? How do you know I looked out of place?"

"Well…" He tilted his head back.

"Well what?"

"You don't really scream 'I'm a millionaire', now do you?"

"What does that mean? Am I supposed to wear a t-shirt or something?"

"That could help." He laughed.

My hands rose and clenched in his face before I dropped them.

"No, but really. You have your own style; you wear combat boots with dresses. That's fine, but don't expect to be treated like an equal by people who live and breathe Prada."

"I have heels."

"But are they designer?"

I crossed my arms. "Why in the hell would I spend that much money on shoes?"

"That is it." He pointed at me. "Your first thought is the price, even though you could afford it. For people like them, their first thought is: does it look nice? You don't fit in because you don't fit in. You don't see the world like they do."

"You say them and they, but last I checked aren't you filthy, stupid rich?"

He shook his head. "My family is rich. I, Eli, am just financially stable."

"You know that's exactly what a rich kid would say, right?"

He shifted, looking back at the television. "So what do you do with all that money you con off...I mean, earn from your art?"

"Don't think I don't know that slip was not by accident, and to answer your question, I run a few charities—what? Why are you looking at me like that?"

"A few charities?" His eyebrow rose. "Really? Who are you, Mother Theresa? You have to have something you use that money on. One thing you splurge for; everyone has something."

"I guess it would be..." I paused.

"Are you going to continue your sentence or just keep staring off into space?"

I turned to watch the sea turtles.

He turned off the TV.

"What do you spend your financially stable money on, then?"

"Nice clothes, watches, mostly cars..."

"Rich." I coughed, placing my hand on my throat. "You are just like them."

"I never said there was anything wrong with them. I just said you were different, and don't pretend like there is anything hotter than a well-dressed man...a well-dressed me, for that matter."

God, could his ego get any bigger?

"So what do you splurge on? Share."

"It's nothing, traveling and..." I drifted off.

"Guinevere I-would-say-your-middle-name-but-I don't-know-it Poe, what do you splurge on?" He sat straighter. "It can't be..."

"What?" I felt like his eyes were piercing through me.

A grin spread across his face like he knew, and he turned on the TV again. "Nothing."

"What?"

He shrugged. "It's just, the only thing a woman like you would be nervous to admit would have to be sex."

"It's not sex!"

"You're getting really defensive right now."

"It's romance novels." I had a collection in my room that would make some women jealous.

"Knew it." He smirked.

"That isn't sex."

"Please, you're telling me you splurge on Dickens? Let me guess, you've got everything from *Pride and Prejudice* to *Fifty Shades of Grey*."

I hate this man so much. "They are books—"

"Oh come on, it's porn on paper, and you had the nerve to knock on my door, telling me I was too loud."

"You won't let that go?"

"Some of us like to actually experience sex in the real world and not just in our heads, thank you very much."

My hands lifted as if to strangle him, but I dropped them.

"At least you're not as prudish as I thought, you're just a closet—"

I slapped my hand over his mouth. "First, whatever you were going to say, don't say it. And second, just because

I'm not screwing men against my wall doesn't make me a prude." I took my hand off his face.

"Why not? You're not married, not engaged, you are a free person. No point in not living it up and enjoying yourself—"

"Those women you slept with, did they make you feel better? And I don't mean while you were doing it or right after. When they left and you were alone, did you feel better? Tell me you did, and I will go out tomorrow night and bring a guy home."

He got up, taking a seat on the coffee table again as he grabbed my ankle and started working on the compression wrap.

I didn't flinch this time. "I guess that's my cue to le—"

"I felt nothing." He looked me dead in the eye, emotionless, his face almost scary. "You're right. I brought them back, stripped them down, fucked them every way I could think of until neither of us could walk, and I still felt nothing afterward. But what would you have me do, Guinevere? Pine after her? Read books about some perfect person who doesn't exist? I was ready to give her my life, my name, everything I was, everything I owned; I was about to give it to her, and she threw it back in my face like it meant nothing. So yes, I fuck women, and in that moment, I feel great. I'd rather have that moment than nothing, because nothing hurts. You should know." When he finished, he gathered up everything on the table and walked into his kitchen.

Getting up, I said nothing, glancing back to him only once before I left his apartment. When I entered mine, Taigi came up to me, rubbing against my legs and following me into my bedroom. The only things in there were the bed and my floor-to-ceiling wall of books. Sitting in the center of my bed, I stared at it all. My books weren't nothing…they were all different little dreams.

He had sex to provide his moment of relief.

I read about it, and the characters' lives.

We were just the same.

Eli

How was it possible? Even with raging music in the background, she was still in my head. When Guinevere left, I got dressed and called Logan, heading to Rue 83, which was currently the hottest club in the city; I figured it had another two or three weeks before people found something new. This was New York; nothing was "cool" for long.

"You were the one who invited me here, and yet I'm having all the fun. What's up with you?" Logan asked, resting against the bar, his eyes on a pretty brunette behind me.

"Don't have fun, be miserable," I muttered to him, downing my scotch.

"Whoa. No seriously, what is wrong with you?"

"Guinevere Poe," I said, grabbing another shot. "By the way, what is her full name? I can't curse her properly when I can't say her entire name."

"How the hell would I know?"

"You were the one who put her in my face. Don't you remember? You invited her fiancé to my wedding, and when they ran off, all that was left was Guinevere and Eli, *les misérables.*" *Why are there two of him?* I felt…drunk. "So you shouldn't be having fun, you should be miserable like us."

"Mom said you saw Hannah today. Is that what this is?"

"No." I smiled, patting his shoulder. "Everything can't be about Hannah. I can't have my life revolve around her. My anger is toward Guinevere tonight, for making me self-analyze when I didn't want to. Now, if you'll excuse

me, I need to seduce a woman because that's what I do."
Spinning around in the chair, I tried to find someone, anyone, really. However, no matter where I looked, it seemed
like all I could see was her heart-shaped face and big brown
eyes everywhere.

Did it make you feel better? Her voice replayed in my mind.

Sighing, I turned back to the bar.

"What happened to seducing—"

"Just go have fun, Logan." I nodded for the bartender to
pour me another glass.

*Note to self: just stay away from women. They can fuck with
your head and heart way too easily. There must be a school for it or
something.*

Chapter Eight
The Cat's Meow

Guinevere

A week had gone by without Eli and I speaking, or seeing each other, for that matter. After that night, we did our best to avoid each other. It rained almost every day, and it was just easier to put a hood up or hide under an umbrella until I was safely within my apartment. I wasn't sure why I kept thinking about him. Every time I closed my eyes, I saw him: laughing at me, or helping me, or just listening. What I missed most of all was him just being there and listening. I felt bad that even though I didn't mean to be judgmental, I often came off so. I couldn't help it, but that wasn't really an excuse either.

I could see him today.

Why do I care?

Because I need to apologize.

"Guinevere, you made it."

The sound of Mrs. Davenport's voice pulled me out of my mental battle. She wore a nice, simple beige dress under a white coat, with her gray-auburn hair pinned back. "I'm sorry it's taken so long for me to get back to you about this mural—"

"It's fine, I wasn't expecting you to drop everything and come straight over to me. How are you, my dear?"

"I'm well, thank you. I was wondering, should I call you Mrs. Davenport, or Dr. Davenport?" She was the chairwoman after all, and she was wearing a white coat.

"Whichever makes you more comfortable. Please, let me show you where I would like the mural." She turned to lead the way.

I followed, closing the distance as we walked. I found my eyes shifting from the nurses, doctors, and patients, to the floors and walls, the different blues, whites, and grays.

Like Eli's apartment. I snickered at that. I was right; he had set up his apartment to match the hospital. *I wonder if he even realized it.* Why do I care?

"Guinevere, did you hear me?"

Crap. "No, I'm sorry, what were you saying? And please, call me Gwen."

Nodding, she repeated herself. "I asked, have you thought of anything to put up? Or done a mural before?"

"Yes, I have done a few, but never for a hospital. My first work was painting a mural at my high school; I think it is still up. I probably won't know what to paint for a while, and my ideas might even change, unless you have thought of something?"

"Sadly, no." She frowned, crossing her arms as we stopped before a large black and white wall with the hospital logo hanging on it. "For years, I've walked past here always feeling like something is missing. It's so cold, but I can never think of what should be here instead. So if you have any ideas at all, I'll leave it up to you."

Having a client tell you to 'do whatever' was both an artist's dream and worst nightmare. Yes, it gave me creative freedom, but what if they hated it? Stepping forward, I ran my hands across the wall before looking up.

"Is it too big? You don't have to cover the whole wall—"

"No, it's fine. I think I can manage, but I will really have to think about this for a couple of days and sketch. And I have two requests."

"Okay."

"The first: do you mind if I walk around the hospital for a while, just to get ideas? I'll do my best to stay out of everyone's way. I usually take photos, but I realize that might be a problem here."

She thought for a moment before nodding. "That's fine, but please be mindful. And your second request?"

"Would it be possible for me to put up a sheet or something?"

Her eyebrows furrowed together. "A sheet?"

"When I start working, I prefer if people aren't watching me, and it helps to keep people back. Oftentimes, people are tempted to touch. I have no idea why, but they are." And it drove me insane.

"Yes, that's fine. When can you start?"

"Tomorrow, but for now I will just measure and think." I pulled out my sketchpad.

"Well, please let me know if you need anything, all right? You have my number, and I'll be walking around—"

"She means spying."

We both turned toward Eli as he approached in his dark blue scrubs and white coat. He handed a cup of what smelled like tea to his mother before drinking from the other one he held.

"I would never spy—"

"Oh please, you hate surprises. I bet she will be down here every other day, trying to get a peek at what you're doing."

"Your lack of faith in me hurts." She frowned, facing me. "I might come down sometimes, but I won't say a thing—"

"You'll just feel her eyes burning a hole in the back of your head—ouch." He stopped when she grabbed his arm.

"I'm going to go before I harm one of my most *precious* doctors. Thank you again, Gwen."

"I still don't think we need a mural!" he called as her heels clicked down the hospital hallway.

"You think of your patients, I'll worry about the hospital." She waved, but didn't turn back as she drank her beverage.

He shook his head. "She didn't even say thank you for the tea."

"Do mothers really ever have to say thank you?" My mother's comeback was always that she deserved it for giving birth to me.

"Do a decent—" He stopped when his beeper went off. Grabbing it, his eyes widened, then he took off running. It wasn't just him. All the doctors around me were paged, one by one, and each ran off in the same direction as Eli.

It was hard not to panic at a sight like that. Part of me wanted to leave, but another part of me, the part controlling my feet, slowly walked down the dark blue line they had run along, gripping my bag as I went.

At the end of the blue line I saw "ER" written above the entrance. Staying toward the corner, I watched as men, women, and small children were rolled in by paramedics.

"How many victims?" A nurse holding bags of bandages and gauze ran past me as if I wasn't even there.

"They don't know," the other nurse replied. "Apparently the truck's tire went down in a sinkhole and caused a ripple effect on the highway, but it wasn't the only one. A summer camp bus flipped trying to avoid—"

"Bunhead!" Eli yelled, lifting a little boy onto the bed.

The girl, who did indeed have her blonde hair pulled into a bun, ran toward him.

"Did you look him over?" Eli questioned, looking into the boy's ears.

"He said he was okay. His nose was hurt, but I checked and it was fine. His sister was worse—"

"Stop talking."

She jumped, closing her mouth.

"Breathe. You said his nose was hurting. Sinus pressure. His eardrums are ruptured, you need to..."

"Page EMT and administer antibiotics for the cuts, and check up every 30—"

He gave her a stern look.

"15 minutes to make sure that was all."

"Dr. Davenport!" another doctor called from the door.

"Bunhead, keep an eye on him," he ordered, already walking over to another room. He and the rest of them were everywhere, moving from one patient to another. Some who were in far worse condition were rushed right out of the room toward surgery. Eli stayed back for most of it.

Even in the chaos I focused on him, running back and forth as wave after wave of new bloody, crying, screaming patients were brought in. It was like he was on autopilot— he had to be. Nothing fazed him, not even when an older woman threw up all over his tennis shoes. Instead of jumping back, he held her gray head until someone brought over a small bucket.

"Sorry. I am so—"

"There is no need to apologize, Mrs. Miller. Do you still feel like the room is spinning?"

I didn't think I would ever admit it to him, but that day I thought he was pretty amazing. All of them were. It went without saying, but seeing it with my own two eyes—and though I loved what I did for a living—in that moment I kind of wished I was a badass doctor, too.

At least now I can think of a way to apologize to him, and a sketch.

Eli

I dropped my shoes in the trash, along with my socks and the gloves I still had on, before falling onto the couch in the attending's lounge. My whole body ached, and not in the way I liked. It had been one of those days that just kept kicking you when you were already down. I had been feeling like crap for a week and I had no idea why.

"God, what is that smell?" I heard someone say as they entered.

I didn't lift my arm from over my eyes. "That would be the trash and my shoes." More from my shoes than the trash, but whatever.

"Yep." He must have sniffed. "Aftermath of the highway accident?"

Nodding, I tried to drown out the voice of Dr. Ian Seo, a plastic surgeon attending of both Korean and American decent whose calm and relaxed voice frustrated me to no end. Every day he enjoyed a fresh, home-cooked lunch he'd had time to prepare...because, well, he was a plastic surgeon. He would take his time, walking through the hospital as if nothing was going on, sucking fat from women who barely had any to begin with, doing a few breast and butt lifts before calling it a day. Every time I saw him, I wondered why I too had not chosen the path of serenity that was plastics.

Because I would gouge out my eyes from boredom, that's why. I laughed at that, sitting upright, then rolled my eyes at him eating his banana-flavored yogurt, his black hair pulled into a small ponytail and his dark-eyed gaze on me. "Why are you still here, anyway? You're usually gone by five."

"Aw, you noticed?"

"How can I not? That's when my headaches stop." I got up and headed to my locker.

"You are hurtful."

"I know." I smiled, pulling open the door. No longer paying attention to him, I was surprised to find a pair of navy and white Nike men's tennis shoes waiting for me.

What in the hell? The note on the laces read:

Dr. Davenport,

Here. Sorry for judging you.

~~You did well today.~~

~~You were kinda cool today.~~

~~I won't be calling you Dr. Asshole again.~~

If the shoes don't fit, sorry again, I guessed, receipt is in the box.

~~See you at home.~~

~~See you back at the apartment.~~

Bye,

Gwen.

She could not be serious. Had she even thought this through before writing it? Oh dear god, why hadn't she used a new piece of paper?

"What is so funny?" Dr. Seo said when I looked up.

"What?"

He pointed his spoon at me. "The smile on your face right now, it's blinding me. What is so funny?"

"I'm not smiling, because nothing is funny—"

"I took a picture." He held up his phone, the photo showing me in profile.

"You what!"

"And I just sent it to everyone in the hospital!" He clicked a button.

I was tempted to cause him bodily harm. "Are you twelve? What is wrong with you?"

"No one would believe me if I said you smiled." He shrugged. "I had to prove it." *What is this, junior high?*

"I smile all the time, you ass," I muttered, grabbing the shoes and undoing the laces.

He snorted, licking the lid to his second yogurt. "That thing you do with your face to patients does not count as a smile."

"You are an—" I stopped when I slipped my feet in, and sure enough, the shoes fit perfectly. My feet relaxed into the soft foam. *How in the hell did she know my shoe size?*

Click. Glancing up, I saw that the asshole had taken another photo of me.

"You were doing it again! Now you've got to tell me."

Putting on the other shoe, I got up and grabbed his stupid phone from his grimy little fingers, walked over to the bin, and dropped it inside.

"Hey! I just got that!"

"Not my problem," I replied, turning to leave, but stopping when he came over to the trash. "Take any more photos of me, and I will tell the chairwoman what you did in the fourth floor lab."

"That's your big threat? You'll tell Mommy?"

I pulled out my phone and began to dial.

He sighed. "Fine."

"Goodnight, Ian."

Leaving the lounge, I tried my best not to make eye contact with any of the staff who I could tell had gotten his bloody photo. They giggled, and it made me want to go over there and grab all of them.

Making it to the front entrance, I stopped when I saw her, still in her dark ripped jeans, yellow v-neck shirt, combat boots, and hat. She leaned against the wall under the hospital sign, bopping her head to whatever she was listening to as she drew.

She's busy. But, I should thank her for the shoes. Without realizing it, I had already walked to her. She was so into her own little world, she didn't notice me until I dropped down in front of her and waved.

"Jesus Christ of Nazareth, you scared me." She jumped, hugging her drawing to her chest. I couldn't deny my eyes were glued to her breasts for a half a second as she pulled out her earphones.

"I scared you?" I replied, sitting next to her.

"All day, no one has seen me." She laughed, closing her book.

"What are you, a ghost? What do you mean no one saw you?" She was kind of hard to miss.

She shrugged. "You doctor *folk* are focused. I spent most of my time floating, looking for ideas for your mother's mural."

"It's not my mother's mural, so don't go painting a giant portrait of her just because she is paying you."

She rolled her eyes. "Don't worry, I've come up with some pretty good ideas. It came a lot faster than I thought it would."

"Let me see?" I reached for her book.

She hugged it again.

"What?"

"No one is going to see it until it's finished. I have a process."

"Jeez, you artists are so emotional." I backed away.

She kicked her foot against mine.

"Watch it, I just got these."

"Hey." She leaned up off the wall, grinning. "You're wearing them! They fit?"

"I wouldn't be wearing them if they didn't fit. How in the world did you know my size, anyway?"

"I was pretty much a tomboy growing up—"

"Shocker."

She glared at me. "I'm sure you were a charmer as a teenager."

"Of course. Just look at me."

"I am—"

"*Anyway,* you were a tomboy?" I pressed on, before she forgot what she had originally been saying.

"Oh yeah. I spent most of my time with this group of boys from my neighborhood. We all basically grew up together, and we were always barefoot in the rivers. I can kind of guess a guy's shoe size when I compare it to theirs in my head."

In the rivers? "Where are you from?"

"Cypress, Alaska, home of the best wild salmon in the country." She raised her head up and nodded.

"Wow." I couldn't stop laughing. "Is that really a place? Cypress? Alaska? You?"

"It is a real place, and it's more beautiful than a city boy like you can handle." She pouted.

"It is the home of *the* best wild salmon in the country... I'm sure I could handle it just fine," I repeated back with a smile.

She got up. "You are such a—"

I cut her off, standing up. "Thank you for the shoes. You didn't have to say sorry for anything, though your note was funny."

"Urgh. I ran out of paper, and I didn't want to bug the nurses any more than I already was to put it in your locker," she muttered.

"So, that's how—" I paused when I saw her come through the glass hospital doors. Her blonde hair was done and she wore a straight skirt and light pink blouse. Since her shift was opposite mine, she was most likely arriving to start hers. I had waited around too long.

"What are you looking at?" Guinevere tried to turn around.

I grabbed her sides, holding her in front of me.

"What are you doing?"

"Do you have all of your stuff?"

"Yes, why—"

Taking her by the hand, I kept my head down, trying to make it out the doors before Hannah faced us.

I almost made it, too.

"She's—" Guinevere stopped.

Damn it.

"Guinevere," I said to her, hoping Hannah would just keep walking, but luck was never on my side.

She whipped her hair to the side as she faced us.

"Let's go," Guinevere replied, allowing me to take her outside again. We didn't stop until we could only see the distant light of the hospital disappearing behind us as we entered the park. Neither of us said anything, and it took me a second to realize I was still holding her hand. I dropped it.

"Do you feel sixteen?" she whispered, looking up at the sky.

I thought about her question for a second. "Running probably was the least mature thing we could have done."

"Screw being mature, it's a pain in the ass anyway," she muttered. "I forgot that was her hospital, too. You told me, I know, but I forgot. What if I see her?"

"Throw paint on her," I joked.

She giggled. "That would probably make her feel better...she would think we're even or something. I guess it would be best to do what you've been doing—"

"Avoiding? Running? No, I'm tired of doing that." I really was, but what I found odder was the fact that I was more worried about her making a scene than anything else. It would just be messy for my mother and the hospital.

As we walked silently, I felt like there was something between us. For the first time, I really thought of her as a friend.

"What is it now?" She moved in front of my face.

"What?"

"You have this weird look on your face."

"Move. I have no idea what you're talking about."

CHAPTER NINE
A CRY FOR HELP

Eli

Looking to my phone, I stared at the background, her painting of a small boy just standing in the rain, an umbrella broken at his feet.

What is she doing right now?

After thinking for a second, I texted her.

'Con artist.'

'I thought we were being civil!'

I grinned. *'Sorry, force of habit.'*

'Yea sure, Dr. Asshole.' … *'Sorry, force of habit.'*

'Are you here?' I hadn't seen her that morning.

'Waiting on supplies. Won't be there til later. You still at the hospital?'

'Getting off now. Drinks tonight?'

'If you're buying.'

'Cheapskate.'

'Think of it as a compliment that I trust your alcohol choices.'

"Sorry," a nurse said as she bumped into me, the charts in her hands dropping to the ground.

"It's fine. I wasn't paying attention," I replied, picking them up when I saw Molly's chart.

"She lost most of her hair this morning," the nurse said as I read through. "It's been a tough day."

"I'll check on her before I go. Thanks." I started walking down the hall.

However, when I got to her room, a few nurses and interns were lingering around along with Dr. Seo, who leaned against the nurse's desk, looking down at his watch a few times before looking back into the room. I checked to make sure Molly was all right from the window and sure enough, she was siting up on the bed, her head covered with a bright blue scarf. She looked pale, but other than that she was fine.

"What's going on?" I moved to Ian.

"TWM is having a huge board meeting at two o'clock today?" He answered like I should know what he was talking about.

"TWM? The computer software and robotics company? And their board meeting means what to you again?" *Or anyone else for that matter.*

He looked at me like I was an idiot. "TWM, otherwise known as Toby Wesley Mechanics, or the company your patient's father is founder and CEO of? It's a coup Eli. It's been in all the papers. They are going to kick him out of the company he started in his brother's living room while his daughter is fighting cancer. It's the most fucked up thing I've heard in a while. Everyone is waiting to see if he's going to go."

Taking a quick glance down at my watch, I saw it was 1:23pm; I looked back to everyone just hovering over them like they were in some sort of zoo.

"I swear, if you all aren't back at your stations by the time I get to that door I will make it my mission to have you fired from this hospital," I stated, already heading to the door.

I heard them scattering and when I turned back, Ian was the only one still standing there.

"Ian—"

"Sorry, I got distracted. Your heart is growing three times in size."

"Go!"

His phone rang and, not answering it, he danced right past me singing loudly to "Feels Good" by his favorite South Korean band Super Junior...the very fact that I knew that bothered me more than I could bear to explain.

I've spent too much time around him.

Concentrating on the task in front of me, I entered the room to find Toby sitting next to Molly watching the coverage of a block party on the television.

"Hi, Dr. Eli." Molly waved and her father stood up quickly, moving to me.

"Hi Molly, how are you feeling?"

"Not sick," she whispered, hugging her bear to her chest.

"That's good. I'm going to talk to your dad for a second, all right?" She nodded, just watching the television quietly.

He followed me out, and no sooner had I closed the door than he started pressing for answers.

"Has the tumor gone down? Can you operate? She's feeling really good today so I was—"

"Toby." I stopped him. "I don't have any news about Molly's condition and I'm sorry if I've given you the wrong message by coming. I came because I'm worried about you right now."

"Me? I'm fine. If you have nothing new then—"

"I heard about your meeting today," I said when he reached the door.

His grip tightened. "That is none of your concern."

"Yes I know. I'm overstepping right now, but I wanted to know if you really want to hand over your company to a bunch of sons of bitches who can't even allow you time with

95

your daughter. I don't know much about TWM, but I remember your motto being all about making life better for others."

"Innovation today for a customer's better tomorrow," he said, letting go of the door and hanging his blond head. He stood there for a moment and finally turned to me. "I dropped out of college, lived off cereal and noodles building TWM. I still remember when I bought my first actual office on top of a Chinese restaurant. It was just me, my girlfriend, and my brother. I thought I had really made it then... Now I have over a hundred thousand employees across the country; believe it or not, I know all their names."

"I believe you, and I believe you don't want to just give up and hand them over to the vultures surrounding you right now."

He shook his head. "Eli, I don't care. If they want to take TWM, let them take it. I won't leave my daughter alone, especially not today. Not the day I lost my wife and she lost her mother. My daughter can't even go to the block party. I won't sit in a board room listening to their bullshit—"

"I'll take her." *Why am I going this far? What the hell is wrong with me!*

"What?" His eyebrows frowned together.

"The meeting will take what, an hour? Two? Molly can't be outside without being monitored, so while you go and beat the shit out of the suits, I will go with her to the party. I'll make sure she has a good time, and then you can meet up with us."

"Eli—"

"It's 1:31. You can still make it. I have your information, and my driver will pick up Molly and me—"

"Why?" He cut me off. "Why are you going this far? We live in the same building, but we aren't friends. You didn't even know me when I came in here. So why?"

I thought about it for a moment, and all I could think of was Guinevere and what she had once said to me.

"Do you know how many crappy people we meet a day in this city? I don't want to be one of them. Sometimes we just need help and it's hard asking for it, so I'm going to offer it. Accept it Toby. Don't give up yet; what kind of example does that set for Molly? Instead of giving up when the world knocks you on your ass, sometimes it's okay to ask for help," I replied, stretching out my hand for him.

He looked down and swallowed. "Please help me, Eli."

"Of course."

As happy as I was to help him, for some reason I wanted to call up Guinevere and tell her I wasn't as much as a pathetic asshole as she thought.

"Molly, you're going to the party with Dr. Eli," he said when he opened the door.

Guinevere

"Stevie?" I said when I opened my door.

"Hi," she replied. She stood there in jeans and a t-shirt, her red hair pulled back and her eyes red and puffy.

I wasn't sure what was wrong with her, but I walked out and hugged her tightly. She cried on my shoulder. There were about a thousand things going through my mind and all I could think was to get her to calm down.

"I have wine and chocolate, which I would rather not eat alone." I took her hand, pulling her into my apartment. Taigi came up to her while I went for the glasses.

"Hey boy, how are you?" She sniffled and laughed, rubbing her hands through his fur. He barked in her face and stood on his hind legs for her, while she took his paw as if dancing with him.

After pouring a glass for each of us, I handed one to her. "You have to taste this, my do-not-covet thy neighbor's father made it and it is to die for—"

I paused, holding my glass as she drank the whole thing without once stopping for air, like a woman dying of thirst. Using her hand, she wiped her lips and held it up for more.

"It's really good." She smiled.

"Could you even taste it?" I questioned, handing her my glass.

She didn't drink, just stared at it. "I'm making a mistake, right Gwen? Marrying Nathaniel…I'm making a mistake."

"Stevie, what happened?" I asked instead of answering, because I didn't know how to answer that question.

"We got in a fight," she whispered, holding the glass to her lips. "More like his parents and I had a fight and he just stood there while they kept going on about how they expected him to marry someone better. I wondered, is this going to be my whole life? I'm going to have to stand there and take their shit because my dad is just an electrical repairman and my mother is a baker?"

"Just an electrical repairman?" I wanted her to rethink that statement. "Remember when we were thirteen and I was staying at your house when Winter Storm Michael came in? Eight and a half feet of snow and ice, it knocked out the power, and it was so cold we shared three blankets. Your mother let us eat all the cupcakes and cookies she'd baked for school the next day while your father put on his snow boots, at least three scarves, two hats, and a ski mask."

She covered her mouth and laughed. "He looked like big marshmallow."

"He did, and he told us to give him a hug before he went out and worked for hours in the snow to get the power back on before nightfall because he was worried people would freeze since there hadn't been any time to prepare. When he came back, we could pull ice off his eyebrows. Your dad isn't just an electrical repairman, Stevie. He's the man that keeps the fire going no matter what."

She dropped her head, putting her glass on the table. "I know. I know. It's just they make me feel like I'm not good enough all the time."

"Then prove them wrong. You know what my dad says. Chin up…"

"Head high!" she said loudly, puffing out her chest before we both broke out into a fit of laughter. "Our dads are something else aren't they?"

"Yeah they are, and they would not approve of us standing here drinking wine over men, which is why we are going out!" I said, going to my living room to grab my bag and camera.

"Going out where?"

"There is this block party happening downtown. I was going to go later to see the fireworks but you and I could both use some cotton candy and laughter." I hooked my arm around hers and grabbed Taigi's leash, dragging us out of my apartment.

She held on to me tightly, and when we got on the elevator she put her head on my shoulder.

"Thank you," she said softly.

"For what? I haven't even done anything yet."

"For not telling me to leave him. I know you aren't fond of Nathaniel, so thank you for not using this as an opportunity to say so," she muttered softly, watching the numbers decrease as we went down.

I wasn't sure if I liked her thanking me for that. I wanted to say the same thing I'd said to her when I first met him: Nathaniel was a spoiled mama's boy. He should have stood up for her and her family. The fact that he hadn't pissed me off. Our families were one of the things that defined us. But if I had told her all that, I could just see our past fight playing out again and us ending up going separate ways. She was marrying him. She was making that choice, and I knew I'd rather be on her side when she needed my help than not speak to her.

Sometimes the best thing you could do for a person was just be there, no matter the circumstances.

Kind of like how Eli was.

Eli

I knew about as much as an ant when it came to little girls. The block party was filled with little children and their parents, balloon toys, and clowns. When I'd offered to bring her there, I wasn't really sure what to expect, but her being quiet, sitting in her wheelchair, holding her stuffed bear was definitely not it.

"Molly? Are you all right?" I asked, kneeling in front of her. She put her chin on top of the teddy bear's head. "Do you want to go back to the hospital?"

"No!" She looked like she was going to cry, which caused a few parents to turn to look at us.

"Okay, we don't have to go back. I'm just asking because you don't look like you're having fun."

"I'm having fun," she lied.

This was the worst idea.

"Eli?"

Turning around I came face to face with Guinevere, wearing jean shorts and a red shirt and cardigan, her camera around her neck and fresh cotton candy in her hand. She looked...just like I would picture Guinevere to look. Molly grabbed my hand, hiding her face behind it.

"Hello?" Guinevere smiled at her.

"Guinevere, this is Molly, a patient of mine. I brought her here while her father went out to work." I wasn't sure why I felt the need to explain that to her.

She ignored me anyway, looking to Molly and crouching down. "Have we met before, Ms. Molly?"

Molly squeezed her bear and Guinevere snapped her fingers and smiled. "I remember now. You were the girl who almost ran me over when I moved into the building. Your dad's name is T…"

"Toby," I answered for her.

"That's right, Toby Wesley. It's nice to meet you, Ms. Molly. You ran so fast last time I wasn't able to say hi. You can call me Gwen. My name is Guinevere, but my friends call me Gwen." She held out her hand and Molly looked at it for a long time before shaking it.

"Do you want some cotton candy?" she asked her.

"No," I said quickly and Gwen looked up at me. "Too much sugar isn't good for her right now."

"Oh, well too much sugar isn't good for me either," she replied, walking over to the trash can and throwing it away before coming back to Molly.

Molly's eyes stared all over her face, and for a split second it looked like she was trying to tell her something in some secret girl code beyond my knowledge.

"Molly, you guys wait here for a second. I will be right back okay? No running off." She held her hands out as if that would hold us in place. "If Eli tries to run, kick him."

Molly giggled and nodded.

"Don't teach violence!" I yelled after her as she ran to wherever it was she was going. She stuck her tongue out like a child, almost tripping over a stroller, much to a nanny's dismay. Molly giggled as the older woman waved her finger at her and Guinevere apologized, running off farther.

"Molly, when you grow up, try to be just a tad more graceful than Guinevere, okay?"

She looked up to me, tilting her head to the side. "Isn't she your friend?"

"Huh?"

"She said her friends call her Gwen. You don't call her Gwen."

She was a sharp little one...and the way she looked at me waiting for an explanation, I knew I couldn't lie to her.

"We are friends, but I like calling her Guinevere more than Gwen," I replied.

"Why?"

Molly, I don't know. "Because Guinevere is a pretty name."

"I like it too! I will call her Gu...in...ev...ere." She struggled on it for a minute.

"Guinevere," I said slowly again for her.

"Guin...evere," she repeated, and I nodded.

"I'm back," Gwen yelled, running back to us with all her might. When she reached us she almost jumped on me, rising up in order to put a hat over my head. Shocked at how close she was to me, I froze as she concentrated on tucking all my hair inside it. It was only when she backed up that I was able to think straight again.

"Looks good," she said as she whipped her head down, packing as much of her hair as she could into a messy bun. She took a silk scarf and wrapped it around her head.

"Better?" she asked Molly, and it for the first time I realized how she must have felt being stuck in a wheelchair with a scarf over her head.

Molly nodded, but didn't say anything.

"Ms. Molly, will you take a picture with me?" she asked her, taking the camera off her neck.

"Yes. Dr. Eli, come on." Molly smiled.

"Yeah, Dr. Eli." Guinevere pulled me around the wheel-chair with her.

"I'll take it, my arm is longer." I took the camera from her hand and both of our hands lingered too long on each other's.

I couldn't help but stare at her, and without thinking I reached over to brush back a strand of hair that had escaped from the scarf.

"Thanks," she whispered, looking away from me and patting down the side of her hair to make sure I had gotten it all.

"Okay." I looked toward the camera, my face next to Molly's. "One. Two. Three."

"Pixie dust," Guinevere said at the click.

"Pixie dust?" Molly turned to her.

"Yep. It's made of happy thoughts and it can make you fly." She pretended to sparkle some all over her face before her brown eyes shot up to me.

Lift her! she mouthed to me.

Following her orders, I did.

"Haha!" Molly giggled, holding on to me.

Thank God she was finally starting to sound like she was having fun.

All thanks to Guinevere.

"Gwen?"

"Stevie, you're back! What took you so long?" she said, walking over to woman with red hair and hazel green eyes, Taigi at her feet.

"I would like to introduce you to my friends Dr. Eli and Ms. Molly. You're going to need a scarf if you are going to hang with us. Right, Ms. Molly?" Guinevere held her high.

Molly nodded happily in my arms. "Yep!"

"I'm gone for ten minutes and you've found pretty attractive friends all by yourself." Stevie put her hands on her hips.

"What can I say? I'm just cool like that," she said, leaning her hand on my shoulder. It felt like she was burning a hole through my shirt, her body was so hot. I was oddly aware of it there and missed whatever they were giggling about.

"Is that okay, Doctor?" Guinevere asked me, standing on her own.

"Huh?"

"Train," Molly answered, pointing. "I can ride the train, right?"

"Sure."

"Let's go before the kid in the Batman t-shirt steals the front." Guinevere lifted her easily from my hands.

I just stood there dumbfounded, watching them, my mind still reeling. Where had she come from? How had she gotten there? And most importantly, how did she have the ability to completely change the atmosphere like that?

"Are you all right?" Her friend Stevie stood beside me, wrapping her head with a green scarf she must have just bought. Taigi sat still on the ground.

"You two seem close. Has she always been like this?" I asked as we walked toward the red, yellow, and black train that could barely fit more than two people in each row.

"Yep. That's Gwen," she said like she knew exactly what I was saying. "I've know her for all my life and I can't explain it. It's like she's—"

"Perfectly imperfect, and the more you at look her the more confused you become but even still you can't look away."

"Wow," she replied.

"What?"

"Nothing, I'm going to catch the next train with them," she said, walking off. She stopped, looked me over again, and shook her head before walking toward them.

"What did I say?"

Taigi barked like he knew the answer.

CHAPTER TEN
SOMETHING BORROWED
AND BLUE

Guinevere

"Why! Why am I like this?" I cried, trying to wiggle myself out of the damn dress. The zipper was broken, and it was not budging for anything. Glancing at myself in the mirror, I sighed. "You're an idiot, Gwen," I whispered as my phone rang. "Eli, this isn't a good time," I answered.

"If you ever beg me for my book, or any of my wine again—"

"Wait!" I tried to move to my door, but I tripped slightly on the hem of my dress, knocking my desk over.

"What are you doing?"

Lifting it up at the bottom, I quickly walked out of my bedroom. "Just put the book and bottle by the door—"

"You want me to what?"

Urgh. "I'm having a moment. Just put—"

"Are you crying?"

"No, I'm not crying!"

"Guinevere—"

Annoyed, and without thinking, I pulled open the door. "Eli, I'm not crying."

His blue-green eyes wandered down the strapless mermaid wedding dress I wore, then back up to my face.

I wanted to slam the door in his face I was so embarrassed, but I knew that would only make it ten times worse.

"Go ahead, laugh." I sighed, waiting in the doorway as Taigi went up to Eli, placing both paws on his legs.

"I don't see anything funny," he replied, handing me the wine bottle and medical textbook I'd asked for before stroking Taigi's head.

"I would prefer if you laughed." *It would make me feel less pathetic.* "Thanks for these, I'll return the book tomorrow."

I was about to call Taigi back inside when I remembered. "We're friends, right?" I asked, though it felt odd for me to call him just a friend.

He looked up from Taigi. "I *guess*."

"So we can help each other without judging, right?"

"Just spit it out."

"This is so embarrassing…"

"Guinevere, you are standing in front of me in a wedding dress. What could possibly be more embarrassing for you?"

He just had to ask.

"I can't get it off."

"You what?" he asked slowly.

"The wedding dress. The stupid wedding dress won't come off, and it's getting harder for me to breathe!" I placed a hand on my stomach. The goddamn thing was like an anaconda wrapping tighter every time I took a breath.

He covered his mouth to stifle a chuckle, but he couldn't take it and laughed outright.

"I thought you said it wasn't funny!"

"It wasn't, until you told me you were stuck in it! How does that happen?"

"I gained a little weight, okay…" For some reason, the more he laughed, the better I felt. "Are you going to help me or not?"

Nodding, he came in along with Taigi and put the things he'd brought on the kitchen counter before closing the door.

I turned around, brushing my hair to the side. I jumped slightly when his hand brushed back.

"You okay?"

"Your hands were cold. I'm fine. Is it coming down?" I asked, feeling him tug harder.

"This is really stuck." He braced a hand on my waist, trying to pull the zipper down. The dress had to be cursed because I didn't feel it getting any looser.

"Can't you just rip it?"

"With my hands? Are you serious right now?" He paused in his attempts.

I grinned, trying to hold in my stomach. "What, you aren't strong enough?"

"If any man can rip a wedding dress off you, please consult a physician before continuing your relationship." His hand shifted onto my shoulder, and once again he tried. "Guinevere, I don't know what to say to you, but this thing isn't coming off."

Lightheaded, I had to brace myself against the kitchen table.

"Guinevere!"

"I'm fine, just felt dizzy for a second—"

"You're turning blue, you are not fine. Hold on." He let go of me and reached toward my knife set, taking the scissors.

"What are you doing—"

"What does it look like? I'm cutting you out of it."

"No—"

Ripppppp.

I took a deep breath, holding the dress up and turning around to face him. "You cut it."

"Can you breathe now?"

I nodded, but looked back down at the gown. "You cut it," I repeated, almost in shock.

"Didn't you just ask me to rip it?"

"I knew you couldn't... Thanks?" I wasn't sure what else to say.

"You're welcome." He put the scissors back and headed to the door.

"Wait."

"What now? Are you stuck in your bra?"

I clutched the dress back up to go to my bedroom. "I just need to ask you a few questions about the hospital real quick. Give me a minute."

After running back into my room, I let the dress fall to the floor after I closed the door, donning jeans and a basic t-shirt before coming back out. When I did, he was already opening the bottle of wine.

"No!" I rushed out, but it was too late.

He poured both of us a glass.

"What? Did you want to drink the whole thing yourself?" His eyebrow went up and he held out the glass for me to take.

"No, Stevie's wedding is tomorrow and I was going to give it as a gift." I sighed, taking the glass from him.

"You didn't think of anything else?" He followed me into my living room, taking a seat with me on the floor near the window again.

"I did, but Stevie...Stephanie now, might not like it. I was thinking of something more sophisticated, so I was going to give the wine to Nathaniel, and give her some earrings," I said, handing him a pillow.

He placed it behind his back as he drank. "Do you mean Nathaniel Van Allan?"

"You know him?"

"New York's elite only mingle with one another. My mother's been 'friends' with Mrs. Van Allan for years. We were both invited, but she just said she would go on her own."

The way he said friends made me wonder how he, from one of the elite families, could be so down-to-earth and relaxed. Yes, he always dressed well, and yes, he owned expensive things, but he never came off as being a snob, at least not anymore. Even in the beginning, when I'd seen him as Dr. Asshole, I still understood that he was acting that way because he was angry and hurt. He genuinely did care about others; I could see it the day I was at the hospital.

"What? Why are you looking at me like that?"

I shrugged, drinking before speaking. "I was just thinking that you aren't like them. You don't care what other people think. Sebas—*he...*"

"You can say his name, Guinevere. He isn't Voldemort."

I giggled. "Well, Sebastian cared a lot. He wanted everything to be...high class. When I was dating him, I knew he liked finer things, and he liked to show off how well he was doing. That he wasn't 'just a trust fund baby'. I felt awkward and a little put on display sometimes, but the good outweighed the bad."

Or at least, I had thought it did.

"Was he the one who picked out that dress for you?" He gazed at the city outside the window.

"How did you—"

"A tight, sparkling-with-crystals wedding dress does not seem to fit your style at all."

Even though I agreed he was right, I was a little annoyed. "He didn't really pick it out. He knew the owner of the bridal store I went into and had them bring out the very best and most expensive dresses. We had gone to other weddings before, and I knew which dresses he thought were ugly. I tried to pick one I knew he would like...wow, that sounds awful. But I can be girly, too."

"Never said you couldn't. It isn't awful, just meant you really wanted to look nice for him. There isn't anything wrong with that."

"I'm glad you cut me out of it." I smiled into the glass. "I would have held onto it like it meant something. I should have thrown it out weeks ago, or at least sold it to someone else, but with Stevie's wedding tomorrow, I just...I don't know. I just wanted to wear it one more time." I was sure there was someone out there that would have fallen in love with it.

"The answer to your non-question about me not being like them is: my father," he replied.

It took me a second to remember where the conversation had started.

"I don't care what they think because they don't matter to me. When my father died, I learned how superficial a lot of them were. Sure, they came to the funeral, held my mom's hand and whatnot, but I remember someone asking, *Who is he again? What did he do? Where did he live?* A few months later, some of the wives even tried to set my mother up. I guess to them, she should have moved on already. I just...I just wanted to hear stories of my father from them. Things they remembered as friends. But then I realized they never did anything more than go to the same parties. It was only the patients he helped that talked on and on about him. I think that's one of the reasons I wanted to become a doctor so badly."

"If your father saw you..." I started.

He turned to face me.

"If he saw you the way I did when I came to the hospital, I bet he would be more than proud. For a second, even I was like, 'Wow, so this is what he does every day.' I thought I wanted to do it, too. This coming from the girl who failed chemistry three ways to Sunday."

He snickered. "Really? I thought I was only 'kinda cool'."

"I scratched it out, didn't I?" *Damn note.*

He laughed, and so did I.

"So, your father was a surgeon. Your mother is a surgeon and chairwoman of the hospital. You are a surgeon, and your brother's working on becoming one, too. I'm almost too intimidated."

He raised his head high.

I rolled my eyes.

"What do your parents do?"

"My mother teaches African American & African Studies and history at the University of Alaska. She immigrated to California from south Africa when she was four and worked her way up the coast."

"And your father?"

"My father is an astronomer. He teaches at the university, too, but during campouts and bonfires, he becomes the chief Native American storyteller. He's half Iñupiat, half English. So technically I'm part Native American, English, and South African."

He nodded his head, thinking for a moment. "I always tried to trace where our family came from, but as far as I can tell we've been in America for generations. I suddenly feel the urge to look into it more."

"You should."

"So both of your parents are scholars and you're the artist...the rebel. You don't have siblings?"

I wished he hadn't asked that. Spinning the glass in my hands, I drank the rest of it before answering. "Not anymore."

Thankfully, he didn't pry.

Eli

Taking off my shoes when I got back into my apartment, I fell back on my couch. I couldn't stop wondering…I wanted to know more, but I knew I couldn't press, not when she was trying so hard to smile about something that was obviously hard. I was starting to realize she had two smiles: her genuine one she gave when she really was happy, and then the other one, her shield. If she felt hurt or upset, she smiled and tried to push it away.

She looked beautiful in that wedding dress—what am I thinking?

"Obviously, I had too much wine," I muttered to myself.

"Where?"

Sitting up quickly, I watched my little brother come out of *my* bedroom wearing *my* shirt, even though the sleeves were too long.

He just rolled them up his arms.

"What are you doing here, and why are you wearing my shirt?"

"I spilled beer on mine," he replied, walking into my kitchen and grabbing *my* last beer. "You should get more of these."

"First question, you still haven't answered it."

"Mom's having the Van Allans over. You know I hate those people." He pushed my feet to the side and took a seat on the couch.

I hit him upside the head with a pillow.

"Hey!"

"Have you thought about getting your own place?"

He looked at me like I had lost it. "And leave Mom all alone in the house? Aren't you the one who told me to take my time leaving? Plus, I like it there."

Saying nothing, I shifted, placing my feet on the coffee table instead.

"So why were you drinking Dad's wine? You usually save that for special occasions." He lifted his legs up as well.

"Guinevere needed a bottle for the Van Allan wedding tomorrow. Apparently, she's friends with Nathaniel's bride. But we ended up drinking together, again." I took the controller, turning on the television.

He kept staring at me.

"What?"

"I'm just processing."

"You do that," I muttered, leaning back.

"Okay, so you drink Dad's wine with someone outside of the family not once, but twice? What is this thing I see between you two?"

"Friendship, that's it. The first time I was a jerk and trying to apologize, this time she asked. I thought it was the least I could do after she bought me shoes—"

"She bought you shoes? Eli, come on, don't lie—"

"We are just friends. We don't see each other in any other way than that. It would be odd if we did. We are the only two people who understand what it feels like, so we talk. Get your head out of the gutter."

He pursed his lips, drinking slowly.

"I mean it, Logan."

"I didn't say anything. I was just thinking how, when I was trying to be friends with her, you told her to stay away from me—"

"Just watch TV and shut up."

He did, but only for about two minutes. "So...does that mean you're coming to the wedding? She is going to be there."

"No. Why would her being there matter to me?"

He shrugged. "I mean, you aren't going because it will bring up memories, but she has to go. It sucks that she's going to have to go through that alone."

"She's a big girl, Logan, but if makes you feel better, you can dance with her if you'd like."

I am not going.

Chapter Eleven
Something New and Old

Guinevere

B ridesmaids dresses were supposed to be ugly.

Yet the dress I wore—and had spent almost a thousand dollars on—was probably better than any of the dresses I owned. The elegant one-shoulder red dress made me feel classy. Stevie had even picked out jewelry and shoes she suggested to go along with it. Yes, it was expensive—well, to me it was—but I had taken what Eli had said to heart and decided to splurge this time around. My longtime friend was getting married, she wanted her day, and if she wanted her girls to look as close to human perfection as possible, then fine. I would get my hair, makeup, and nails professionally done, and I couldn't even lie about it not being fun. I felt a like a Barbie, but in a good way.

I walked into the waiting room looking for the rest of her bridesmaids, and when the four of them looked to me, their mouths—well, all except for Josephine—turned up in the widest grins, so I took it as a good sign.

"Gwen, you look amazing!" One of the women gasped, coming up to me. "From now on, just walk around in red. It is definitely your color."

"Thank you. I was trying my best." I laughed.

"Ladies." Josephine stepped up. "Stephanie will be coming out any second. Let's remember it's her day."

Their smiles dropped, and they took a step away.

I wanted to ask Josephine what I had done to make her so angry with me, but then again, I remembered that after that day I was never going to see her again, so I really didn't care.

"Ladies." Stevie's mother came out of the dressing room, holding the doors closed behind her with a smile so wide it could crack her face. "May I present to you, the future Mrs. Van Allan!" She pushed open the doors.

Stevie turned to us, and in my head it was like she did it in slow motion with romantic music and lighting, that's how beautiful she looked. Her hair was pinned up in a loose bun with a red rose in it, and she wore the best princess wedding gown I had ever seen, with little lace and sparkle accents.

"Gwen?" she called out to me.

I realized I was the only one who hadn't moved close. "I'm sorry, I'm just in awe right now. You look so beautiful, Stevie." I finally walked up to her. "So beautiful I'm going to cry."

"Don't cry! If you cry, I'll cry." She laughed, hugging me.

"Oh, and we can't have that." Stevie's mom came up, giving me a small hug as well. "We are already running late. Hurry girls."

Eli

Why am I here?

No, honestly. Why?

Ever since I had entered the hotel, I kept wondering, why?

Logan grinned beside me like he knew something I didn't, and my mother was proud because I wasn't afraid of a wedding...which, as a grown man, should not have been that surprising, but whatever. For some reason, that afternoon I had put on the best suit I owned, polished my shoes, and combed my hair…like I was going to prom. Nevertheless, I was there, at Nathaniel and Stephanie's wedding, sitting on his side as everyone chatted about how wonderful the wedding hall was. In my mind, not only was the place annoying because the air smelled like one too many damn roses, but it also looked pretty modest in comparison to a lot of the things Hannah had done for ours.

"Oh, don't they look nice?" My mother smiled at Nathaniel as he and his groomsmen walked in, taking their place at the front under the arch of white and red roses.

"I guess. With those tails, they look like stuffed penguins," I muttered.

She elbowed me. "If you were going to be sour, why did you come?"

Good question.

"He wants to see someone," Logan whispered.

Reaching behind my mother, I smacked him on the back of the head. *Bad answer.*

"You are both grown men, can you act like it, please?" She smacked both of our legs. "Lord in Heaven, help me."

"Sorry," we both said, though I still glared. He kept trying to tell me something was going on between Guinevere and me, and in all honesty, it wasn't. I thought of her as a friend, nothing more, nothing less.

"Oh my god, is that Gwen?" my mother whispered when we all stood up at the sound of the music.

"Can't be," I said to myself, watching the person come forward. The Guinevere I knew wore little to no makeup ever, her brown hair was always down or to the side and she didn't think that much about it, and she barely ever wore jewelry other than her feather earring cuff…which was on that woman's ear.

"It's her," I whispered. *Just a dolled up version of her.*

"She looks amazing," my mother said as she walked right by us.

"Yeah." For some reason, trying to think about it made my head hurt.

"The bride is that way." Logan snickered behind me, and I knew he meant for me to stop looking at Guinevere.

We are just friends. And what kind of friend would one be if they didn't think their pal had the ability to be attractive sometimes? She looked nice, and there was nothing wrong with saying it or thinking it. I noticed Logan had switched places with my mother to do what all little brothers are born to do: annoy the hell out of me. But, I cut him off before he could say anything. "People like you are the reason why men and women can't just be friends without anything else going on. She looks nice. You're thinking it too. What is the big deal?"

He said nothing.

I smirked.

"I was just going to ask if you had gum," he whispered with a smile.

Trying my best to ignore him, I looked up front. For some reason, most likely because I didn't know Nathaniel or Stephanie that well, my eyes kept drifting to the only person I did know, standing up front in red. She didn't look fazed at all, just smiled a small, real smile for her friend. When her eyes shifted and looked out over the crowd, she finally noticed me. Her smile grew, taking up her whole face.

She looks so silly right now. Jeez. Anyone who saw her would think she had won the lottery or something. Lifting my finger, I pointed at her to look back where she was supposed to be looking.

She made a quick face before looking back.

Guinevere

"I'm so happy you're here," I said, all but running up to him now that I'd finally managed to rip my face from the photo session as everyone entered the reception hall.

"Why?" he asked casually as the woman in front of the seating chart table handed him a place card with a key dangling from one of the edges.

"You know why. I know you didn't come for me, but I'm glad someone else is as—"

"Miserable?" He smirked.

"Not miserable, just…" I wasn't sure how to put it into words, really. I didn't want him to hate it there, but—

"I understand, Guinevere. Don't think so hard, you'll pop a vein."

"You know I've always wondered, is that really possible?"

He shook his head, searching for his table.

Shifting my head to the side, I looked him up and down. He wore a black bowtie with a classic-fitted black tuxedo that had a nice sleek lining. "You look nice."

He stopped, looking back at me.

"What?" I asked.

"Nothing. So do you. You put in a lot of effort, it—"

"Hey, I can doll up like the best of them. Tonight, I won't even drool."

He snickered.

I walked with him.

"Where are you sitting, at the head table?"

"No, the head table is Nathaniel and Stevie, plus both their parents on either side. I'm at table—" I stopped when I saw my name card on the table next to Logan's. "Well, it's here. She must have put me here after I told her I knew you all, since I know no one else."

"Gwen, are you sitting with us?" Logan spoke up, his mother on his arm and a cocktail in his hand. He was dressed up just like his brother, bow tie and everything.

I had to admit, they were quite a pair. "Good evening, Dr. Davenport, and it's nice to see you again, Logan. Yes, apparently I am sitting with you all, if that's all right?"

"Of course, and you look absolutely stunning, my dear." She pulled me into a small hug.

"Stunning? Gwen, you're smokin'." Logan grinned, hugging me as well with one arm.

"You're not bad yourself." I laughed when he came around and pulled out my chair as Eli pulled out his mother's. "What gentlemen."

"I know, it makes me so proud. If only they could always be like this."

And, like sons, they both groaned under her gaze.

It was funny to watch the three of them.

"How long have you known Stephanie, Gwen?" Logan questioned.

"Since I was six. We met when—well, you'll hear all about that. I'm doing part of their toast, so I'll save our story until then. Hopefully I don't panic."

"Why would you panic?" Eli asked.

I met his eyes across the candlelit table covered in rose petals. "I get nervous when I talk to big groups of people."

"You did fine when we were at the university."

"The university?" his mother asked, looking between us.

I nodded. "We basically fought over which is the better career path: art or the sciences. I won." I grinned.

He scoffed. "If anything, it was a tie, but that is only because you brought up the 'you need me and I need you' argument. I'm pretty sure I got at least a few of them to see reason and come over to my side. Remember how *kinda cool* I am?"

I clapped slowly for him. "I tell you that you are a decent doctor one time and—"

"It sounded more like amazing to my ears." He drank his water.

"And it goes to your big, egotistical head. Sorry, Mrs. Davenport," I said to her. After all, the fathead was her son.

"No." She smiled, looking between the two of us. "It actually reminds me of when I met his father. The man could praise himself. 'Meryl, you should have seen me today, I'm telling you there is no better doctor than me in this state. Meryl, did you see how fast I laid that stitch?' Oh, gosh. I didn't call him egotistical, I called him Dr. Brainiac."

I thought about it for a second. "Isn't that a super-villain in the DC comics?"

"That's why it annoyed him so much." She giggled.

So did I. I didn't know why it was that funny, but just seeing her laugh so happily at her memories felt nice. Wasn't that what was normally supposed to happen at weddings?

"What did he call you back?" Eli asked softly, watching her as he drank his scotch.

Leaning over, she put her hand on his arm. "You know, I never found out. I'm sure he called me something in his head, but no matter what, when he was cross he would just say *Meryl*, like I exhausted him and he couldn't even put up any more of a fight."

"My father just makes faces." I ran my hand over the rim of my water glass. "My mother would get upset about something he either forgot to do, or something he totally messed up, and he would just sit in his chair and watch her as she tried to fix it, which made my mom angrier, and then he would look to me and start making faces. He could even guess what her next words were. When I was a teenager, I would wonder, 'Why is he just sitting there? Mom's gonna lose it.' Then I realized he just knew her too well. My mother likes things to be done a particular way. The best help he can offer is to keep his hands off and wait until she actually gives him directions."

"Where are your parents now?" Mrs. Davenport questioned.

"*Cypress, Alaska,*" Eli said in a strange voice.

"Is that a real place?" Logan asked beside me.

"It's the home of the best wild salmon in the country," Eli and I said at the same time, though he was a lot less serious than I was. I could only give him a look from across the table.

He shrugged.

"Ladies and gentlemen, please welcome Mr. and Mrs. Nathaniel Van Allan," the announcer said, and we all stood, clapping.

I clapped as loudly as possible, not caring who saw me.

Logan joined in, raising his glass.

Eli

After everyone settled down and the champagne was brought out, Guinevere walked to the front of the ballroom. The lighting changed slightly, focusing on her. She didn't look nervous at all to me, but maybe she had just gotten used to covering it up. She moved to the side, and an old picture was projected onto the wall, showing two little girls dressed in jean jumpers, their hair in pigtails and their arms around each other. Little Guinevere made a peace sign as young Stephanie appeared to be squeezing the life out of her.

"The day I met then Stephanie Murray was the first day of kindergarten. The first grade boys had decided to mess with us, and I, being the rebel I always was, was not going to have that. No one backed me up."

Stephanie and her parents groaned together, trying not to laugh, when all of a sudden the picture changed to one of them sitting on two boys and high-fiving each other.

Oddly, she took a long pause as if considering something before blinking and turning back to Stephanie. "No one but Stephanie. Safe to say, no matter what happened in my life, when I turned back, she was always there. She was there when, at fourteen, we decided to hitchhike cross-country, but only made it as far as the bus station before panicking and running back home. She was there when, at sixteen, we thought dyeing our hair white would make us look more mature. And she was there every step of the way, encouraging me to follow my dreams. So when I first met Nathaniel, I was a little jealous. I kept wondering: who is this boy, trying to take away my best friend? It took me a while, but I saw it, the way she smiled so wide it looked like her face would break. How he was always so willing to jump into whatever she was doing…with slightly more logic than we had together. How he made her world ten times bigger, and it made me so thankful." She tried not to cry. "Because my best friend was with the best person for her, and she was going to get to laugh and smile like that for the rest of her life, the way she deserved to. You're one lucky guy, Nathaniel, and thank you. Please never stop what you're doing."

When she was done, she took a deep breath, handing the microphone back as Stephanie came over to give her a tight hug.

"Do you like her?" my mother asked.

Her question forced my eyes back to her. "No."

"Yes," Logan answered. "If you don't, why does it bother you so much when I say you do? If you didn't like someone, you wouldn't even think about it. It's because you like her and would rather not admit it that you get angry."

"We just met each other—"

"I knew your father for two weeks before we dated. Four when he told me he loved me," my mother added, giving me a look before she drank her water.

"For the last time, we are just friends."

"Okay." Logan raised his hands. "Keep staring at your *just friend* like she's the only woman in the room. I'm sorry."

When she came back to our table, she took the empty seat by me, not Logan.

I hated how she now smelled like roses because of all the damn flowers. She always smelled like fresh rain... *What am I thinking?*

"Your speech was beautiful, dear," my mother said to her.

"Thank you." She smiled, but it wasn't real.

"What is it?" Something was bugging her, I could tell.

She leaned over, putting her hand on my arm. "Whatever you do, don't look back. Hannah and Sebastian are sitting two tables over."

My first instinct was to turn, but she squeezed.

"Don't look. I was just going to leave, but I didn't want you to not know. Seeing them together will just make us upset, and with the alcohol we will make a scene. Please, not tonight."

Grabbing the water, I nodded. Attending had been a bad idea, I'd known it all along.

"Have you taken all your photos, Gwen?" my mother asked, leaning toward us.

She nodded.

"Then Eli, take her home. I will tell them you weren't feeling well. It's all right to not be here."

"I'm fine, thank you. I did nothing wrong. Why should I run away? Today has nothing to do with either of them, that's old news. I wish them the best." Gwen watched as Nathaniel's best man did his speech.

"Oh, thank you, but I didn't ask for this," she said when a waiter came over with a plate of steak.

"I did, for you. You didn't like the fish, right?" She hadn't eaten anything but bread and the broccoli off her plate while sitting with us. I figured she didn't want to tell them to take it back and get something else.

She looked at me.

"What, don't you like meat?"

"No, I do. Thank you, I was starving," she replied before cutting into her food.

Even though I'd heard her tell me not to, I couldn't help but tilt my head to the side slightly, scanning the room for them.

"Don't, Eli," she said, not even looking up before taking a bite.

How did she know?

Whatever. Sighing, I sat straighter. I hated weddings. They brought up both old and new awkward situations to fall into...like now, when everyone was getting onto the dance floor at the end of the speeches.

"Mother, would you like to dance?" Logan extended his arm, stealing my idea before I could act. He gave me a wink, and of course our mother accepted.

"Yep, this is going to be my last wedding for a while," Guinevere whispered.

"The only other one I plan to attend is my brother's." I glanced to them on the dance floor. "And that might take a while."

She snickered. "I don't know, your brother would be a catch."

"For whom?"

"Oh, come on. He's young, attractive—"

"Are you asking me to set you up with my brother?"

"God, no. He's like my little brother; I'm just saying he has charm. Just wait, some girl is going to have him falling hard, faster than you can blink. That's how love works."

"You still believe in all that love stuff?" I'd hoped she would be more cynical to the whole thing. *Like I am.*

She pointed to Nathaniel and Stephanie on the dance floor. "Of course. I was unlucky. People are sometimes unlucky in love, but I'd rather be unlucky a dozen more times than close myself off and never have the chance to have that with someone."

"I blame your books," I replied.

She grinned. "I know, a woman who *reads.* Gosh. Ha, but, if you want to borrow any—"

"No, thank you."

"Shame. I find guys who read sexy."

"So you're saying you want me to fit your idea of sexy?"

She froze and looked directly at me. "That came out wrong."

"You sure sounded pretty clear to me. What book would you start me off with?"

"You want me to see you as sexy?" She looked confused.

"If everyone woman within my presence does not find me worth drooling over, I've failed as a man."

She pretended to gag.

"Cute," I replied.

She just drank, looking back at the crowd on the dance floor.

"Please don't tell me you want to dance."

"I don't," she lied.

Sighing, I stood up, taking her hand.

"No, seriously, I don't—"

I spun her toward me. "When will you realize I can tell when you're lying to me? You have to dance at least once at a wedding. Do you know how waltz?" I asked her when the music changed.

"Don't underestimate me, Dr. Davenport. I took ballroom dancing 101 *and* 102 in college, and I passed with an A+."

"I'm so intimidated right now," I mocked. "Just keep up."

"Do your worst," she said, and immediately lifted my arm into the right place.

She always had to challenge me. We started off slowly, her feet following my lead as we moved first right to left, then left back to right.

"How am I doing?" She smirked at me.

"This is basic," I replied, speeding my footwork with the music.

She never lost her footing or even stepped on my toes, she just followed perfectly. Spinning her out, her dress came up slightly before she came back in. "Still basic?"

Again we sped our moves, and it was like the music was following along with us as we kept going, spinning around the floor. I did notice she was a lot closer to me than she generally should have been, but neither of us was focused on that. I watched her, trying to see if she at any point couldn't keep up, but her big brown eyes stayed focused on me, a small grin on her lips. She kept up with me in every way, even when I tilted her back unexpectedly. Her face was so close I almost lost my concentration.

She looks beautiful. Dear God, what am I thinking?

Finally, when the music slowly came to a stop, we did as well...to a welling round of applause.

Both of us glanced around to see the whole floor had been cleared, and now everyone stood on the outside, even Nathaniel and Stephanie.

"How do we escape?" she whispered, nodding to them.

"Just keep walking," I replied, helping her off the dance floor.

We didn't go back to the table, instead ending up walking until we were out the double doors and in the main hall of the hotel. Holding on to me, she stepped out of her shoes.

"Oh, thank God." She sighed happily. "I have flats back in the dressing rooms. I'll be right back."

Why did I care? "I won't be waiting."

"Whatever," she said, holding her dress up as she ran.

When I was alone, I took a deep breath. What was this? Why did I feel like this?

"You looked happy."

I froze at *her* voice. *I knew this day was going to come, but why now?* "Hello, Hannah."

I turned to the woman wearing the light pink gown. "You look nice."

"Wow. Even now, you're always the gentleman." She smiled sadly. "And here I thought you were avoiding me."

"No, sorry, I just don't have anything to say to you. You should head back in. Your boyfriend, fiancé, or whatever, might get the wrong idea."

"We aren't together. We just came for appearance's sake," she said as I was about to turn. "He still loves her, and I—"

"He still loves her?" *Who gives a damn if he still loves her? He can't have her... What am I thinking right now?*

"Eli, Eli please hear me out. I—I think I made a mistake. No, I know I made a mistake."

She made a mistake? Is she kidding me right now? There were a million things I'd figured she could say to me, just to spite me—that he was the better lover, the better man—and I would have preferred any of them to that reply.

"Your mistakes aren't any of my business, Hannah." I turned from her.

She held back my arm. "Eli, wait—"

"Is everything okay?" Gwen asked, coming close but keeping her eyes on Hannah.

Guinevere

My feet didn't really hurt that badly, I just needed a moment away from Eli. He had been so close to me, closer than I had been to any man in what felt like forever. That, and the way his eyes stayed trained on me like I was the only person in the world...it was hard to even hear the music with how quickly my heart was beating against my chest. For some reason, I trusted him; even when he said he wouldn't wait, I knew he would still be there when I got back. I just wasn't expecting *her* to be holding on to him, and for some reason the sight bothered me to no end. "Is everything okay?" I asked when I reached them.

Eli pulled her hand off him. "It's fine. Did you get the shoes?"

"Yes. I'm just still trying to figure out why you are standing here." I pointed to Hannah.

She sighed. "I know what I did to you, the both of you, was wrong. I'm so sorry—"

"Will your 'sorry' make everything better?" I smiled at her. "I mean, you only destroyed two people's dreams in what, thirty seconds? Not to mention all those phone calls and emails I had to make to family and friends, trying to figure out how to explain my that fiancé ran off with another woman...on her own wedding day."

"We aren't together—"

I just looked to him in shock.

"Hannah, you are not helping." Eli sighed.

"Let me hit her," I said to him. "Please, let me hit her."

"You don't want to make a scene—"

I stepped toward her.

Hannah didn't back up. "I deserve it."

"You do deserve it. I should curse you out, throw water in your face, and so much more, not just for hurting me, but for hurting him. What makes it worse is you didn't even have the decency to make your affair last. Should I feel better about that? If you two were soulmates, at least I could say 'they really fell in love.' I'm a romantic like that. I thought I was the pitiful one, but the truth is, you are. How stupid you must feel right now for throwing everything away. I feel sorry for you." I took a step back and turned around.

Chapter Twelve
Mistake or By Design

Eli

Not just for hurting me, but for hurting him.

Her words repeated in my mind as the driver held open the car door for us at our apartment. She hadn't even argued with me, just got in the car and didn't say a word or even look at me during the drive. In the elevator, she kept her head down, and when we reached our floor, she slowly walked to her door.

I don't want it to end like this.

She unlocked the door, and I came up behind her, pulling it closed. "Say something," I whispered.

She didn't turn around.

"Guinevere, please say something. Anything."

"Eli, I'm tired. Please let it go."

"She said he's still in love with you. Will you go back to him if he calls?" I didn't know why I asked, but I just knew I had to. I couldn't let it go.

"Do I look that desperate?"

She still wouldn't face me. "I don't know how you look right now. Turn around and ask me again."

"I can't."

"Why?"

"Because you are confusing me."

"I feel the same."

Her hand tightened on the doorknob. "We've had too much wine. Let's call it a night, Eli."

"All right. If that's what you think it is." I let go of her door, waiting for her to head inside.

But, she didn't. She just stood there.

"Why are you confused?" she asked, finally turning. "When you say things like that, it comes off like—"

"Like I like you?" I said, and it felt like a relief to say. "Maybe it's because I've talked to you more than anyone else. Maybe because I was heartbroken after Hannah, and you could see right through me, and it didn't seem like a big deal anymore. Maybe it's because you make my whole family seem brighter. I don't know what it is. I don't know how I got here. One moment you were just that other woman who got hurt too, and then you were Guinevere. Funny, weird, talented, beautiful Guinevere, and I'm thinking about how you smell like rain, and whether you've eaten. I don't know how it happened, all I know is that I'm thinking about you, and not just like a friend."

"Hannah is—"

"Not my problem. Nor is she yours. I really don't want to spend right now talking about them; we've done that. I want to talk about you and me, and this thing between us." I took a step forward.

She took a step back until her back was against her door.

"Tell me, Guinevere. Am I crossing a line? Am I the only one going down this road?"

"We will hurt each other, Eli. This is just going to be a rebound—"

"I'd rather get hurt a dozen times, remember? Or was that just talk?"

"Eli—"

"I'll ask again, Guinevere: am I mistaken? Am I the only one who feels something here?"

She looked to the side and shook her head.

"You have to say it." I needed to hear the words.

She licked her lips, took a deep breath, and looked me square in the eye. "No. Happy? I've been trying to tell myself we are just friends, but I keep...I keep hoping to see you, and talk to you, and be around you...you are slowly taking up all the space in my head, and I—"

I kissed her. Not like the peck on the lips I'd given her at the university; I kissed her like I meant it. Her mouth was soft against my own and opened slightly for me when I licked the bottom of her lip. I held onto her waist and pressed her up against the door, her hands went up into my hair, pulling me closer.

I felt my fingers crawling up the length of her, cupping one of her breasts.

Shit. I didn't want us to start like that. I forced us apart.

"What?" she said.

We both took deep breaths, though neither of us had moved, our bodies still pressed together.

"This is what I do when I just want to screw a woman, Guinevere. I said I wanted to see where this is going with you, and a one-night stand is not where I want it to go, so we need to stop."

"Okay." She nodded, pushing me away.

But I didn't like that either, leaning in and kissing her again. She bit my bottom lip and I moaned into her, her tongue in my mouth, tempting me more.

"Fuck. No," I said again, taking a step back. "You weren't supposed to be this good."

She laughed. "What does that mean?"

"I don't know." She just had this innocence about her; the fact that she was so passionate already was throwing me for a loop.

"So let's call it a night?" she said to me.

I found myself staring at all her curves but, biting my lip, I nodded.

"Okay then. See you tomorrow?" She opened her door.

"Wait."

"Eli! You're killing me here."

Good to know.

"I just wanted to say, knowing you, tomorrow you're going to want to get all dressed up again to make a good impression...but don't, okay? Let's not put on a false façade that we are anything other than who we were two days ago."

She frowned. "You only confessed when I got all glammed up—"

"I confessed because after Hannah spoke to me, I realized I didn't want you beside any other man. I'm a tad bit possessive like that."

"Don't worry, I will whip that right out of you."

"We're on to whips now?" I couldn't stop myself.

She laughed, shaking her head at me. "Goodnight, Dr. Davenport."

"Goodnight, Ms. Poe."

She closed the door slowly, never breaking eye contact with me until it finally shut.

"Oh, shit," I whispered to myself, hurrying into my apartment. My hard-on for her was killing me slowly. Pulling off my clothes, I couldn't help but wonder how we were going to be now that we had crossed this line.

I was a little too excited.

Guinevere

"What just happened?" I asked Taigi, sliding down to sit right in front of my door. One of my hands went to my lips and the other to my chest, where my heart was trying to escape.

I hadn't just kissed Eli. I had made out with him to the point where I wanted to do so much more. He tasted like vanilla ice cream: sweet and chilly.

"What am I doing, Taigi?" I whispered, running my hands through his fur. His tongue dropped out of his mouth. "If we do this, we are going to complicate everything. Right? It won't just be us hanging out, it will be dates, and...sex."

It was all supposed to be negative, yet the more I spoke, the more I wanted all of it. Even now I shivered, just thinking about how his hands had gripped me, how strong they were. How strong and hard all of him felt against me...

Stop it. I'm not going to think about it until tomorrow. We weren't officially starting until then, right? Did our relationship have an official date?

I was going to give myself a headache. *Stop thinking about it.*

Yet even after I had showered and changed, I couldn't let it go. Sitting on my bed, I rested against the wall, grabbing my book from the floor beside me.

Is he asleep? This is useless! I wasn't going to be able to get any rest, and it was his fault!

"Stupid, sexy, egotistical, kissing doctor," I muttered, grabbing my pillow and burying my face in it. I heard my phone buzz, even though I couldn't see it.

"Where are you?" I jumped up onto my knees, my hands patting down the surface of my bed.

Taigi barked, using his nose to push the phone for me.

"See, this is why I love you, Taigi," I said, reaching to pick it up.

He barked two more times before rolling himself into a ball in his smaller bed at the foot of mine.

It was a text.

'Are you sleeping?'

'*Yep.*' Urgh, I should have come up with a better reply.

'*So you are dream-texting me? That's new.*'

'*Why are you awake?*'

'*Why are you asleep after messing with my head?*'

What? Me! Sitting up and crossing my legs as if that would help, I typed harder, as if he could feel my emotions through the phone.

'*Me messing with your head? Says the guy who drops the 'I like you' bomb and kisses the life out of me to the point where I was thinking of asking you in, only to be a gentleman and tell me he doesn't want to just screw me. I'm not messing with your head, Dr. Davenport, it's you who is messing with mine.*' I felt proud the moment I hit send...until I realized how crazy I must sound.

"I hate trying to date," I said, falling over to the side, not wanting to see his reply. There should be a take-back button on messages.

Peeking at his message when my phone vibrated, I prepared myself for his reply. '*But it feels nice, right? Me messing with you. You messing with me. You want this, right?*'

'*Yes.*' I answered without overthinking, because it did feel nice.

'*It does for me, too. I don't like talking to you via text. I prefer seeing your face when we talk, so I'll just wait a few more hours. Sleep well, Guinevere.*'

'*You too, Eli.*' Falling back on my bed, I remembered that his bedroom was just on the other side of the wall. If he was in there texting, he was right behind me. I wanted to knock on the wall, but that just seemed a little bit creepy, so I rolled over, holding onto my pillow.

I felt like I had only closed my eyes for a few minutes before Taigi started to bark, coming over with his leash and dropping it beside me. I glanced at the clock: 5:32 AM.

"Taigi, it's too early. Can we go later?" I rolled over.

He jumped onto my bed.

"The sun isn't even completely up yet!" I begged.

He just pushed the leash toward me and barked.

"Okay, okay." I felt like an old woman getting up. Stretching out my back, I grabbed my running capris, though I hadn't run since I was kid. I usually took him to the park and just waited for him to wear himself out chasing squirrels or his ball.

"Give me a second, boy," I said when he followed me into the bathroom, whining as I took time to brush my teeth.

He whined again, his paws on my leg.

"We're going, we're going." I put on his leash and exited my room, and he ran toward the door. "What is up with you—"

I paused when Eli came out, adjusting the mp3 player on his bare muscular arm, wearing black loose-fitting running pants and a hooded shirt. Only when Taigi went up to him did Eli glance at me, wide-eyed as he took his earbuds out.

"Morning," I said quickly, even bringing my hand up and doing a small wave like an idiot.

"Morning." He grinned. "Do you usually go out this early? I've never seen you."

"No, usually we go out later, but for some reason, he wouldn't let me sleep this morning." *Now I look like a stalker, thank you.* I glared at Taigi, who walked on his own toward the elevator. "See, he really has to go." I followed, walking past Eli.

"Where are you guys going?" he asked.

He was already next to me as I pressed the button. "Central Park," I replied, getting in with him.

We both reached to close it, our hands grazing each other.

"Sorry." I quickly dropped my hand.

He snickered, closing the doors. "He looks excited."

I glanced down to Taigi, whose tail waved back and forth.

"I was so busy with the wedding yesterday that I could only give him a short ten-minute walk, which is nothing; he really needs a good run." I petted his head.

"You run, too?"

He sounded excited as we reached the bottom floor. "Yeah." I had no idea why the hell I said that; it just spilled out of my mouth. I only ever either let Taigi run by himself or biked next to him. Running was not my thing.

"I usually do the Hudson River route, it's almost nine miles, but Central Park is good too. Do you start your run from here?"

Almost nine miles every morning? Are you shitting me right now?

"We—" Before I could finish telling him to go on without us, Taigi ran forward, pulling me with him. What made it worse was I could feel Eli running beside me.

Why, Taigi, why? I screamed in my mind, running with them. I couldn't get out of it now. It was early enough that the sidewalks toward the park were mostly empty; there was still even early morning fog out.

When we made it to the park I hoped, prayed one of them would slow down, but they were in their own little world, running farther and farther along the path while I could feel my calves tightening up.

Come on, Guinevere, you can do this. Just make it a half hour. I pushed myself, breathing in slowly through my nose and out my mouth.

I thought I was doing pretty well for a little bit too, until my whole left leg went numb and I had to slow down, much to Taigi's annoyance. I slowed, finally stopping at a bench and grabbing my leg.

"Are you all right?" Eli came over.

I noticed that while I was sweating like crazy, he just looked like someone had sprayed him with a damn mister. Sighing, I just sat, trying to catch my breath.

"I'm not a runner." I threw up my hands. "I have no idea why I said I was. I take him on walks, and if he really needs to go for a run, I take my bike. I'm a great cyclist, but running...yeah, not my thing. I think I'm dying. How long have we been going for?"

"Twenty-four minutes—"

"Really?" I was surprised I had made it that far. *I should have kept going!* "See? I can't even make it thirty minutes. That's bad, right?"

He knelt down in front of me. "Which leg is stiff? I'm guessing you didn't stretch?"

"All of me is stiff, but my left leg is worse. I stretched my back when I got out of bed, but other than that, no." No point trying to hide my embarrassment. I wanted to go back home and close my eyes. Maybe I could restart the day.

He took my left leg and massaged my calf. "Guinevere, when you're with me, I have one rule: don't lie, especially if it leads to hurting yourself for no reason...or for any reason. I don't really care if you are a runner or not."

"I'm sorry," I whispered, trying not to focus on his hands. "You looked excited when I said I ran, too, and—"

"I was excited I could spend time with you." He glanced up at me. "Even if we didn't say anything, you were still going to be next to me. I spent the whole night wondering how I was going to approach you today. Running seemed like a good way to break the ice. I was excited about that."

"I won't lie, I'm sorry," I said softly. "But I thought you said you could tell when I'm lying."

He frowned. His hands had worked their way from my calf to my knee, and he froze right before reaching my thigh, his eyes looking up at me. "I was distracted and didn't notice. Should I stop? Does it feel better?"

It did feel better. "Don't stop." It wasn't a lie. I wanted him to keep touching me.

He smirked, his hands working up and down my thigh slowly.

Doing my best to keep my mouth closed, I kept my eyes on him and he kept his on me. I swallowed when his fingers worked farther, pressing down harder through my tights, and I could feel myself breathing hard.

He bit his lips, took a breath, and stopped, his hands not leaving my thigh. "You are really good at seducing me," he whispered under his breath. "Last night, this morning. Guinevere, we *just* started, you can't put me in positions like this. I want to be a gentleman before I'm the fiend."

I placed my hand on his, leaning down to kiss him just as hard as he'd kissed me the night before, our mouths opening for each other, both his hands now gripping my thighs as if he was forcing them to stay where they were.

Breaking away, his eyes dropped to my lips and he swallowed, taking a deep breath.

"If you think I'm seducing you now, you're in for one hell of a ride, Dr. Davenport."

"I look forward to it, Ms. Poe."

"Go for your run, you look like you need it." I nodded down at his...problem.

"It will have to do...for now." He got up, as did I. "Are you going to be at the hospital today?"

I nodded. "For this mural, I'm going to be there for a while."

"If I distract you, will it take longer?" He grinned, already preparing to run again.

"Don't distract me!"

"You say that now." He winked, waving at me before taking off.

I noticed he was going much faster than he had when running alongside me. *He must have been holding back.*

Falling back on the bench, I noticed Taigi had finally settled down, sitting next to it without a care in the word. He barked at me.

"Fine. Fine. It's all thanks to you."

He barked again and put his head down.

"You're still my favorite, I swear." I laughed, petting through his fur. It really was all thanks to him that today was starting off well...even though my legs felt like jelly.

Yep, definitely going to need ice.

Chapter Thirteen
Winners and Losers

Eli

Twice in less than twenty-four hours, I was forced to subject myself to a cold shower thanks to Guinevere Poe. Two days before, I wouldn't have thought of her like that; I wouldn't let myself. However, the second I admitted it, I felt like a barrier fell down and I could see her in ways that…left me feeling hot. My mind put all the pieces of her together like a puzzle. I hadn't realized I had already felt so much of her. I knew she had dainty feet from the time I wrapped her ankle, smooth skin from the time I tried to take the wedding dress off her, which was also how I remembered what her back looked like, and how full her breasts were.

Not now. I groaned to myself, grabbing my bag, though I smiled at the shoes she had given me. When I came out into my living room, I saw Logan sitting on my counter, eating my cereal. "Shouldn't you be at class?"

"It's Saturday. Why were you smiling when you came out?" he asked mid-bite.

"None of your business—" I stopped, wanting to ask him a question. "What do you think of Guinevere? As a woman?"

He grinned wide.

"Before you start with your foolishness, just answer my question."

"Honestly?"

"No, lie to me. Yes. Honestly."

"She's super hot," he said seriously.

I kind of wished he had lied. "You're just saying that to see if you will get under my skin."

"No." He shook his head. "When Sebastian first introduced us, I thought that too. She has a really nice smile. I thought she was actually one of the models for his magazines, and then realized her body was way too sinful for that. I mean, how full her bre—"

"Stop," I snapped at him. *Before I beat you over the head with that bowl.*

"What? You asked."

"I asked you to tell me what you thought of her as a woman, not give me a rundown of her body."

"Aren't bodies pretty much a big part of what makes up a woman?"

Why am I talking to this kid? "Just forget it, never mind."

I moved to grab fruit from my fridge and a water bottle when he spoke again.

"Fine. Everything except body: she's smart, and kind, a little odd but in a funny and cute way, successful on her own, and lastly, but most importantly, Mom's already in love with her. If you didn't like her so much, I'd probably ask her out."

I stopped to look at him. "You like her?"

He shrugged. "Not as much as you do, and before you use me as an excuse not to date her, know that I said I would ask her on a date, not confess to being in love or anything like that. She's a nice and pretty cool woman to be around. Of course, any straight male would want to go on a date with her. Just because you're blind doesn't mean we all need to be."

"We both just got out of pretty serious relationships. This could blow back up in our faces badly. Maybe we should wait longer before doing anything." *Anything more.*

"If you know she likes you back, what are you waiting for? The people you both were in relationships with didn't."

I didn't even want to think about it anymore. "Don't eat all my cereal," I told him, walking to the door.

"Don't let her see the stingy part of you for a while—if you actually go for it." He snorted to himself.

"I already did." I grinned when his head whipped back to me, and I closed the door.

"Wait, what?" he yelled.

I knew he would follow, so I quickly got on the elevator. Just as it was about to close I heard her voice.

"Please hold! Thank you." She came in, not even bothering to look up, cell phone in one hand while digging through her purse with the other. "No, I'm going to need double that amount of paint. Yes. Thank you so much. Also, can you get me the same art students as before? You're an angel with six wings, Suzy. Bye." She hung up, taking a deep breath. "Thanks for holding the—" She stopped, turning toward me.

"You're welcome," I said just as the doors opened at the ground floor.

"I thought you would already be at the hospital by now," she said when I let her out first.

"My shift starts in twenty minutes. I'm usually early, but I'll make it right on time."

"Is it because of me? I messed up your schedule this morning, didn't I?"

The reason I was running later than usual *was* because of her and our morning, but not the way she was thinking. "It's fine, I promise. Ride with me to the hospital?" I asked her when my driver pulled up.

She looked at the town car, then at me. "You have a driver take you to work every morning?"

"Not every morning. How were you going?"

"The bus."

"What kind of millionaire uses the bus in this city?" I opened the door for her.

She hesitated. I wasn't sure why.

"Aren't you sore?"

"True," she said, getting in.

Nodding to the driver, I took a seat beside her.

"Do you have rules?" she asked, putting on her seatbelt.

"Rules?"

She nodded. "Like not to talk to you at work? Or pretend we aren't close, or—"

"Who has rules like that?" I knew who already.

She didn't answer, just glanced out the window.

I brought her face back to me. "I told you my one and only rule this morning: don't lie. That's it. If you want to talk to me when I'm not busy, then talk to me. I'm not going to broadcast that we are…a couple, but if people find out, I really don't care. I'm not Sebastian, and I would hate it if I were being compared to him in your mind."

"You don't compare me to Hannah?"

"I don't think about her. I think about you, just you. That's why I'm here. Can't you tell? I grow more attracted to you with each passing second. Catch up."

"How are you doing it?" she whispered, her eyes dropping to my lips. "Why am I all of a sudden thinking about you like this? We should be going slow, getting to know each other…"

"Maybe it's because we've already been doing that for weeks," I told her.

"I should still make you work for me, right?"

She is too close. "Fine. I get off at eight. Late dinner? I'll cook."

"It's our first date, then," she said, taking off her seatbelt as we arrived.

Opening the door for us, I took her hand to help her out and thanked the driver.

She glanced at our hands and smirked, but didn't say anything.

Only when we were inside the blue and white building did we break apart.

"Let me know before you leave?" I asked.

She nodded, waving. "Looking forward to it, Dr. Davenport," she replied, heading to the wall.

I watched as she grabbed her headphones from her backpack and placed them over her ears. She danced as she walked like she didn't care who saw her, just kept bobbing her head.

"Is that the artist your mother brought in?" Dr. Seo asked, coming in on my right. As we watched, she took off her jacket and dropped it to the ground beside her, leaving her in just a tank top and jean shorts.

"Yes—"

"Interesting." He tilted his head to the side, watching her. "Go ahead, mate. It looks like I need to go introduce myself."

He stopped when I put my hand on his shoulder.

"What?"

"You can say hello to her, but if you try to go beyond that, you'll regret it. Enjoy your day of facelifts and silicone breasts." I turned, starting up the stairs.

Sadly, he followed me up two at a time. "She's not even your type."

"Female is my type, didn't you know?" I replied, heading to the locker room.

He snickered, pulling his hair up into a ponytail. "I bet you I can get her to go on a date faster than your cruel, stiff self."

"Really? How much are we talking about?" I lifted my shirt and pulled out my scrubs.

"The usual $5K, and this time the loser has to dye his hair."

Idiot. "Fine. Shake on it." I offered my hand.

When he took it, I said, "I think pink would look nice. How about you?"

"Fine, as long as you are willing to bleach that dark hair of yours." He still didn't get it. Pulling out my phone, I video-chatted her.

"Eli?" She stared, confused.

"I was just wondering, what should I make for our first date tonight?" I smiled as Dr. Seo's mouth opened and closed before he flipped me off.

"Anything is fine, I'm only allergic to—"

"Coffee, I remember. Sorry for bothering you."

"No problem. Bye." She laughed, hanging up.

"Sometimes man, I can't believe I'm your friend," he muttered.

I tied my laces. "I warned you if you tried to go any further you would regret it, didn't I? Listening is what makes you a good doctor." I patted his arm, heading to the door.

"One of these days I'm going to win against you. I'm donating the money to the children's ward again?"

"At least someone will just think you are a remarkable guy," I replied, walking out. When I did, I noticed Dr. Stretch, Dr. Four Eyes, and Dr. Bunhead were only then running up to me.

"You're late," I said, glancing down at my watch.

"Only by two minutes!" Dr. Stretch raised his hand.

I glared at him.

"The pit?"

They sound so sad. It was nice. I didn't answer, just nodded, heading to my first patient. That day I felt amazing.

Guinevere

Taking a step back, I stared at the wall in front of me. I had been at it for the last four hours and had only traced out the left corner. Stretching my arm and fingers, I kept stepping back.

"What is it?"

Turning around I saw no one, but I felt her move toward the wall. Placing my hand on her shoulder, I stopped her from kneeling down. Her head was covered with a small hospital cap with a bow on it. Her white skin was so pale it was eerie. She didn't even really look alive.

She hugged her teddy bear to her chest.

She shouldn't be walking. "Ms. Molly?"

"Hi Guinevere."

"Molly, shouldn't you be in your room or something—"

"No!" she yelled, pulling herself from me and running. She didn't get very far before tripping...or maybe her legs just gave out.

"Molly." I rushed over, picking her up. "Molly, can you hear me?"

She wrapped her arms around my neck, taking deep breaths. "I want to go outside." She started to cry. "I hate it here. I want to play."

I walked quickly to the nurses' station. Three doctors came running toward me, their eyes glued to the little girl in my arms. However, it was...what was his name...that man from apartment 32C who called out to her.

"Molly!" he yelled, trying to take her into his arms. "Molly, come on. Stop this, let's go back."

"No!" she screamed in my ear.

I winced. Her grip on me tightened. "I found her at my work station. She's not letting go."

I tried to take her off of me, but she just wrapped her legs tighter.

What is this?

"Molly, if I promise to come play with you, will you go with your doctors?" I hoped she would loosen up.

She shook her head. "Grown ups lie, you won't come. Daddy lied, he said I would feel better. The doctors lied, saying the other doctor would me fix me. I want to go home!" She cried harder.

I glanced at her dad, who just looked broken. His shirt was rumpled, his shoulders hunched, and his five o' clock shadow seemed to be working on its tenth hour.

"Okay. I won't lie then," I said, shifting her. "You are sick, Ms. Molly, and these people are trying to help. Running away won't make you feel better, and you won't win in the end. You liked the drawing, right? I can't come to play, but I can paint you any picture you want. Just tell me."

"My mommy," she whispered. "Can you draw her?"

I smiled, nodding. "I will have it to you in a week, and if you don't receive it, you can tell everyone I am a liar too. But right now, will you go with your doctors?"

She frowned, but nodded.

I handed her to a dark-skinned doctor with glasses. "We will take her to get her labs done, and then she'll be back in her room," he said as the trio escorted her away.

Her father—Toby, I now remembered—stood wringing his hands, watching her go. "I know this is a very dumb question, but are you all right?" I asked.

He picked up his head some, turning.

His blank look was like he'd forgotten I was there, which was understandable.

"My daughter called me a liar, and she is in pain. I'm the furthest thing from all right." He put his hand over his face and took a deep breath. "I'm sorry to dump that on you."

"It's okay, I said it was a dumb question. You look like you need a mental break. Would you like to sit with me? You're Toby Wesley, right? From my building?"

"Oh, that's why you look familiar. Yes. Ms. Poe, correct?" He followed me to sit in the chairs by the wall. "Is this your work station?" He glanced over at the light sketching on the wall.

"Yes. I officially started on it today." I leaned back in my chair and followed his gaze. My sketch was pretty hard to see with the naked eye, so I wasn't worried about anyone figuring it out yet. When the paint came in, that's when the screen was going to have to go up.

"What's it going to be?"

"It's a secret for now. Which reminds me, do you have a photo of your wife? Is she here as well, so I can work on Molly's painting?"

He sat taller in the chair, not looking at me. "She passed. It's all right, you're busy. I wouldn't want her to—"

"Mr. Wesley, if there is anything I would hate to be called, it's a liar. I promised her a painting. I have to give her one before the week is out, or else that's what I would be."

He glanced back, a small smile on his lips, before pulling out his wallet and handing me a worn photo. "If it's not good enough—"

"It's fine." I brought out my phone and snapped a photo of it. I didn't want to take it from him.

"Mr. Wesley?"

I turned, and there was Eli in his blue scrubs and white coat, holding a large cup in one hand.

"Is everything all right?"

"Yes, Dr. Davenport. Molly ran off, but we found her. I'm going to head back to her room now and wait with her, if that's okay."

"Of course. I'll be there momentarily."

Toby nodded and turned back to me. "Thank you again."

"Any time." I stood when he walked away and turned to Eli, who also watched him go.

"Nothing was going on," I said quickly.

He turned back to me, eyebrow lifted.

"I found Molly. Well, Molly found me, and I promised her a painting—"

"Why are you explaining this to me?" He looked completely confused, stepping up to me.

"I just didn't want you to get the wrong idea and get upset—"

"You're doing it again. I'm not sure if you realize it, but you are basing what you think my reaction will be on what Sebastian's was." He sighed, taking my hand and giving me the cup.

He was right, and I hadn't even thought about it. "I'm sorry."

"Don't be. I'm just going to have to work harder to make sure you see the clear difference between him and me." He smirked, nodding to the drink in my hand. "It's hot vanilla. Since you can't drink coffee, I wasn't sure what to bring you."

"You didn't have to bring anything, but thank you."

"I know, but if I didn't, what excuse was I going to use to come see you?"

Smiling, I took a sip, and my eyes about popped out of my head. "This is really good."

"Good to know. I have to head back. See you later?" he said, partially turned.

Taking his arm, I stopped him from going any farther by kissing his cheek. "Thanks."

"You're welcome. And I'm just going to be honest: your ex sounds like one hell of a douchebag." He waved, walking away.

When he was gone, I sat again and couldn't help but wonder if all guys were really like Eli. Sebastian was the only man I had ever seriously dated. When he got jealous over me speaking to other guys, I just thought he was worried about losing me. When he said he didn't want people at work to know we were going out, I thought it was because he was worried I would be looked down on for dating the boss. The more I thought about the situation, the more it felt like I should have never stayed with him. But hindsight was always twenty-twenty, and it had been hard to see the flaws when I was always staring at him through rose-colored glasses.

Eli

Turning away from the room where Molly lay resting beside her father, I faced the interns in front of me, trying my best not to holler. "She ran away?" I asked softly.

"She's been through so much chemo, we don't even know how she got up," Four Eyes said, and they all nodded along with him.

Bunhead stood straighter. "Besides, we were only gone for a second. We thought the nurses would watch out for her."

Do not lose it, Eli. "Why didn't you let me know? I had to find out from her father," I managed to say through clenched teeth.

Dr. Stretch shrugged his skinny shoulders. "We didn't want to bother you with something—"

"Stop talking!" I snapped. *I'm going to kill them.* "I'm going to go in order, so pay attention, because if I have to repeat myself, not only will you be off this service, you will be off this floor. Dr. Four Eyes, the reason why you must watch children who have received chemotherapy is because they are more resilient than adults. Some days can be horrible, even downright painful, but some days they feel well enough to get up and move. Dr. Bunhead, that is the reason why I asked you three to keep an eye on her. Unlike you, the nurses are not my interns. Unlike you, they have over a hundred patients to see to. Dr. Stretch, if you ever fail to inform me about my *missing* patient's whereabouts, or anything of the sort, I swear you won't just be off this floor, but you'll never be able to practice medicine in this state again. Any questions?"

None of them spoke.

"I will ask again. Any questions?"

"No, Dr. Davenport," they all replied.

"Great, which means you all will pull a night shift here to make sure that not only is Molly all right, but also that you get updated scans in the morning, along with any written thoughts you have on my procedure. For now, just check her blood work."

Nodding, they ran as fast as they could the other way. In the wrong direction.

I didn't even bother to stop them, just went to the station up front where Dr. Seo, who seemed to have a lot more free time, leaned back, shaking his head.

"You are so mean to the kids, honey." He laughed.

"The kids need to stay in school," I muttered, filling out my chart. "I'm not even sure how they got this far. Who doesn't tell their attending that their patient is missing? Idiots."

"So, you excited for your date tonight?" he asked.

"I am not talking about this with you." I signed my name before putting the chart back and walking away.

He followed. "We've been friends since medical school—"

"No, we went to medical school together. You just kept telling people we were friends."

He sighed. "What do women see in you? You're such an ass."

"Handsome and successful, what more do they need to see?"

He muttered something under his breath. "Look," he said when we stepped into the elevator. "I'm just shocked you're seriously with someone after—"

"Stop." I sighed. "I don't completely know what Guinevere and I are yet. We like and are attracted to each other. I feel nice when she is around, and after the year I've had…the year we've both had, feeling nice isn't something we take lightly. So yes, to answer your first question, I'm looking forward to tonight. I really hope it works out. But if it doesn't, it doesn't." Getting off, I turned back to him as he was about to go back up again. "Your hair better be dyed tomorrow."

"You are just being spiteful now." He frowned as the elevator doors closed.

Pulling out my phone as it vibrated, I smiled at her text.

'*I left for the day. Let me know when you're back.*

Go be 'kinda cool'.

Guinevere'

Chapter Fourteen
Much Ado About Nothing

Eli

I felt like I had been at the hospital forever. My whole body ached, and I was more than ready to just relax with Guinevere. However, when I got off the elevator, I noticed the person waiting at my door was Logan.

He leaned against the wall, looking down at his feet.

"Logan, I'm really busy tonight, you are—"

"I need to talk to you," he said seriously, his hands in his pockets. "I'm sure after you hear it, I'm not going to be here long."

"Logan? What is it?" I put my things down, giving him my full attention.

He took a deep breath, looked to me, and then dropped his head again. "I dropped out of medical school today."

It was like he had pushed me in front of a moving train. "I'm sorry, you what?" I asked slowly.

He nodded. "I dropped out of medical school—"

"Have you lost your damn mind?" I yelled. "What do you mean, you dropped out? You have the highest grades in your class, I spoke to your professor a week ago!"

"I don't want to be a doctor, Eli!" he hollered back at me. "I've been trying to figure out how to tell you this for...years."

"I can't believe you are saying this right now. Where is this coming from? Logan—"

"That's right, me! It's coming from me, Logan, your younger brother. I don't like hospitals, Eli. I don't like sick people. I don't want to save people's lives with a scalpel, and I don't want to be like you or Dad. I'm not—"

"Then what *do* you want? Huh? You seem to have yourself all figured out, big kid, so tell me, what are you going to do with your life?"

"I want to make music."

God help me. Turning away, I tried to find words, tried to keep calm, but I could feel my pulse quickening at the side of my neck. "Please tell me you are messing with me again." I finally managed to say. "Please tell me this is just some stupid joke."

"It's not stupid or a joke. It's what I want to do. I've already met with a record label and was asked to tour, and I'm going in a week."

"Like hell you are—"

"Eli, maybe you don't get it, but I'm sick and tired of waiting and hoping for your blessing! I'm an adult. I'm able to make this choice on my own, and I've made it." He walked around me, back to the elevator.

"So what, you are just going to throw away all your hard work? Drop everything and go sing for a living?"

"Yes, and the only reason the work was so hard was because I hated it so much. I did it because I wanted my big brother to be proud of me. I wanted him to be happy, because I knew he did everything in the world for me growing up to make up for the fact that I never knew my father. You taught me how to play baseball and soccer. You went to NYU, even though you got into the best schools in the country, because you wanted to be near me and Mom. Even after we told you we were fine, you still only chose Yale for medical school so you could drive home every few days to be with us. You've always taken care of us, and I wish I wanted the life you want for me. I really do. I wish I wasn't letting you down right now, but I'm not like you, Eli. I can't live my life for other people. I just can't." He got into the elevator.

I wasn't even sure what to say. Grabbing my stuff and entering my apartment, I was tempted to go back after him. He was throwing his life away. Why didn't he see that?

Taking an aspirin, I lay down on my couch, trying to breathe and get a hold of myself, but my headache would not stop.

Guinevere

I waited until about ten before I finally worked up the courage to knock on his door.

It took a while, but he finally opened it, wearing the same clothes he'd worn to work that morning, only more rumpled. His eyes widened as he stared at me, and then down at his watch. "Guinevere, I'm so sorry!" He put his forehead on the back of the hand holding the door.

"Can I come in? I brought Chinese." I lifted the bag for him to see.

He tried to smile. "Guinevere, I'm in an awful mood—"

"I know. I heard you and Logan. I'm sure the whole building heard you and Logan. I was just going to let it go and pretend I didn't hear anything if you called. But then I felt like I was lying. I was looking forward to spending time with you so, bad mood or not, I'm here with food."

He moved aside for me to enter.

I walked to the kitchen, putting the bag on the counter and pulling everything out. "I wasn't sure what you wanted, so I kind of got one of everything that sounded good. Stevie swears by the place, so I—what?" He was just staring at me when I turned around.

"Nothing. I'm just a little annoyed with myself for falling asleep, and you went through all this trouble. I'm sure you overthought everything, from ordering the food to coming over here," he replied, moving to get plates.

"I wasn't overthinking. Wondering what to get is a valid concern. You eat mostly healthy anyway, so I wasn't even sure about Chinese. But it's better than pizza, right?"

He snickered, shaking his head at me. "Chinese food is worse for you, but it's all right, I'll eat anything."

I should have gotten pizza!

"And now you're thinking you should have gotten pizza." He laughed, dishing out the food for us both.

"Stop doing that."

"Stop making faces and I wouldn't be able to know. Rice or noodles?"

"Always rice," I said.

His eyes paused on the small gift I had brought over as well. It was wrapped in plain brown paper from my apartment.

I saw him reach for it, so I took it back.

"Food first," I said, holding it behind my back.

He gave me an odd look but said nothing, handing me my plate and reaching into his wine fridge.

"Oh no, you're almost out of your dad's wine? I feel like it's my fault."

"I'm nowhere near being out. My mom has a whole cellar full at the house. Besides, we know how it's made. We can always have more produced if we really want to," he replied, grabbing glasses and following me to the living room. He sat close by.

Once more, I smiled at his soft couch. "One day, when I move into a bigger place, I'm going to get myself this same couch."

"Are you still using your apartment as a makeshift studio?" He took a bite and stopped, looking down at his plate. "This is amazing."

"When it comes to food, no one knows better than Stevie. Wasn't the food at her wedding great?"

"I thought you disliked the fish?"

"I did, but I'm pretty biased against all fish not from back home. I'm not even sure why I bothered," I said, taking a bite.

"Do you miss it? Cypress?"

I nodded. "Some days more than others. I love New York. After you've lived here for a while, it's kind of hard not to. But I miss the open spaces, and the nature. Once, when I was nine, we ran into a herd of baby deer, and I remember wanting to take one home with me so badly that I cried when my dad told me to leave them alone. His reasoning was, he would be sad if someone thought I was pretty and decided to take me home, which was really horrid now that I think about it, but I understood what he meant."

"The photos you showed at Stevie's wedding were cute. It's completely how I envisioned you. I'm sure you must have given your parents one hell of a time." He laughed.

"Not really." I sighed. "My parents never really tried to tell me no, so I always tried to do my best around them."

"Why?"

Putting my plate down on his coffee table, I faced him. "I'm going to tell you something sad, but please don't worry about if I'm still hurt or anything like that. For the most part, I'm really okay." I could tell he felt a little lost. "I'm only saying this because you fought with your brother. So when I was twelve, my brother came back from college and told my parents he didn't feel like a guy. He said he hated looking at this person in the mirror that wasn't him. It was killing him on the inside. He planned to become a female, and my father lost it." I whispered that last part.

"He was so angry he almost had a heart attack. He told my brother to never come back to his house ever again…not until he 'got his head on straight'. My brother, he tried. He tried as hard as he could to change himself to be more like what my father wanted, but that just made him hate himself more. No one talked about it. Then, a year later, he committed suicide, and only a few days after that, we each got letters in the mail from him. Mine was him telling me how much he loved me, and wanted me to be the best Guinevere in the history of Guineveres, and also to take care of his puppy, Taigi. To my parents, he said that he loved them, even though he knew he disgusted them, and that he hoped they could one day forgive him. My father cried for weeks, and my mom couldn't even get out of bed." I hated talking about my past. I had told no one this, not even Sebastian.

"When I go home and hug my father, I always wonder if he regrets what he said to my brother, if he would have preferred to have two daughters instead of one daughter and a dead son. The only reason I'm saying this to you—and I'm sorry for making this evening so depressing—is because hearing Logan felt like I was hearing my brother. The same thing, just this time it's about music. Is it really the same? No. Yes. I'm not sure. All I know is, we all get one life, and it's hard enough without the people we love trying to stop us from completing our dreams. Could he go out there and completely fail as a musician? Sure. It happens to millions of people, and I'm sure there will be more than enough people who will tell him he isn't any good, or that he will never make it. Believe me, I know, because I've met all of them."

Many of them were still waiting for me to fail.

"He just needs his big brother to love him anyway. I get that you love him and want him to be happy, but whether he fails or not, he just needs you to be in his corner." When I finished, I handed him the present I had wrapped.

Unfolding his arms, he took it, not looking up at me.

"I lied to you and your mother...well, and the world before. When I painted my *Whispers of the East*, it wasn't for my grandparents. It was for my brother. I've just never told anyone about him, and I didn't want my parents to be hurt if they ever saw it. The anniversary of his death is Friday, and your mom said your father died a week after that. So, I made a large-scaled one to give to her, and had small copies made and framed for you and Logan."

Eli

My hands shook as I unwrapped the paper, and when I saw it, I felt like someone was squeezing my heart. The painting was so good it looked like a photo, and she had drawn a picture of Logan and I all grown up alongside my mother and father. We were all laughing at something, and it felt so real, like he had actually lived it along with us.

"Guinevere..." I didn't even know what to say, so I put the frame down next to the lamp and kissed her. My mind was racing, I felt ten million different things, and the greatest of all was just to be with her...for as long as she would let me.

She shifted onto my lap, and my hands went under her shirt as hers gripped my hair.

"Eli..." She moaned as I kissed down her neck. "I want this with you, but I want you to want it, not just in return for the painting."

Flipping her onto her back, I stared at her. "I want this for all of that and more, because you make me feel...you make me feel things I can't describe. If you tell me to stop, I will stop."

She pulled open my shirt, smiling to herself. "I see all that running does a body good."

I reached for a condom in my back pocket when she stopped me.

"I'm on the pill," she replied, and it was music to my ears.

Grinning, I kissed her once more, biting her bottom lip. Returning the favor, I ripped open her shirt, kissing both of her breasts before I trailed my tongue down her stomach, pulling off her jeans and underwear as I went.

"Ahh..." she moaned, reaching up to hold the couch when two of my fingers slid into her. She rocked against me. "Eli!"

She shivered when I licked her. Her leg on my shoulder, my tongue buried itself in her, tasting, drinking all of her in, my fingers never once stopping.

"Eli...ahh, Eli... I...I—ahh...I can't," she said.

Or at least I thought she did, but I wasn't sure between all of her moaning and her hands pushing on my head, keeping me going.

"Eli!" She came, her body arching up.

Sitting up, I wiped the corner of my mouth, grinning at the sight of her underneath me, her chest rising and falling with each breath.

"Kiss me," she demanded.

How could I deny her? Her tongue rolled over mine and I moaned, knowing she could taste herself on my tongue.

With a slight push, she was able to get me onto my back, hopping on top of me. When she did, she took off her bra, dropping it on the ground next to me. Sitting up slightly, I grabbed her breasts and took one into my mouth. She gasped when I bit her nipple.

"Eli...I...I want you," she said, undoing my pants and reaching for me.

I twitched in her warm hand. When she stroked me so slowly, I lost my train of thought.

"Guinevere," I gasped, letting go of her breast and thrusting into her hand.

"I want you in me." She kissed my lips quickly and repeated each word.

Holding her waist, my breathing shallow, I almost came when she lowered herself onto me.

"Fuck," I hissed.

She was so damn tight, all of her clenching around me. With her hands on my chest, she rode me, her hair falling to the side, mouth partly open, moaning my name over and over again as she did.

I couldn't take it. At this rate I was going to lose it. Pushing her onto her back, I lifted up her leg, pounding myself into her, her breasts bouncing with each fuck.

"Oh, god," she cried out, hands on my shoulders. "Eli... fuck yes!"

The more she screamed out, the more I needed to hear it and the faster I went, to the point where the lamp next to the couch fell to the ground and the couch shifted with us, but I didn't care.

Her body arched up, and I was on my knees, gripping both of her thighs. I could barely see straight. "So good..." It was more than fucking good; her body was driving me toward madness.

"Eli!" she screamed my name, reaching her second orgasm.

Picking her up, her arms wrapped around me, I slammed into her, and she kissed the sides of my face. And, because she was either the cruelest woman I had ever met or the very best, she spoke dirty to me.

"Fuck me hard, Eli," she moaned, biting my ear. "Don't let me stop screaming, baby.

"I want more! Fuck me more!" she cried out, her nails running down my back.

She's killing me.

"God, ever since you kissed me, Eli, I've wanted you to fucking take me like this."

"I will, repeatedly." I spread her legs wider, enjoying how body her tilted up to the sky and, hugging her to me, I couldn't hold back any more.

"Ahh!" I came, my eyes closing to keep the room from spinning.

We both stayed there, neither of us moving from each other, her arms around my neck and mine against her waist as we took deep breaths.

When she finally relaxed, she sat atop me, making sure I could see into her eyes.

"Next time, you need to scream my name," she whispered, kissing my lips softly. "I want to hear you cry out Guinevere when you come."

I grinned, placing my hand on the side of her face. "You are not at all as innocent as you seem."

She ran her finger over my lip.

I took it into my mouth, biting it.

"Some people become different when they drink or get high. For me, it's sex. It's like something clicks in my head, and I want nothing more than for you to keep going. Thank you, I had forgotten how much I missed this."

"You are a vixen...my vixen." I wondered what else I would find out about her.

"Fuck me like that again, and I'll be anything you want me to be, Dr. Davenport," she said softly as we kissed again.

Thank God for her.

Chapter Fifteen
What's Said In Bed

Guinevere

I woke up, and the first thing I noticed was how soft the bed was. I ran my hand over the blue satin sheets and the memories flooded my mind. I could still feel his skin under my fingertips. Sitting up and taking the sheet with me as I did, I heard the shower running. The clock beside me said it was only 1 AM.

I can make my escape now...or I can join him. My heart rate quickened. I knew my answer and let go of the sheet.

I wasn't sure why I was like this. If I went a while without sex, it was like I forgot how great it was, and then when I had it again, it was all I wanted...like a child who had candy for the first time. Odd was the fact that I had only ever had sex with one other man, Sebastian. He had been my first, and I had thought he was good. I'd had nothing to compare him with, but Eli...I now understood why my bedroom wall had shaken like it did.

Everything in the marble bathroom was coated with steam, and yet I could still see the way water dripped down every muscle and toned ab right down to his legs, and how he had cute dimples on his white ass.

"Eli," I whispered, just loud enough for him to hear me.

He turned, wiping the water from his blue-green eyes and brushing his black hair back. His eyes wandered down my naked body, taking it all in and, opening the shower door, he held out a hand for me, using his body to shield me from the hot water until I got used to it. He held me, his hands resting on my ass.

"Did you just get up?" he asked.

I nodded, running my hands up his stomach. "I thought about leaving before you came out."

"You made a much better choice," he replied, one of his hands coming up to cup my cheek.

I leaned into it.

"We've crossed a bridge, and there's no going back. I don't want to. I want what happened last night to happen repeatedly."

"Which part?" I kissed his chest. "The part where you made me come with your fingers and tongue? Or the part where I rode you...no, it has to be when you flipped me down and fucked me like a whore on your couch." I kissed his chin. "Whatever part, I'm more than happy to do it again."

He pushed me up against the wall, his hands on either side of my face. "Keep talking like that, Guinevere, and you won't be able to walk out of this shower, or my apartment, for that matter."

I smirked. "You promise?"

His lips crashed down on mine, his hand cupping between my legs, and as I moaned he broke away slowly, his hand never stopping...not that I would let it. I held on to it, rocking right into the palm as he watched me.

"You are sinfully beautiful, Ms. Poe," he whispered.

With my free hand, I grabbed him, enjoying how he throbbed in my hand.

Holding on to the wall and to me, Eli grinned as he closed his eyes, lips parting as I stroked the length of him.

He let go of the wall, gripping my hand, his eyes sharp and focused as he stared at me.

"You have me in the palm of your hand, Guinevere."

I moaned, feeling another of his fingers slip inside me.

"And I can't have that."

"Do your worst," I told him.

He let go of me, raising his hand to my lips and, as I knew he wanted, I licked up slowly. Grabbing my waist, he spun me around.

I braced myself against the wet tiles, feeling him press up against my ass.

He kissed the water on my back up to my shoulder where he bit softly.

Tilting my neck, I welcomed each one of his kisses and love bites, grinding myself against the length of him.

He bit the top of my ear. "You have a way with words, Guinevere, has anyone told you that?"

"No." My lids felt heavy and when he grabbed one of my breasts, I couldn't help but close my eyes and just give in to him. "Eli."

"God, I want to fuck you so hard your knees give out right here, right now," he whispered into my ear, squeezing both of my breasts.

"Eli—"

"Can you feel how hard I am for you? Only you?" To prove his point, he took my hand and made me hold him. "That is because you have to be the sexiest woman I have ever met."

He is torturing me with words. "Eli, please…" I said when he let my hand go.

"Please what?" He put one hand on my breast, the other moving back between my legs. "Please screw you? No, that's not what you said last night. Fuck you, right? Fuck you until I scream only your name."

"You aren't playing fair." I bit my own finger when he massaged me slowly.

"Why would I play fair when I can feel how *wet* you are, how much you enjoy it like this?"

He's right. Damn it. "Eli, I need—"

"You need what? My head between your legs? You tasted so good on my tongue." He bit my ear again, his hand working faster.

Between that and his words, I had to clench my legs closed.

"That won't help you, baby. I feel you. Beg me, I want to hear you beg for me to fuck you the way you need...the way you deserve."

"Eli, please. I'll do anything, please, fuck me," I begged him, almost screaming. "Fuck me hard!"

"As you wish," he said, grabbing my ass as he, in one powerful thrust, entered me.

My mouth dropped open in the sheer pleasure of it, and I rested against the wall in front of me. "Oh god!" My voice shook with each thrust, deeper and harder into me.

"I like the way you sound when I fuck you like this, Guinevere. Hear yourself?" He kissed my shoulder.

I could barely hear anything, because my ears were ringing.

"God, and I thought you were tight last night," he moaned behind me and slapped my ass, pinching my nipple.

"Yes! Eli! More, please," I begged.

"As you wish." He slapped my ass over and over again as he buried himself deeply inside of me.

"Eli!" I screamed as I came. I couldn't hold back any more.

Holding my hips, his pace quickened. "Gwen...Guinevere!" he cried out as he came, holding me still in front of him, the shower water now running cold against our hot skin.

"You almost called me Gwen," I managed to say.

He kissed my back. "You are my Guinevere; Gwen is for everyone else."

I could live with that.

He moved from behind me, and I realized it had only been only him holding me up. My legs gave out.

"Guinevere!" he called, turning off the shower.

I laughed, trying to cover my mouth. "You really did fuck me 'til my knees went weak. You're amazing."

He snickered, reaching out of the shower enclosure to grab two towels, one for my hair and the other to wrap around my body when I stood again. Only when I was taken care of did he grab one for himself, tying it around his waist.

"I was watching that," I said.

He laughed. "Careful, Ms. Poe, or we will never leave this bathroom." He gave me his hand, helping me out of the shower and back toward his bedroom.

"Are my clothes still in the living room?"

"Over there." He pointed to the dresser by his closet. He had folded everything nicely. "But your shirt is damaged beyond repair. Have this."

"Thank you." I took his shirt. "I'll head back and bring it with—"

"Don't go yet," he said.

"What?"

"It's only 2 AM. Stay, sleep here for now. I can make breakfast when we wake up in the morning."

For some reason, I wasn't sure. "I don't want to be that girl who never leaves, Eli—"

"I'm the one asking you to stay. Believe me, if I need space, I'll let you know. But our relationship is more than sex. Or at least, that was my plan before last night," he confessed, rubbing the back of his neck. "Remember what I told you about Hannah and Sebastian?"

"We said a lot about them. You're going to have to refresh my memory." I took off the towel and put on his shirt.

Coming over to me, he helped brush back a few strands of my hair, which were starting to curl from the water. "I said that any two people with working organs can have a great screw, but that a relationship based only on sex won't last. I was right. They didn't. I don't want to be like them."

"I was going to tell you this during dinner, before everything happened last night." I looked up at him. "You might not have noticed, but I'm a little weird. I have full conversations with my dog, and honestly sometimes I think he's a secret mastermind. I make weird faces because I'm having a conversation in my head. I change into this super polite doll when I'm around adults, even though I am one. I'm still a little jaded from my ex and worry I'm going to ruin this because I suck at dating. Like you said, I snore...I still will never admit I drool though. There are times where I hate getting dressed up and just want to eat ice cream and watch Netflix until the sun comes up. Because I like you, I lie, and say crazy things like I run nine miles every morning, when in reality I think the fact that you do that every day is insane. Oh yeah, and I ramble...apparently."

"So what you are saying is, you aren't perfect and you're a handful?" he said slowly.

I nodded. "I will drive you crazy, which is why I wanted to warn you last night, before we went further."

He laughed and kissed my forehead. "Maybe you forgot, but I knew all that from the beginning. It still didn't stop me from liking you. Any other warnings you have for me?"

"In the morning, my hair will look like a French poodle. Don't worry, I will fix it. It's the price I pay for shower sex."

He just shook his head. "Do you want anything to eat before we go to bed? I'll bring it."

"Anything is fine," I told him, falling onto his bed...I was so sleepy.

Eli

Safe to say she was by far the most unique girl I had ever been with in all my life. Her list of faults...I believed every one of them, and yet I didn't seem to care. She made me happy. Next to her, because of her, I smiled and laughed more than I had in any other period of time. Even in the beginning, I got a kick out of her just getting worked up over my words. Now her rambling and mishaps just seemed to be part of her charm. Taking the tray, I headed back in to find her buried under my sheets, blissful, her eyes closed.

"That smells good," she whispered, sitting up in the middle of the bed.

"Here." I handed her the glass of orange juice, which she happily took, before setting the tray of sandwiches between us. "Turkey or ham?"

"Must I really choose?" She pouted.

"Both works, too." I had made more than enough.

Smirking, she took the turkey first. "Thank you."

"You know"—I grabbed a sandwich for myself—"I'm not perfect either, right? I'm a controlling neat freak who gets his kicks torturing young interns, and I only have one friend whom I'm an ass to, for the most part."

"If I found out you were perfect, I would feel uncomfortable," she replied, licking the mayo off the side of her lip.

I tried not to focus on it.

"Besides, after last night, I have a better understanding of what type of person you are."

"And what type of person am I?"

"A rock," she said.

I looked at her, completely confused.

"My dad always classifies people in terms of nature. People who are rocks, like you, are always at the base of people. Helping people, taking care of people, no matter the cost. You don't realize it, but when Logan was saying how much he wished he could pay you back for always being there for him, I saw it. You are willing to sacrifice everything for the people you care about."

"Isn't that everyone?" I took another bite.

"Yeah, but not everyone plans their lives around their little brother and mother, where they go to school, where they start their careers. Not everyone calls their brother's professor just to check up on how he's doing. You do it because you love them enough that worrying about yourself makes you feel selfish. Even when we first met again at the hospital, I was wrong; you weren't telling me to leave because my presence bothered you, you really were worried that Logan was going to keep blaming himself. You are your family's rock. It's not a bad thing, it's amazing," she said, eating as her brown eyes watched me carefully.

I wasn't sure how I felt about her reading me so easily. "What does your father call you?"

She laughed. "I'm the rain because, as he would say, I'm vital to his life. The world would be a horrid place if it never rained. My mother says it's because I can be a summer shower or a hurricane. And my brother...my brother used to say it was because I was a wonder. No matter how many times you see the rain, if you just sit and watch, it's wondrous. As you can tell, they were all biased."

I didn't think so, but said nothing anyway.

"And what I told you about my brother." She bit her lip, glancing back up at me. "Do you mind never talking about that with anyone? Besides you and Stevie, you're the only person outside of my family who knows."

"You never told anyone else?" I wanted her to say she never told him.

She nodded. "It's not something you can bring up in casual conversation."

"I won't say a word. Thank you for telling me. I'm still not a hundred percent okay, but I'm going to try my best to support Logan. I guess part of me is annoyed because I can't help him in any way. He has to do it on his own, and I have to let him. It's a first for me."

"He's doing well already," she said, taking her phone off the bedside table. "He already has a lot of followers on social media, and his song was in the iTunes top one hundred."

"What?" I took the phone from her, and sure enough, there was Logan onstage at some concert. "When did he do all of this?"

"I don't know. I remember Sebastian talking about his music career once, but I never followed it closely. I googled him after he left; as you can see, I'm a little nosy."

"I had no idea he was already doing this," I said, more to myself, scrolling up and down all the messages he had from fans, people he didn't even know who supported him more than I did. Sighing, I gave her back the phone, resting against my pillows.

She took the tray off the bed and put it on the ground beside her. Wrapping her arm around me, she rested her head on my chest.

"I only wanted to make sure he was okay. When our father died, Logan was so little. I felt bad because I had all these memories, and he didn't, so I've always tried to do what my father did for me: set a good example, make sure he was doing everything he was supposed to, going to all his games. I didn't realize I was suffocating him." It hurt to think about.

"You weren't," she said softly as my hands rubbed up and down her side. "I'm sure he's happy he has all those memories, and besides you wanting him to be a doctor, he wouldn't change anything."

"I knew he liked music, but I never thought it could be his career. It's just—"

"His life now depends on whether or not other people like what he does." She looked up at me. "That's the difference between your career and ours. Yours is by education and training. In many ways, it is in your own hands. But, like you said, for us, it all rides on whether or not we are popular. We can go to school and train too, but if, at the end of the day, no one buys anything... It was scary at first for me, but when you do make it, and you give someone a painting, and he looks at you like you created a miracle... it's worth the risk."

There was silence between us for a while and I remembered her painting. How it *was* a miracle. There were no family photos of us all together, and with her hands, she had created one on her own.

A smile spread across my face when I heard her soft snore.

Rolling her over onto her back, she then shifted onto her side, facing me.

Behind her, I saw the time and realized we had talked for another hour. She was just so easy to listen to and speak with.

"What are you doing to me, Guinevere?" I kissed her head, feeling myself drifting. I was pretty sure I was going to dream of her; she was slowly taking up a bigger part of my life.

CHAPTER SIXTEEN
TROUBLEMAKERS

Eli

I held Taigi's leash as we walked back to the apartment. Guinevere had to rush to meet a paint supplier since we'd both overslept, so I offered to take Taigi out. I could only get in a thirty-minute run, but I wasn't bothered; I felt more than worked out, anyway. Before we could turn the corner, Taigi stopped, sitting his gray ass on the sidewalk.

"Come on," I said, tugging on his leash.

When he got up, he tried to walk in the other direction.

Kneeling in front of him, I scratched behind his ear. "We can go for a good run tomorrow, but I've got to go to work."

He barked, trying to walk back again.

"Taigi," I said like I was talking to a naughty child.

He whined, but followed me.

The moment I turned the corner, I wished I had listened to him.

He hunched over, looking almost like a wolf, and growled at the man standing right in front of our building, holding a bouquet of red and white poppies. The fact that I knew what they were proved I had gone flower shopping with my mother one too many times. When we reached the man, Taigi's growls grew louder.

"Taigi?" Sebastian turned, looking down at the dog.

Taigi barked, baring his teeth at him.

Good boy, I thought, tempted to "accidentally" loosen my grip on his leash.

"Eli—"

"To you, it's Dr. Davenport, and why the hell are you standing in front my building? Would you like for me to actually bust your face in? Hannah isn't here to threaten me with the cops."

He looked back at the building above. "You live here?"

"And you don't, so why are you still in my face?"

"That's Gwen's dog—"

Taigi jumped as if to bite off the finger he had dared to point in his face.

"You should leave before I let him go," I threatened, giving Taigi some slack.

The husky jumped closer to Sebastian, causing him to back up quickly.

"Taigi, it's me, Bash—"

Again, he bared his teeth.

"Apparently he doesn't want to see your ugly face, either." His whole presence was pushing my buttons, especially since I knew why he was there.

"I came to see Gwen—"

"Why?" I asked him calmly. "You miss her? You know you made a mistake? Those all seem like *you* problems, because she's fine. Haven't you been selfish enough for one lifetime?"

He dropped his head, running his hands through his sandy brown hair. "I can never say sorry enough for what I did to you. You have every right to hate me, but I need to see her. I know if we talk, if we just remember the good, instead—"

"What good could possibly overshadow the fact that you ran off with the woman who was supposed to be my wife as she walked down the aisle? What universe do you live in?"

I could tell he was getting angry from how tightly he held the bouquet in his hands. His whole body tensed.

"This is none of your business, *Dr. Davenport*. I still love Gwen, and I'm going to make my universe her universe again—"

"You sound more like a crazy stalker, and not her partner," I said, moving toward the door, but stopped when I was at his shoulder. "But then, how could you be, when she's with me?"

"What?" he snapped. "What the fuck do you mean you are her partner? You couldn't possibly be in—"

"In a relationship? Why not? Come on, use that peanut-sized brain of yours, Evans. You both dumped us. Who else were we going to look to but each other? So when you say it's none of my business, you are sadly mistaken, because Guinevere is with me in every sense of the word. And if you, in any way, upset her or try to contact her, I won't just bust your face in, I will make sure you spend the rest of your life being fed through your nose."

He was steaming, his body shaking. "Are you scared she'll go back to me? Is that what this show of manhood is for right now? What, you guys have known each other for a little while and you think that compares to the years she has spent next to me? Do you know anything about her? She's in love with me, I was her first!"

"Are you trying to make me jealous right now?" I snickered. "Please understand, I don't give a rat's ass about what you both *were*. She knows you broke up with Hannah, and you know what she said? She wished you two had stayed together. That was right before she took my hand. So stop yelling about how you were her first and she wants you, because the truth is neither of us wants anything to do with you people ever again. We're enjoying our lives way too much for your bullshit."

Taigi took this time to lift his leg and piss all over Sebastian's Italian shoes.

It took everything I had not to laugh.

"You fucking mutt!" he screamed, trying to kick the wetness from his shoes.

Taigi happily sat beside me.

"Try your luck at something new tomorrow, Evans. It looks like you really won't win today," I replied, heading inside.

Only when the elevator doors closed did Taigi relax, lying down on the elevator floor.

Kneeling down, I petted his stomach. "I see what she was saying about you being a little mastermind. That's why you wanted me to turn around? So I didn't waste my time with him?"

He looked up at me lazily, only to put his head back down—like I shouldn't have even bothered asking, since I knew the answer. *Great. Now I'm guessing at the thoughts of a dog.* This was all Guinevere's doing…but I couldn't help but wonder if Sebastian had really been her first. She was just so…sexual. The fact that any man had thrown that away made me wonder about his sanity.

When I got off the elevator, there was Logan, once again leaning against my door. He looked like he'd had one hell of a night.

"Are you hungover?" I asked him, opening my door and letting Taigi in; I would drop him back at her place once I left for work.

He nodded. "I was just so upset at myself… I was so determined yesterday, and then when I left, it all disappeared."

He sat down on the arm of my couch, burying his head in his hands.

Grabbing an aspirin and water, I handed it to him. "You didn't let Mom see you like this, did you?"

He shook his head, throwing the pills into the back of his mouth and drinking half the bottle at once. "She was fast asleep when I got home this morning. I didn't want to wake her up, so I came here. Cause where else am I going to go?"

"Here is fine."

He sighed, not looking up at me. "If it doesn't work out, I promise I will go back to med school. I won't ask for you to help get me into a good one, either. I will work hard and get in on my own—"

"It will work out," I said to him.

He looked up at me, his blue eyes confused. "What?"

Taking a seat, I drank my water. "Don't think of medical school as a fallback plan. If you don't want to be a doctor, Logan, then you can't be doctor, no matter how hard you force yourself. Make music. Your songs aren't half bad; I listened to them while I was running this morning. You have talent."

"Who are you, and where is my older brother? God, how drunk am I?" he muttered, falling into the seat beside me.

I smacked him over the head.

"Yep, it's you," he groaned, rubbing the spot. "I don't get it. Last night you were one minute away from killing me. You looked so disappointed."

"Logan." I sighed. "I'm sorry. Over the years, I've never asked you what you wanted to do with your life. I just made decisions for you and forced you to do what I thought was right for you. You aren't me, and I'm not you. I can't keep coaching you, nor am I going to stand in your way. So, I'm just going to be your brother on the sidelines. My only job is to cheer you on, no matter what. It might take me a while to adjust, so be patient with me, but I promise I will try."

He didn't say anything for a few minutes, just took a deep breath. "Thank you, Eli."

"I have no idea why you are thanking me." I tried to brush it off, taking the frame from the side table and giving it to him.

"What is this?" He stopped, just staring at it. "Is that—"

"Us, plus Mom and Dad. Yeah, Guinevere painted it. We have copies; apparently she's giving the original to Mother."

"It looks so real. For a second, I thought: when did we take this?" He laughed. "She's amazing."

"She really is," I said to myself.

Guinevere

I bit my spoon and opened my yogurt as she came over to me, her heels clicking on the floor before she sat down, placing a cup of coffee in front of me.

"Mrs—Dr. Davenport, good afternoon," I said once I put the spoon down.

She smiled. "Gwen, you can call me Meryl, it's fine. How are you?"

"I'm fine, thank you. I'm taking a small lunch break before starting my first round of painting."

"I went by to have a sneak peek, but sadly your curtain is already up. I think I saw a few younger students here with you last night?" She stirred her coffee.

"Oh yeah, they helped me finish tracing it onto the wall. At first I thought I could do it alone, but that would have taken me weeks. I promise, when I'm done, I will let you be the first to see it."

She nodded, holding her cup.

"Is everything all right?"

"My sons. They often think I don't know or don't see everything that happens to them. For the most part, I just let them think I'm clueless. What neither knows is that they, like their father, have a tendency to ramble when they're drunk."

What? Why was she telling me this? "I don't understand…"

"Last night—well, early this morning, Logan stumbled into our home an absolute mess, and he was upset with himself. He kept asking why couldn't he just be like Eli, and saying he didn't want to let us down. Then, thirty minutes ago, he comes to my office, clear-minded and sober, with his brother, telling me he's dropped out of medical school and is going on tour." She giggled.

I wasn't sure if it was a nervous giggle or a happy one. "Are you upset?"

She shook her head, just staring. "Not at all. Whatever my son wants to do, I will always support him. I knew he wasn't passionate about medicine, so I wasn't too surprised. What caught me off guard was Eli. I was expecting to have to calm him down and remind him he can't control his brother's life…but for some reason I didn't need to do that. And I got to wondering, besides me, who else can break through that thick head of his? Next thing I know, I'm looking for you."

Why was I so nervous? Brushing my hair back, I nodded. "I heard them fighting, and I talked to Eli afterward—"

"Thank you, Gwen." She put her hand on mine. "Thank you for being there for him. At first, I told myself he was only pretending to be all right for our sake, and then I realized he really is happy. So thank you. I hope I'm not putting too much on your shoulders. I know you two are friends, right?"

I felt like she was trying to read me, and I took a bite of my yogurt, looking away. Only I wished I hadn't, because then I saw Hannah and her pretty, curled golden hair as she held her tray and sat three seats behind us. Her eyes met mine, and I was forced to look back at Meryl. She glanced over, and Hannah's head dropped, eating her soup.

"She must still bother you. I never said I'm sorry for what you had to go through on that day. I can't even imagine."

"You have no reason to be sorry. None of that really bothers me. Part of me feels like I should be more upset, but I'm glad I'm not. I keep thinking I'm so glad we ended before I married him, or everything would have been much worse."

"Good for you," she said, drinking some of her coffee. "I, for one, am glad I do not have to worry about her and Eli again."

"What do you mean?" I stopped eating.

"Once Eli cuts you out of his life, he cuts you out completely and never goes back. When I visited him three days after the wedding, I noticed he had already gotten rid of everything that once belonged to her. It's just the type of person he is."

I knew that wasn't a hundred percent true. He might have thrown out everything physical, but he had still held on to her phone number for a while before finally allowing me to delete it.

"Who is what, Mother?"

Speak of the devil.

Turning, he came alongside us with a man with silver-pink hair pulled into a short ponytail, both of them holding trays of their own.

Meryl winked at me, standing up. "Nothing, we were talking about her work. How are you, dear?"

"Why do I have a hard time believing that?" He gave her a look, taking the untouched coffee from in front of me and giving it to his friend.

"Eli—"

"She's allergic to coffee." He kissed her cheek, taking a seat in front of me.

She gave me a look, and all I could do was nod.

"And if it was nothing, why don't you stay?"

"Eli Philip Davenport, you don't believe your own mother?"

"No, I know you were talking about me. You only throw out my middle name when I've said too much, or you have." His eyebrow raised and a smirk crossed his lips.

She looked to the pink-haired man. "How you are his friend is beyond me, Dr. Seo."

"I only endure his torture because you are his mother, Madam Chairwoman."

She patted him on the shoulder, nodding to me before taking her leave.

At her exit, Dr. Seo tried to take a seat with us, but Eli gave him a look…a look he ignored, pulling a chair close. "Dr. Ian Seo. It's a pleasure to meet you, Ms.—"

"Guinevere Poe, but you can call me Gwen. I like your hair." I shook his hand.

"That cruel man made me dye it after cheating in a bet. Thank you, though." He frowned at Eli, who spread jam on his bagel, not paying any attention to him.

"What was the bet on?"

Eli stopped mid-bite and glared at him.

"He was just trying to warn me not to touch something that was his. Lesson learned. Do you have any friends who like Asian men with pink hair?"

"All my friends are taken." I laughed, shaking my head. He sighed.

"I'll keep an eye out," I added.

He looked to Eli. "Must God bless only you?"

"That sounds like a conversation between you and whatever god you believe in. Can you take the coffee and go? It's giving her a headache."

It wasn't, but I knew he was just saying that to get him to leave. I noticed he had started drinking tea instead whenever he was around me.

Dr. Seo winked at me before getting up. "I hope to see you around more, Ms. Poe."

"I'm working here, so I'm sure we will meet again."

He nodded, patting Eli on the shoulder, much to Eli's annoyance, before leaving.

"So, what were you and my mother talking about?"

"What was your bet against Dr. Seo?"

He licked his lips, swallowing before nodding. "Fine, it's a draw."

"How's your day?" I asked, continuing to eat.

He shrugged. "Saved a few lives here, saved a few lives there—"

"Wow, I am surely in the presence of greatness. Should I bow?"

"If it pleases you." He winked. "Your mural?"

"It's good. Only planned to be gone for a few minutes, but people just keep popping up."

"I know what you mean," he said seriously.

I could feel something was off. He didn't look happy, nor did he look like he wanted to tell me what was bothering him. "Eli, what is it?"

"This morning when I came back with Taigi, Sebastian was waiting in front of the building...with flowers."

"White and red poppies?"

He nodded.

"I'm guessing you didn't just walk past him?"

"Words were spoken."

"Just words?"

Again, he nodded. "Though Taigi did piss on his shoes."

"Oh, I love my dog." I laughed, brushing my hair back. "He didn't say anything to upset you, did he?"

"Not in the least."

"Good, then if you aren't worried about it, I'm not." I stood, grabbing my tray. "I really should get back if I want to get to where I was hoping today. Dinner?"

"I'll actually cook this time," he replied, but before I could leave, he called out once more. "Guinevere?"

"Yes?"

"Three questions: do you like poppies?"

"Yes, they are my favorite flowers. Your second question?" I knew he was asking because of Sebastian.

"What's your middle name? After all, thanks to my mom, you know mine."

It seemed like a boring question, but I told him. "It's Aurora. Guinevere Aurora Poe. And your last question?"

"Will you go on a date with me tonight, Guinevere Aurora Poe?"

"Yes."

"Pick you up at the arts and crafts corner?" He smiled.

Rolling my eyes at him, I waved before heading out. I walked back down the grayish-blue hall while stretching my arms, preparing for the work ahead of me. Then she came out in front of me at the end of the hall. "Hannah." I nodded, trying to walk around her.

She called out to me. "You should stop now."

"What?" I turned to her.

She put her hands in her scrub pockets, walking forward. "Whatever is going on with you and Eli, you should stop before you fall in love with him and he actually hurts you. Eli doesn't fall in love."

"I'm sorry, what's going on between me and Eli isn't any of your business—"

"I cheated because he didn't love me." She cut me off. I wanted to slap her across the face, but she just kept going.

"Eli is a planner. He sets goals and has this whole layout in his mind of the way his life should be. I wanted to get married at the end of the year, but Eli wanted to get married by his 31st birthday. Why? Because his father did. He dated me because I checked all the boxes for what he wanted in a woman. There was no passion in anything we did; it was all just logical for him. I wanted passion. I wanted to be loved the way you see in movies. So I cheated. And—"

"How's that passion working out for you?" I asked. "Maybe you forgot who you're talking to, but I really don't give a shit, Hannah. If you don't feel loved, you leave before you are in a white dress, walking toward someone. You want me to feel pity—"

"No. Like I said, I just wanted to let you know, because I hurt you already. You should be with someone who can love you, who's not messing around—"

"Stop talking to me!" I snapped at her. "I don't want to hear your words of *"wisdom"*; you aren't my sister, or my friend. You are the last person in the *world* I would ever take relationship advice from. Mind. Your. Own. Goddamn. Business. Hannah!" Walking away from her, I went straight to my corner, closing the curtain behind me. Why couldn't they just leave us alone? Why must we be as miserable as them?

CHAPTER SEVENTEEN
THE OFFICIAL FIRST DATE

Eli

"**H**ave you thought about where you're going to take her?" Ian asked me as I changed. "She seems like a down-to-earth type of girl to me. I'm not sure taking her to the opera will be her type of thing."

"Ian—"

"Plus, she's been working all day, I'm sure she would feel out of place... Oh no, you aren't going to do an Edward Lewis and take her shopping and let her buy anything her heart desires, right? It might seem nice in movies, but she might take it to mean you dislike her current style."

Closing my locker, I looked at him. "Who the hell is Edward Lewis?"

"*Pretty Woman?* How have you never seen that movie?"

"How often do you remember the characters' names when you watch a movie?" I asked, placing my watch on my wrist.

"That's beside the point right now. Have you thought this out? First dates are important." He was starting to get on my nerves.

"Not really. Other than asking her out, I haven't thought it through too much. I don't overthink with Guinevere, I just do, and it feels amazing. So go get yourself a date, my friend, and leave me alone," I told him, grabbing my bag.

He grinned like he was high, and with his silverish-pink hair, it wasn't a hard sell. "You called me your friend. It's like she's melting your frozen heart—"

"Goodbye Ian," I said, already out the door. I wasn't sure why he was so happy I was going on a date. He hadn't been that excited when I'd gone out with Hannah. I had taken her to the opera and she had loved it, but Guinevere wasn't Hannah, and I didn't want her to be.

"Eli."

This is what I get for even thinking about her. Sighing, I turned around to see her standing there, still in oversized scrubs and a sweater. "Yes?"

"Can we talk?"

"Sorry, I have a date," I said, turning toward the exit.

"Seriously Eli, four and a half months ago, you were about to make me your wife. Please, give me five minutes!"

I stopped, clenching my coat. Facing her again, I walked right up to her. "But the thing is, you aren't my wife. You aren't my anything. I gave you two years, Hannah. I gave you a ring. I don't want to waste giving you any more of my time."

"If you had given me your heart, you wouldn't be able to go on a date. Not with some other woman, not yet."

Wow. I huffed to myself. She really was that selfish. "So what you're telling me is I should be suffering? I should be a wreck, right? Because then at least you could see how badly I was in love with you?"

She crossed her arms. "I didn't mean it like that—"

"Yes, you did, and I'll give you an answer. The first month, I was like that. And then I met her, and without realizing it, I stopped thinking about you. Even when we were actually talking about you and him, you were both just blurs, and I could only see her. Maybe because she knew exactly how embarrassed and stupid I felt. The reason I'm not miserable like you were hoping is because when I..." I smiled, not really able to stop myself. "Because when I think about her, I can't stop smiling, and it's about the dumbest things, like why the hell does she not buy furniture, or how can she think vanilla ice cream is the best flavor in the world? So. Please stop asking me for a moment of my time, Hannah. I don't want to go back to you. Have a good night."

I didn't care if she called after me a million times. I wasn't going to turn back. Heading toward the front of the building, I felt lighter. Glancing up at the giant curtain, I shook my head. God only knew what she was painting in there. "Guinevere?" I was tempted to knock on it.

She popped her head out. "You're here already!"

"Do you want me to go and come back?"

"No, give me ten—no, five minutes. Sorry, I got carried away and lost track of time." She went back in her corner. There was a small clink, and she let out a soft curse.

"You okay?"

"I'm great."

She sounded like she was hopping. *This is what I am talking about.* I just never knew what she was going to say or how she was going to react. Sitting on the chairs, I waited.

Sure enough, when she came out five minutes later, she had changed into a long white dress, green jacket, and her military boots. "Is this okay for where we're going?" She spun around for me.

"Are you telling me you changed back there?" It was taking my mind a little while to catch up. Her bare legs were distracting me—that, and the knowledge that five minutes before she had been naked.

"Yeah, no one could see, right? My plan was to go home and then change, but I forgot while I was working. What?"

Standing up, I took her hand. "Nothing, you look beautiful."

"Really?"

She laughed like she didn't believe me. "I wouldn't say so if you didn't. Let's go," I said, walking out to where the car was parked, waiting in front of the hospital. My driver handed me the keys before heading back to the town car.

"This is yours?" she asked, running her hand on the car. "Tell me this is yours."

"It is. It's a—"

"Black 1965 Aston Martin DB5 Vantage Convertible. It's James Bond's car," she finished for me in total awe.

"You know cars?" I asked, opening the door for her and heading around to the front seat.

"I told you before, I grew up with boys. And I know there are only twenty-one of these in the world."

"Well, I'm one of the twenty-one," I said, pulling out onto the street.

She bit her finger, looking at me with a large smile on her face.

"What?"

"Don't mind me, I'm just watching your hotness level rise."

I snickered. "What level was I on before?"

"Does it matter now that you've broken the scale?"

It was my turn to bite my own finger, looking over at her. The way she rested back in the seat, her hand out, flowing with the wind, the way her dress hiked up even farther... "Guinevere, I swore to myself I am never having sex in this car, and you are testing me."

"All right, not in it, but what about on it?"

Dear Jesus, give me strength, I prayed, focusing on the road in front of me. I could hear her giggling at the effect she had on me.

Her hand grazed mine, and I took a deep breath. "Guinevere—"

"I'll be good, I swear."

But I didn't want her to be good. I enjoyed her exactly the way she was: happy, fun, free, sexy, and beautiful.

"The aquarium?" she said when we pulled up in front. "Isn't it closed?"

"Not if you ask it not to be," I said as we took off our seatbelts and I stepped out. After walking around the car, I opened her door for her.

"You rented out the aquarium?"

"Really isn't that hard." I took her hand, placing it over mine.

She looked back to my car, though. "Are you sure it will be all right? Can you leave it here?"

"It will be fine, believe me. Mr. Raymond will look after it." I nodded to the man who came out of the town car.

"Rich people," she whispered under her breath.

"Said the rich woman."

She gave me a look, then froze when I snapped on all the lights in the tanks all around us. The place glowed soft blue, and she gravitated to the tanks. Smiling, she followed the fish with her hands.

"Like it?"

She looked to me and grinned. "It's beautiful. I love it."

"I remembered when we watched Animal Planet, your eyes were glued to the sea turtles." I took her hand, leading her toward the tunnel.

She lifted her head, her eyes following the sharks swimming over us. "Hello." She laughed, turning so her back pressed against my chest as she watched the stingray hover right above her.

Wrapping my arms around her waist, I kissed the side of her head. "You look beautiful when you smile like that," I whispered.

She held on to my arms. "Thank you, and thank you for this. It's really romantic."

"Like something out of your books?" I teased.

She turned back to me, her eyes serious. "Exactly like that. I'm just waiting for you to kiss me."

"Happily," I said before my lips brushed against hers. Her hands went around my mouth and I held her waist, pulling her as close to me as possible. I loved how she fit against me, how she moaned against me even then. Breaking away, I rested my head on hers.

"How long can we stay here?" she asked me.

"Until you get hungry. Then I plan on making you a late dinner."

"You don't have to do all of this."

"I want to." I kissed the top of her head. "Let's go, we have to see the sea turtles at least once."

"I'll race you," she said, breaking free of my hand and running.

"You want to race?" I chased after her, catching her with absolute ease, lifting her up and over my shoulder.

"Damn it, I forgot you run."

She laughed hysterically as I held her. Spinning us both around, I laughed too.

Guinevere

It was around eleven when we got back to his place. He said he was off the next day, so he didn't care if we stayed up until dawn. His driver, I had found out, wasn't just his driver; he was responsible for all of Eli's cars because Eli was a collector. I thought he had showed me the coolest one, but he said he would save those for another date—I was just glad there would be other dates.

When I told Stevie I was dating Eli, she was both happy and worried about me. She was worried I was moving too fast and would get hurt, but at the same time happy I was moving forward at all. I couldn't explain what it was about him, me, us together—we just worked, and yet it felt like everything about us was totally opposite.

He stood in front of me in simple jeans and a nice button-down shirt, a towel over his shoulder and an apron around his waist as he fried some of the tomatoes. He had a whole master chef thing going and he looked so sexy that way.

Taigi stayed by my feet, just resting, already fed and now fighting sleep.

"If you are trying to impress me, it's working," I said, reaching for one of the fresh sliced tomatoes he had cut.

"Did you think this kitchen was just for show?" he asked, readjusting the heat of the oven and sliding the chicken back inside.

"Honestly, yes. When do you have time to cook, anyway?"

"I have days off. Why don't you cook?" He continued slicing the ham as thin as possible.

"I cook decently, especially if I have a set recipe to follow, but I'm not as talented as you, it seems." I tried to grab another tomato but he beat me to it, eating it himself.

"I could teach you…for a small fee."

"A small fee?" I opened my mouth as he fed me a small bite of the bread he had hand-seasoned. Safe to say, I moaned, it was that good.

"Yes, you have to promise to make those sounds afterward…all night." He kissed me, quickly licking his lips.

"Are you trying to seduce me, Doctor?" I wiped the corner of my mouth.

His eyebrow went up. "Is it working?"

"I think I'll just keep you guessing." I grinned, reaching into my bag when my phone rang. The number looked familiar but there was no ID. "Guinevere Poe."

"Gwen, it's me. Please don't hang up," he shouted into the phone.

I did anyway and dropped it beside me, looking back to Eli, who just stared at me.

"Is everything okay?"

"Yep. It was no one important—" Before I could even finish, my phone rang again and vibrated against the counter.

"Do they know they aren't important?" he asked softly, placing the fresh cut lettuce in a bowl.

"It's Sebastian."

"I figured. Want me to answer?" he questioned.

I couldn't tell at all what he was thinking. The phone stopped, and I let out a sigh of relief, only to have it start ringing again.

"Please make him stop. He called before, and I told him I didn't want anything to do with him. For some reason, he doesn't believe me." I grabbed the phone and handed it to him.

He smirked, wiping his hands before taking it. "How can I help you, Sebastian?" he questioned.

I wished I could hear him on the other side.

"I'm going to have to stop you right there, because we had this conversation already. What my girlfriend and I do is none of your business."

I walked around the counter to Eli. He looked at me oddly as I squeezed between him and the counter, kissing up his neck. He pressed up against me.

"Eli…" I moaned, louder than necessary.

Eli placed his thumb on my bottom lip, his eyes never off of them. "Sebastian, if you'll excuse me, my girlfriend is begging for my attention."

"I'm begging for a lot more than that," I said to him, and I was sure that was the last thing Sebastian heard before he hung up.

I watched Eli's hands go on either side of me after returning my phone to my bag. "You called me your girlfriend."

"Aren't you?" he asked, gripping my breast. "You are only seeing me, aren't you?"

Licking my lip, I nodded.

"Then by definition, you are mine. Just like I'm your boyfriend. Now I am tempted beyond measure to take you right here. But, I promised you dinner." He moved his hands back down. "So you are safe until then."

"Are you sure?" I said, reaching for him.

He bit his lip, glaring at me.

"Because what your body and mouth are telling me are two different things right now."

"Thank God," he muttered to himself when the timer went off.

Laughing, I backed away, allowing him to finish with his cooking. "Saved for now, but the night is still young," I said, moving to get the wine.

"When I first kissed you, I thought my appetite for sex might put you off. Yet, you are enjoying yourself as you tempt me every step of the way," he said, grabbing plates.

"Would you prefer me to be nervous? Pretend I don't like the way you bend me over and—"

"You are evil." He kissed my lips. "I like it."

I kissed him back, and bit his bottom lip. "Good. I'm too stubborn to change now."

"Let's eat, we can talk about that later," he said, moving to the dishes.

I watched as he took his time, like the perfectionist he was, putting everything together elegantly on the table.

It looked better than if we had ordered it off a menu at a five-star restaurant and tasted just as good.

"Grab the salad?" he said, moving toward his dining room.

"We are eating in your dining room?"

"That is where people usually eat dinner, Guinevere," he said, placing my plate on a silver mat on top of his black wooden table. The whole table was already set up for two, with wine glasses and a pitcher of water in the center.

"You really went all out," I whispered when he took the bottle and salad from me, placing them on the table before pulling out my chair.

"There is even vanilla ice cream in the freezer."

"Don't you hate it?"

"But you believe it is the cornerstone of ice cream, remember? And this isn't really going all out. When I go all out, you will know."

"Honestly, I thought you would make hamburgers and we would watch Animal Planet together again. What is this? It smells good."

"It's just chicken with prosciutto and tomatoes over polenta," he replied.

I was tempted to point out that he had said *just* before that description.

"What kind of first date would hamburgers and Animal Planet be?"

I shrugged. "You've just done so much today—"

"Good, you'll always remember how amazing I am." He winked.

There's that ego. Saying nothing, I took a bite. I kind of wished it didn't taste as delicious as it did. I could feel him staring at me, waiting. Chewing slowly, I reached for the glass of wine.

"You are trying so hard not to compliment me right now, aren't you?"

"I really am. It's so good." I caved, cutting into more of it.

Eli

Because I'd cooked, she refused to let me help clean up. Instead, she made me sit where she had at the counter, placing the gloves on her hands and getting to work.

"Guinevere, it's fine—"

"I had a really amazing night. You wouldn't let me do anything, so please at least let me clean up."

Raising my hands in defeat, I sat back down, noticing the book that hung out of her bag. "What are you reading?" I asked.

"A collection of poems by W. H. Auden." She scrubbed.

"May I?" I asked, already reaching for it.

She nodded.

Taking the book out, I flipped to the page she had dog-eared. I noticed how worn the spine was, to the point that if I closed the book, it would still open right back to this page. *She must really love it.* Smirking to myself, I cleared my throat, and out of the corner of my eye, I saw her look up at me. I read, my voice barely over a whisper.

"And down by the brimming river I heard a lover sing under an arch of the railway: *Love has no ending.* I'll love you, dear…I'll love *you* till China and Africa meet, and the river jumps over the mountain, and the salmon sing in the street, *I'll love you…*till the ocean is folded and hung up to dry and the seven stars go squawking like geese about the sky…"

Even with all my dramatic pauses, it took only two minutes to read. When I looked back up at her, she had stopped doing the dishes. Her brown eyes were warmer than ever before, and the corner of her lip turned up slightly.

"You win."

"What?"

"This date. It's officially the best one of my whole life. You win. I admit that you, Eli Philip Davenport, are remarkable," she whispered before looking back down to scrub away at my plates.

I walked over and came up behind her, grabbing her hands. I pulled off the gloves myself and she didn't stop me. She had long since taken off her jacket, forcing me to stare at her shoulders and chest all night long. Brushing her hair over, I kissed the base of her neck, sliding the straps of her dress and bra off her shoulder. Her dress fell to the floor with ease, the bra still cupped to her chest.

"Come to bed."

Chapter Eighteen
Miracles and Tragedies

Guinevere

I t had been a week since our first official date, and I still couldn't get it out of my head. Whatever he'd wanted from me that night, he could have gotten, but instead we only made out. Yes, it got…passionate, and lust poured off us both in waves, but we just had stripped down to nothing but our underwear and kissed each other. There were times where we talked about random things, like his childhood home and things he enjoyed doing—apparently he really enjoyed swimming, too. We talked until I fell asleep with his arms around me. His reason for not sleeping with me was simple: it was our first date. He said you don't sleep with the girl on the first date…at least, that's how it worked for him. People often say that dating is a game, and if it was, Eli had mastered it to an art form. It was funny though, at least to me: the fact that we didn't sleep together made the night all the more memorable.

"Dr. Davenport, please do the surgery."

When I turned the corner, I heard a sob.

There stood Toby Wesley, gripping Eli's white coat.

His three interns all tried to help, but he just waved them off. "Toby—"

"She's all I have left. She's my little girl, there has to be something else you can try. We've poked and prodded her, we've pumped her veins full of poison! You have to do the surgery!"

"The tumor is—"

"Fuck the tumor!" he yelled, releasing Eli's coat and pushing him away. "Fuck the damn tumor! I want it out of her, and if you won't do it, I will find someone else who will!" He walked back into the room, the door slamming behind.

Eli took a deep breath, saying something to the doctors around him before heading toward the stairs.

Only when they were all gone did I head to the patient's door, gripping the painting in my hands. Unsure whether or not I should go in, I put the painting by the door, but before I could leave, it opened again. "Sorry." I backed up quickly. Toby looked understandably worse than the last time I had seen him; the dark circles around his eyes made me feel like he hadn't really slept in years. His gaze shifted down to the painting that had fallen into the room.

"Did you bring it?" Molly waved behind him.

"I made a promise, didn't I?" I smiled, bending down to pick the painting off the ground. Without a word, he moved over for me to enter.

I walked up to her bedside. Her skin looked almost gray, and she couldn't even lift herself up. Her scarf was the brightest sparkling pink I had ever seen, and she wore a bow on her arm where her IV was.

Pulling up a chair, I sat, placing the painting on my lap. "Can I open it for you?" I asked her.

She tried her best to nod.

Pulling the brown paper off, I held it up closer for her to see. "What do you think?"

"Daddy, it's Mommy and the baby." She reached up to touch it and smiled to her dad, who leaned against the window with his hand over his mouth, looking at the family portrait of them. Swallowing a lump in his throat, he knelt by her bed, taking her hand. "Yes…yes sweetheart, it is," he whispered.

Seeing them, I felt my eyes burn.

"What do you say to Ms. Poe?"

"Can I really have it?" she asked.

Laughing, I nodded. "Of course you can have it. I made it for you…the both of you."

He glanced up at me and stood on his own two feet again. "Molly, you still need to say thank you," he said to her.

"Thank you!"

"You're very welcome. Keep looking at it, and hopefully it makes you feel better, okay?" *If only it was that easy.*

"I feel better now." She touched her mother's face.

"I'll come visit you later, all right?"

"I'll walk you out," her father said when she nodded.

He didn't have to, but I felt like he wouldn't take no for an answer. The moment I stepped out, he closed the door behind us.

He stood there, fighting back tears, but failing. Taking a deep breath, he smiled at me. "I know you don't know me too well, but can I hug you?"

Nodding, I wrapped my arms around him.

He let out a small cry, but stifled it to the best of his ability.

It felt like he was falling, or just crumbling in my arms.

Finally he let go, then wiped his eyes. "How did you know about the baby she was going to have?"

"I heard a few nurses whispering about it. It's all right—"

"It's more than that. Thank you. Thank you so much." He took my hands and turned back to look into her room. "I'm so scared. I'm not sure what to do. She's suffering so much, and I can't do anything but sit here and watch.

She collapsed this morning, she's dying, and her doctors are saying they can't operate. I should go, right? I should try for other opinions, right?"

I wished it was a rhetorical question, but he was really asking for an answer. "Toby, I'm not a doctor, I don't know."

"But if it was your child—"

I sighed. "I'm so sorry, Toby, I wish I could help you. I really don't know what to say. I can't answer that because I don't have children. I can't understand the position or pain you are in. All I can do is tell you to trust yourself. Do what you think is right for Molly. That's all you can do, isn't it?"

He was silent, and it was almost as painful as him speaking.

"Go in, she's calling for you." I waved back to the small girl inside.

"Thank you again," he whispered, his hand on the door.

"Of course."

I stayed there for a little while longer before walking back to my station. If I felt this bad, I wondered how Eli felt. I couldn't imagine having that much pressure on his shoulders, and that was just one of his patients. How did he do it? How did he deal with it all? When he was home, it was like the hospital him was switched off. He never went into detail about anything. He would always just say 'saved one'...but what about the people he couldn't save?

Does he not tell me because he doesn't think I can understand?

I knew he couldn't break doctor-patient confidentiality, and I didn't want him to—I just wanted to know how he was doing.

"Gwen!" Logan came up to me, dressed in dark jeans and a pretty nice leather jacket.

I had noticed that after he had declared he wasn't going to be a doctor, his fashion was changing slightly. I guessed he was just finally being who he really was. He'd even gotten his ear pierced.

"Hey, aren't you going on tour?" I asked when he reached me.

He frowned. "Can't wait to get me out of the way, can you?"

"That's not what I meant." I laughed.

"I know. I leave tomorrow. Just came to have lunch with my mother and ask you a small favor."

"What?"

He nodded behind me to the mural. "I won't be back for the unveiling, and it's been killing me wanting to see what you're doing back there. I swear some people have already peeked in."

"Everyone is so impatient. You can't see the full effect of it until you back up some, anyway—"

"Please, Gwen."

"You're just going to use it to torture your mother's curiosity, aren't you?"

He grinned. "How do you know me so well?"

Shaking my head, I lifted the curtain, allowing him to come inside.

He looked down at the paint all spread across the ground and the once white shirt I wore while painting lying next to it before glancing up. He took a step back and bent his head as best as he could, looking up at the whole mural. "Is that the—"

"Yep." I didn't want him to say it out loud.

"They are going to love this." He dropped his head and looked back to me. "I love it."

"Thank you. I'm always a little nervous, but if I know you really like it, I can go forward with no fear." At the vibration, I pulled my phone out of my pocket.

Katrina had texted me.

'We have a slight problem.

Are you at the hospital? I will come pick you up.'

"Is everything all right?" Logan asked.

I nodded, texting her back. "Can you do me a favor?" I questioned, reaching for my other painting.

"Sure, what's up?"

I handed him the painting.

He looked at me, confused.

"You remember the painting I gave to you and Eli? Well, this is the original. I wanted to give it to your mother today, but something just came up and I don't know when I will be back. Can you give it to her for me?"

"Of course I can. She will most likely cry and hunt you down to give you a hug later, though."

"I've been giving them out for free lately, so it's all right," I said, stepping out with him only to find Eli walking toward us.

He looked between us both.

Logan put his arm around me. "I confessed my undying love for her—"

"Hey!" I pinched his side.

He winced, backing away.

Eli grinned. "Apparently she didn't accept."

Logan made a face at both of us, walking away with the painting under his arm.

I got another text message.

'I'm here.'

"You showed him the mural?"

"Yeah, since he begged. He's going to miss the grand unveiling and whatnot. But, do you mind if we talk later? I'm so sorry, my lawyer has been trying to get in touch with me, and she never calls unless it's important. She even came here."

"That's fine. I got what I needed," he said.

"What?" I hadn't done anything.

"I got to see you."

Grinning, I walked backward toward the doors. "You are smooth, Dr. Davenport."

"Aren't I? Good luck." He waved.

"You, too," I said, pushing the glass door open. When I did, I saw Katrina was already standing outside her town car, wearing a blood-red dress and suit jacket. In her hands was a letter.

"What's going on?"

She handed me the letter. "Your ex-fiancé is suing you."

"For what?"

"Breach of contract. Apparently you aren't answering any of his calls, and thus you haven't been able to do any of the projects he needs."

I groaned, wanting to slap myself. "I bit myself in the ass by not terminating my contract, didn't I?"

"Isn't it obvious? This is the only way he can get to you, and being the controlling son of a bitch he is, of course he would go this low," she replied, pulling out another letter from her white Louis Vuitton handbag. "Option one: we try again to break your contract, but believe me, this will be a hell of a fight, and you might lose millions. He will not be as generous as he was in the beginning. I'm not sure what happened, but he is being a prissy little bitch. You don't have any leftover feelings do you?"

"No, he's doing this because I'm seeing someone else."

"You are?" Her blonde eyebrow rose.

"Yes," I said proudly. "And I don't want to lose millions, or be in a fight with him for months or years. What is my other option?"

She took a step to the side and opened the door to her town car. "We can go meet with him and see how to work out a schedule, since you are working on other projects. Your contract ends in a few months anyway; there is no point in going to war now."

"Fine. But try and stop me from murdering him while we're there," I muttered, getting in the car.

"If he gives me an opening, I will sue for anything I can think of."

She was trying to make me feel better, and it was working. Sebastian Evans was a spineless little prick.

Eli

I walked into my mother's office, and the first thing I saw was her crying in Logan's arms. "What in the—"

He nodded to the painting on the table and mouthed 'Guinevere'.

She strikes again. I had gone by Toby and Molly's room again to see them both staring up at her painting, laughing and talking together about it. They were so happy, I almost forgot she was even sick. It was why I had wanted to go see Guinevere. Taking a seat across from them, I tried to touch the painting.

My mother smacked my hand away.

"Mom!" I yelled, pulling back my hand.

She wiped her eyes. "No one is touching it until I can have it framed and put up in your father's study."

In all these years, she had not moved any of my father's things from the house. Like he was coming back at any moment. She knew he wasn't, but she said she liked to close her eyes and sometimes just forget.

"Is she still here?" she asked, looking down at it.

"No, she had an appointment," I said to her.

"Let me know if she comes back," she whispered, nodding to herself. "It looks so much like him. She even got the little scar on the side of his chin he got from playing soccer."

"She said when she came to visit you in your office, she got a good look at all the pictures in here, and she was able to look him up online," I said with a smile.

"When you guys are all around like this, grown up, I can really see it. You both are like him in so many ways. Did you know he wanted to give up medicine, too?" She glanced between us.

"What? No, he didn't." I couldn't believe it.

She nodded. "He was an amazing saxophone player. He was really into jazz. But in the end, he said it would always be a nice hobby."

"Point one for the musicians." Logan nodded to me, leaning back in the chair.

Ignoring him, I looked at her. "Why didn't you say anything?"

"Because you always wanted to be just like him. I knew you, like me, couldn't play an instrument to save your life, so I just let you focus on your books."

Logan laughed so hard he snorted.

She smacked him on the leg.

"Ma!" he yelled, rubbing his thigh, and then smiled.

"Don't laugh at your older brother. If it weren't for him setting a good example for you, God knows you would have been living in dive bars."

"Thanks for the vote of confidence, Mom." He frowned, glaring my way.

"Oh Eli, I have something to tell you. Hannah asked to be transferred to one of the inner city clinics for a while. I have no idea why. What did you say to her?"

"The truth," I said, pulling out my buzzing pager. I stood, already at the door. "I have to go." I didn't wait to hear their reply, or even wait for the elevator. Pushing open the stairwell door, I ran down three steps at a time, spiraling downward until I got to their floor. A nurse headed toward the room, right beside me. "What happened?" I yelled, moving toward the bed.

Molly's tiny body wouldn't stop shaking, her eyes rolling into the back of her head. And then she just went still.

"Molly! I need a crash cart in here!" I yelled.

"Molly! Molly, sweetheart, wake up! Molly—"

"Get him out!" I hollered over her as the nurse handed me the defibrillator.

Come on, Molly.

Guinevere

After Sebastian left me, I told myself to listen to my instincts from then on. I had known something was off that day, but I'd ignored it. I wouldn't make that mistake again. I would listen to my gut, no matter what happened. And sitting there with him, everything within me told me not to stay there any longer than I needed to.

His office was filled with the same overly done, pricey bullshit as before. He had floors done in marble, his walls finished in the nicest wood, and all his awards hung up behind him proudly. On his desk was a pompous nameplate, his name carved in glass with *Founder & CEO* right under it.

I walked in.

He stood up, buttoning his dark navy suit, and walked in front of his desk, his arms over his chest. "You came—"

"This place reeks of bullshit. Mr. Evans, can we just get down to the point?" I said, taking a seat.

Katrina stood right beside my chair.

"Gwen—"

"Ms. Poe would like to apologize for not getting any of your requests, though I do believe the fault lies partly with you and your office for not going through the correct channels. If you have work for my client, you should speak with her agent, who will filter the request to Ms. Poe. I'm sure any judge will agree with me." Katrina threw his lawsuit back onto his desk.

He didn't look at her, only stared at me. "I'm sorry I hurt you."

"Can't you see this smile? I'm fine, Mr. Evans. How could a man such as yourself hurt me?"

"Gwen!" he yelled.

"Mr. Evans, yell at my client again, and I will not only sue you for harassment, but will make sure to add emotional distress to the list. Do you feel emotional, Ms. Poe?"

I frowned. "Now that you mention it—"

"Gwen, please." He sighed.

Katrina was about to say something, but I shook my head. "Say what you want to say, Sebastian."

He sat up straighter, moving to stand right in front of me. "I know what I did was horrible. I hurt you, and I truly am sorry, because there is no woman on earth whom I love as much as you. I couldn't see it. I was just so nervous about us...worried we wouldn't make it, like my parents. Remember? My mother walked out on us, and I just didn't want to be hurt like that again. Every time I close my eyes, I see you. I remember how you held on when I took you to see Cirque du Soleil, how you would fill the fridge for me, even when I told you not to, and how you would rearrange the apartment and dance in the living room. I miss you, Gwen. I will spend every day of my life trying to make it up to you. You are the only woman in this world for me."

Katrina looked down at me, her eyebrow raised.

"Bash," I said softly, sitting up onto the edge of my chair.

"Gwen." He smirked.

"I was so blind when I was with you that hearing you speak right now makes me want to slap myself. I remember Cirque du Soleil. I held on to you because I have a fear of heights, and I thought I was going to have a panic attack watching it. The reason I filled your fridge all the time was because before I moved in, you never did it yourself. And if you did, not once did you buy anything I liked eating. I had to rearrange the apartment because you bought big-ass furniture after I told you I didn't want anything in there. You only care about yourself. You are not the only man in the world for me. So, please. PLEASE. Stop. The shades are off. I'm not blinded by the great Sebastian Evans any more. Don't use stupid lawsuits to draw me here. Don't call me in the middle of the night. Stop, because if you don't, I will get a restraining order against you. I'm sure that would kill the last few months I have on contract, right, Katrina?"

"You should have told me he called you in the middle of the night. I would have filed a restraining order with Judge Banks that very night," she replied.

I stood. "Anything you need me to do, please work it out with my agent. Tara will make sure I have it scheduled. Goodbye, Mr. Evans," I said, closing the door.

Only once we were in the elevator did Katrina speak. "We will only do this once," she said to me, raising her fist up for me to bump it.

Grinning, I knocked my fist against hers.

"Now we will never speak of it again."

"Of course." I tried to sound as cool as ice, just like her, but it was too funny. Walking out of the building, my phone rang. When I checked, I saw it was none other than Stevie's mother. "Mrs. Spencer? Is everything okay?"

"Hi, Gwen. I'm so sorry to call you out of the blue like this. I was trying to call your mother, but it kept going to voicemail."

I knew why. My mom hated talking on phones for long periods of time, and Mrs. Spencer could go on for days sometimes. "What can I do for you, Mrs. Spencer?"

"Well, quickly, do you know the name of your father's doctor? The one he went to after the heart attack? I want to make sure to get Ryan to go. I swear, that man doesn't believe me when I say all this food of his is killing him. Do you know what he had last n—"

"Wait. I'm sorry, did you say my dad had a heart attack?" *What?* Maybe she was confused.

"Yes. It was about three weeks ago, wasn't it? Ryan, honey, when did Masoa have his heart attack?" she yelled, forgetting to move the phone away. "Yeah, it was about three and a half weeks ago—"

"Mrs. Spencer, I'm going to have to call you right back."

Eli

"It's a miracle she survived," Bunhead said behind me as I stared at the charts up on the wall.

"What is our next step, Dr. Davenport?" Dr. Stretch came up beside me, and when I turned to him, he took a step back. "Dr. Davenport—"

"Stop talking!" I snapped, and they all jumped. "Stop talking. Stop saying the fact that she is alive is a miracle, because it isn't. Close your mouths and look at her x-ray. Does that tumor look odd to any of you?"

Dr. Four Eyes adjusted his glasses and stepped forward. "Looks like it moved to the right some."

"Isn't that good? You couldn't operate because of the location, but if it moved or shrunk—"

"It didn't move," Dr. Stretch whispered, looking between her old x-rays and her new ones. "She has two tumors. The chemo helped the bigger one shrink, but she has a second one right next to it. Her kind of medulloblastoma makes up less than 12 percent of all brain cancers," I said, stepping forward and putting up more of her scans. "Chemotherapy and surgery were long shots for her from the beginning. Now, the cancer is spreading. Her body is dying, and we brought her back today, but we are working on borrowed time. She won't make it to the end of the week."

"Are you going to tell her father?" Bunhead whispered.

"I did." I faced them. "Get them their discharge papers and fax all their information to Dr. Birell at the Comprehensive Cancer Center at Johns Hopki—"

"Dr. Davenport!" A nurse came in.

I already knew why, and I ran toward the room I had only just been in two hours before. This time I was watching Ian, who had given up on the defibrillator and now was just using his hands.

"How long has she been down?" I asked him.

"A little over three minutes." He sighed, stopping himself because he knew what I knew.

"What are you doing?" Toby yelled at me. "Save her! Save her! What are you doing?!"

"Mr. Wesley, your daughter collapsed this morning, she had a seizure two hours ago, and her heart has given out now. Anything more is torturing her. Her body can't take it any more. I'm so sorry. I truly am. I'm so sorry for your loss, but she's gone." Looking to Ian, he nodded, then glanced at his watch as I unplugged everything from her body.

"Time of death, 8:43 PM," he whispered.

Toby collapsed at the side of her bed, sobbing on top of her body.

My chest felt like it was on fire. I felt like I had stripped this man of everything he had left. Because I wasn't good enough, I had cost him his daughter. Exiting the room, I didn't stop for anyone, just walking, maybe running—I couldn't tell what my body was doing any more. Everything passed in a blur until I found myself outside, breathing heavily under the pouring rain.

I failed. God. Why I did I fail? "Ahh!" I screamed up into the rain.

"Eli!" Guinevere ran closer to me, her hand overhead, as if that would stop the downpour. "Eli, what is it? What's wrong?"

For some reason, I tried to smile for her, but I couldn't. "Me. I'm what's wrong. You should go home alone today—"

"Eli, talk to me."

"I don't want to talk! I'm tired of talking. All I do is talk all damn day!" I yelled. Sighing, I ran my hands through my hair. "Please don't wait or look for me."

Walking back into the hospital, I tried to ignore how bad my head and chest hurt.

Chapter Nineteen
The Oath We Make

Guinevere

"How long will he be like this?" I asked Dr. Seo, watching as Eli stitched up an old woman's arm in the ER. For the last 96 hours, I wasn't even sure if had really eaten anything. He was basically living at the hospital and, from the looks of the hair growing on his chin, he hadn't thought to bring a razor.

Dr. Seo bit into his apple, leaning against the wall. His pink hair was now back to black and in a half ponytail. "It depends. If you haven't noticed, Eli doesn't handle death well. He thinks just because he's a doctor, he can save everyone if he's just a little better. When he and I were interns, we lost an older man. He came in with his son after they had been in a car accident. His son appeared more hurt, so Eli focused on him, not realizing the boy's father was bleeding internally. It wasn't his fault; his son really was hurt. After the man died, Eli barely ate or even left the hospital for a month. He only slept because his mother threatened and swore she would bar him from the hospital. So he made a makeshift bed in the on-call room. No one else dared sleep in it, either."

"What can I do for him?" He looked like a ghost...worse than he had after Hannah.

"Wait for him to move on again? For as long as I've known him, nothing else works. Some big save snaps him

217

out of it, but who knows how long he's going to be like this. It's weird when he doesn't insult me back." He pouted.

I snickered. "You are a sucker for pain, aren't you, Ian?"

He winked, then got a page. "I have to go. I'll see you later. Don't stress too much about it, all right?"

Easier said than done.

Nodding, I waved, glancing back to Eli, who was on to the next patient, changing his gloves as he rolled over.

He nodded and smiled at the patient, but even then, he still looked dead.

I wanted to grab the sides of his face and scream at him, wake him up. But, did I really have the right to? I thought of Molly and Toby...I wondered if him getting over it would be right.

Turning back, I left him and headed to the mural wall. I was finally done with it and was supposed to reveal it that day, but I felt like there was a dark aura around the hospital. I wanted to wait until everyone was in a better mood.

"Gwen!"

"Stevie?" I said when she came close, dressed in a white and black polka dot dress, pink coat, and sunhat. "Nice outfit."

"Oh, don't start with me." She took my arm, locking it under hers and heading toward the curtain. "I came to see your masterpiece. Are you giving a speech?"

"I hate public speaking."

"You keep saying that, but you've always been good at it," she replied, taking a seat in front of it. "And what's wrong with the outfit? Is it the hat?"

I laughed when she took it off and strands of her red hair stood up. Brushing it down for her, I shook my head. "No, you look fine. Eli told me, as a rich person, I can no longer be prejudiced against the rich."

"I've been saying that for years. I guess it just had to come from your sex—"

"Don't finish that sentence."

"I was going to say sexy boyfriend." She ignored me, looking around. "Where is the good doctor, anyway? I haven't been able to give him my best friend stamp of approval yet."

"Working. Did you get this dressed up for me?"

"Sadly, no. We are going to the Hamptons tonight. One of these days you really have to go, Gwen. It's so beautiful living right off the beach."

"You lived off the lake in Cypress."

She rolled her eyes. "Yes, that was nice, but I'm telling you, the Hamptons have a sense of romance to them. Have your doctor boyfriend take you."

"He's working."

"So you aren't taking him to go meet your parents?" She frowned. "I heard about your dad's heart attack. Why didn't you tell me?"

"For me to tell you, someone was going to have to tell me." I was still annoyed about that. "My mom and dad decided not to 'worry me' and apparently he is 'fine now, sweetie.' They have been driving up the coast. They should be home by Wednesday, and I hoped to fly in on Saturday, but..."

"But?"

I sighed. "What do you do when Nathaniel is dealing with something hard? I mean, he dealt with things on his own before you were in his life, but now that you are with him, you should do something, right? Not just let him work it out?"

She thought about it for a moment, then shrugged. "It depends. When it's family issues, I just tell him I'm there if he wants to vent, and then try to be around as much as possible, just kind of waiting. When he's really not in the mood, I make him dinner and get him drunk. Sex usually follows, and after that, I can't get him to shut up."

I laughed, shaking my head at her. "Man have you changed, Stevie. Remember when you said you would never kiss a boy?"

"Remember when you said you were going to marry Mario Lopez, then Orlando Bloom?" She elbowed me. "And then who was it you wanted to marry after that... Prince Harry, you really liked Prince Harry."

"I would have made an amazing princess, thank you. It even sounds nice: *Princess Guinevere of Cambridge*," I said, slowly stretching it out for her sake.

"Safe to say, neither of us was in the right frame of mind."

"I can agree with that." I laughed, looking toward the curtain. "If I asked him to come with me, do you think he would?"

"Only way to find out is to ask. Now, what are you going to wear?"

She was helpful.

Eli

"He's suing me," I said softly, standing behind the chairs of her office.

My mother nodded. "He's grieving, Eli. He doesn't know who else to blame. I looked at the chart. I spoke to almost every neurosurgeon in this hospital. You did everything right."

"Then why?" I snapped. "If you do everything right, everything by the book, why does this still have to be the ending? That man has no one else left."

"It's not your fault!" She stood up, placing her hand on my face. "Sweetheart, I've told you this before: you can't save everyone. You aren't God. They come in broken, and we do the best we can as humans, with everything we have to fix them, and sometimes it still isn't enough. You didn't kill her. You aren't the reason his family is gone. That is not your doing."

Sighing, I nodded. I knew she was right, but it still didn't help.

Taking a step away from me, she grabbed her coat. "You are going to take a week off."

"Mom—"

"You are being sued, Eli. No matter how unjustified, the lawyers will handle it. But you can't be here like this. Look at yourself. I'm saying this as the chairwoman: you need to go and get your head on straight, Eli. Don't stay here. Don't see patients, because if you slip up in this state in any way, everything will be ten times worse."

"What am I going to do for a week, Mom?"

She shrugged. "I don't know. Shave, eat, sleep, talk to your girlfriend."

"You know—"

"Of course I know. Just because I'm your mother doesn't mean I'm blind. I could tell the moment it changed and you two weren't pretending to fight anymore. Have you spoken to her since?"

I said nothing.

"So for all you know, she might not even be your girl-friend any more."

I sighed, not really wanting to have this conversation.

"Did you know she was done with her mural? I'm heading to see it now. Or did you forget that the world keeps spinning, even when you stop?" She opened the door. "You coming or not?"

"I'm coming," I muttered, holding the door for her to walk out. In all honesty, I hadn't realized Guinevere was done. She had kept trying to meet up with me, talk with me, but I'd pushed her away. I wasn't ready to feel better yet.

"Well, isn't this a production," my mother said, glancing around at the doctors, nurses, a few well-enough patients, and even some press.

Guinevere stood in front of them, gripping her hands together tightly, her nervous habit. She had changed into a simple pink skirt and black v-neck shirt, her hair pulled into a braid on one side.

She looked cute. She had put in a lot of effort, even wearing makeup. When she saw my mom she nodded to herself, and then her eyes shifted to me and she smiled before facing the rest of the crowd.

"Thank you all for coming. For many of you, I know the chairwoman didn't really give you a choice," she said, getting a few laughs.

My mother only crossed her arms, eying those who laughed.

"When she first asked me to paint this mural, I honestly had no idea where to begin. So, I wandered the halls of the hospital, sometimes noticed, but for the most part not so much, because everyone had eyes only for the patients. And being doctors, isn't that what you want? In the weeks I've been here, many have gone, sometimes happily and sometimes on sad terms. The people who remained no matter what were the doctors. I hope this serves as a reminder of the promise you all have made, and how thankful we are for it." She spun around, nodding to the people above the curtain.

It came down in one swift motion and left us all speechless. She had drawn patients at different points on the wall with the background of a park, the older ones in wheel chairs and another with a cane resting on a park bench, teenagers listening to music, parents holding their children, all of them coming from the far distance. At the corner of it all, from top to bottom, was the Hippocratic Oath, which explained why she had needed my textbook. My mother, myself, and the rest of us could not help but read again:

"I swear to fulfill, to the best of my ability and judgment, this covenant: I will apply, for the benefit of the sick, all measures which are required, avoiding those twin traps of overtreatment and therapeutic nihilism. I will remember that there is art to medicine as well as science, and that warmth, sympathy, and understanding may outweigh the surgeon's knife or the chemist's drug. I will not be ashamed to say "I know not," nor will I fail to call in my colleagues when the skills of another are needed for a patient's recovery. I will respect the privacy of my patients, for their problems are not disclosed to me that the world may know. Most especially must I tread with care in matters of life and death. If it is given me to save a life, all thanks. But it may also be within my power to take a life; this awesome responsibility must be faced with great humbleness and awareness of my own frailty. Above all, I must not play at God. I will remember that I do not treat a fever chart, a cancerous growth, but a sick human being, whose illness may affect the person's family and economic stability. My responsibility includes these related problems, if I am to care adequately for the sick. I will prevent disease whenever I can, for prevention is preferable to cure. I will remember that I remain a member of society, with special obligations to all my fellow human beings, those sound of mind and body as well as the infirm. If I do not violate this oath, may I enjoy life and art, respected while I live and remembered with affection thereafter. May I always act so as to preserve the finest traditions of my calling and may I long experience the joy of healing those who seek my help."

"Thank you all for allowing me into your hospital, and thank you to the students and the NYU art department for your help; I couldn't have done it without you," she said to them as we all clapped.

My mother walked over, wrapping her arms around her. People called to her for photos and press work. The more her attention was divided, the more jealous I became, because they all had the chance to congratulate her and shake her hand before me. She was amazing and talented and beautiful, and I just wanted to hold her and tell her that.

"You aren't thinking about walking through the crowd and kissing her, right?" Ian came over to me, pulling off his K-POP scrub cap.

"And if I was?" He looked back toward me like he was impressed, even leaning back.

"Welcome back, Dr. Davenport. I wasn't expecting you to return from the dark side for another few days. I guess all you needed was a GP boost."

"A GP boost?"

"Don't pretend like you don't know whose initials those are. Now, if you will excuse me, I'm going to go take a selfie in front of the mural." He smiled, walking past me.

"You're an idiot."

"You love me anyway!" He put up a peace sign as he walked.

Shaking my head at him, I stayed in my spot. I would wait until the crowd was gone and the excitement went down, and then I would go to her. For the moment, I was more than happy to just watch her shine.

Guinevere

I felt like I had been smiling and getting blinded by flashes forever, but watching a few patients take photos in front of the mural made up for it all. I sat down, staring up at it, practically amazed with it myself. Not really the painting, but with the oath on it. I felt like whoever read it would really believe in the love affair between art and science. Both were in each other, really.

"Is this seat taken?"

Looking toward him, I shrugged. "My boyfriend might beat you up."

He snickered. "Your boyfriend does deserve to have his ass handed to him for pushing you away, and for yelling at you in the rain. It's only romantic if the kiss comes afterward, right?"

He was trying to joke, but I could tell he didn't find it funny.

"I'm sorry, I was just upset about—"

"I know," I finished for him. "At first I was confused and upset, then I heard, and the first thing I wanted to know was if you were okay...well, that's a lie. I wanted to know if Toby was okay, though I knew he wouldn't be. But I was worried about you, too."

He laughed, taking my hand, holding it in his and kissing the back of it. "I'll be fine. Toby, he's in pain. Will be for the rest of his life. I just need to remember there will be more Mollys, and to try harder to help them in the future."

"In the future, will you tell me more?" I asked softly. "I know I can't understand everything, but I would hate if you felt the need to give me a censored version of what your day is really like. You've never talked about your work in detail to me before."

"I'll try, but the reason I don't say much is because when I'm with you, I like that I forget about everything else."

"Then do you have time to run away with me?" It sounded so cheesy saying it like that. From the look on his face, I could see he agreed.

"Run away with you?"

"That came out wrong. Actually, no. It came out right. My father had a heart attack a few weeks ago and didn't tell me. So I want to go home, and was kind of hoping you would go with me...if you want."

"When did you find out? About your father, I mean."

"The same day Molly passed. A lot of things happened. If you don't want to go, it's fine. I just thought I would offer, but you have work—"

"I'll go," he said, squeezing my hand. "Let's run away to Cypress."

CHAPTER TWENTY
CYPRESS, ALASKA
WELCOMES YOU

Eli

I couldn't take my eyes off her. I was sure no one else could, either. She held on to the arm of the chair like a cat held on to a shower curtain, her eyes closed shut. The plane shook again and she bit her bottom lip, taking deep breaths.

"You don't fly home often?"

"I drive."

"You drive from New York to Alaska?" She had to be kidding me.

She nodded. "It's not that bad. It takes about three, almost four days, and I stop to take pictures of scenery and whatnot." The plane shook again, and she looked like she was going to cry.

I need to calm her down, I thought, placing my hand over hers. Only then did she open her eyes for the first time since we had taken off. She hadn't been that bad on the first plane—the ride was so smooth she went to sleep—but since this was a much smaller one, she could now feel every bump through the clouds. "Why is your acrophobia this bad?" Talking often helped.

"When I was eight, my father and brother went hiking up the mountain trail. I was angry they'd left me behind, and even more upset that they thought I couldn't do it. So I packed my bag with Skittles—the purple kind, two water bottles, my flashlight, tissues, and a compass. I figured I was only about an hour behind them, and left while my mother was finishing up some work. I felt so proud of myself as I walked through the woods alone. I wasn't scared of anything in the *day*. I was halfway up the trail when the sun went down, and then I started to panic because I couldn't find my dad, and wandered off the trail. Long story short, I was lost up there for seven hours, staring down at all of Cypress, petrified I would slip off and no one would ever find me. So, heights make me think I'm on top of the mountain again."

"So let's think of some other place else to be in your head." Leaning over to her, I brushed her hair back and whispered into her ear, "You aren't on top of a mountain. You're with me, in bed—"

"Naked?" Her eyebrow rose.

"Not yet," I said softly. "I slowly unbutton your shirt, kissing from your neck down between your breasts. At my touch your nipples are hard, and when I take them between my teeth, you moan so loudly our neighbors are jealous. You clench your legs closed and I don't know why, baby, because you want me to touch you there…kiss you there…lick every inch of you. Don't you?"

"Yes," she whispered.

"I can hear you now. You're screaming my name, 'Eli… Eli,' and God almighty, Guinevere, you taste so good I don't ever want to stop. I could spend hours between your legs, just teasing you…tasting all of you. I love how wet you are for me, baby, how your body trembles at my fingertips. You think I control you? With every moan, I am at your mercy. You would not believe the things I want to do to you, your body. It makes me so hard it pains me. Please, let me have you. Let me fuck you 'til you can't see straight any more, Guinevere."

She gasped. "Please."

"Your body is mine tonight?" *Every night.*

"Yes."

"And so I spread your legs, slowly filling you... Fuck," I moaned in her ear. "Jesus, baby, you are so tight."

"Eli." She bit back a moan.

"Gripping your waist, I'm not stopping until I can count on both hands how many times you come for me. I moan at the sight of you biting your finger and grabbing your own breast...goddamn, you are beautiful. It drives me insane when you look at me with those big, beautiful brown eyes of yours. You come, screaming my name, and it's still not enough. Why do you torture me like this, Guinevere? How is it possible I want you even more? With every thrust *deeper* and *harder* inside you, I want you *more.* God, and that sound, you're moaning, I'm moaning, the bed is shaking under us, slamming against my wall. Can you hear it? When I kiss your lips and you grab my hair, moving along with each fuck, I lose control. Your lips, your tongue: that is what real ecstasy tastes like. Ramming myself in again, and again, and again, until you cry out, your nails working their way down my back—"

"Ladies and gentlemen, this is your captain speaking."

"No," she cried desperately, her eyes fully open, her hands still gripping the seat, but for a whole different reason.

Grinning, I turned back up front as we prepared to land.

"I will find a place for us to continue this, Dr. Davenport, and it will be more showing than telling." She said before leaning back again, clearly frustrated.

I placed my hand on her thigh, squeezing lightly. "If I fuck you in the forest and no one is around to hear it, how loud will you sound?"

She bit her lip, but didn't say a word.

She was so fun to torture, and I couldn't wait to see how she decided to pay me back...because after talking to her like that, I was in desperate need for her again.

"So again, your parents' names are?" I asked as if nothing had happened when we got off the plane, grabbing both her carryon and mine.

"My mother's name is Ankia and my father's name is Masoa, but you should just stick with Mr. and Mrs. Poe," she said.

We headed toward the front desk where Taigi rested in his carrier on the ground, waiting for us to pick him up.

"Gwen. Guinevere!" The woman in charge of him waved.

Guinevere stopped, tilting her head, trying to remember the woman with short auburn hair and hazel eyes. "Yes?" she said, still confused.

"It's me, Chloe. Chloe Drake," the woman said.

Guinevere's eyes almost fell out of her head. "No way." She stepped back, looking over the woman again. "You look amazing, Chloe."

"Thank you, I lost 97 pounds since we last saw each other." She lifted her arms.

Guinevere clapped for her, then turned to me. "Eli, this my old high school friend, Chloe Drake. Chloe, this is my... boyfriend, Eli Davenport."

She looked at me wide-eyed, then shook my hand when I extended it.

"It's a pleasure to meet you," I said to her.

"The pleasure is all mine, Mr. Davenport. Welcome to Cypress." She handed Guinevere Taigi's leash.

He just yawned, licking his nose.

"Your parents are already waiting for you out front."

"Thank you," Guinevere said to her.

"So, I'm guessing you didn't tell anyone we were dating?" I whispered to her as we headed to the front exit.

She shook her head. "I told my mother...so I'm sure my father knows. I'm not really sure how they feel about it, though. I was supposed to be married to someone else."

The thought of that bothered me. "Did they like Sebastian?" I wished the man would just disappear, along with any memories of him.

"They weren't thrilled about him. I guess they clearly saw what I didn't. So they'd better like you."

"No pressure." My mother and brother were already in love with her; I wondered if her parents would be that pleased with us.

The second we stepped outside, all I could see were tall, deep green trees, around the bottom of which grew more green grass and wildflowers. In the distance, a mountain range stood high against the cloudy white and blue sky. None of the buildings anywhere stood any higher than the trees. The whole place looked like it was taken out of *Nature Magazine*, or at the very least belonged as someone's screensaver. It was beautiful.

"Gwen!"

We both turned to our right.

Taigi broke free of his leash, running with everything he had into the older man's arms and licking all over his face.

Her father stood around the same height as me, maybe an inch taller. His skin was tan, his black and gray hair cut short, his face clean-shaven, and around his neck hung a beaded necklace with an arrowhead.

Beside him, a woman shorter than all of us with short black dark hair that stopped at her shoulders and smooth brown skin pulled Guinevere into a hug, kissing her cheeks. "Welcome home, sweetheart," her mother said, unable to let go of her arm. She looked young to be a mother and Guinevere had at least five inches on her, obviously getting her height from her father.

"And this one might be?" He nodded to me, brushing back Taigi's fur. His dark eyes stared—no, glared into me, starting from my feet up to my face, and then back down again.

"Mom, Dad, this is Dr. Eli Davenport, my boyfriend. Eli, these are my parents," she introduced us.

Before I could speak, her father spoke up again.

"You moved on pretty quickly, don't you think?" He looked to Guinevere.

"Would you prefer I cried and ate ice cream every day for the rest of the year?" she challenged him.

"Don't mind them." Her mother took my hand. "Welcome to Cypress, Eli. I hope the trip wasn't bad. Gwen here has an awful fear of heights."

"Thank you, ma'am, and no, it was all right. We just talked. I was actually nervous about coming here, especially for the reason your husband brought up." I addressed him directly, saying, "It's nice to meet you, sir."

"I don't like him, he's all city boy. I can smell it. Come on, Taigi." He frowned and turned, taking Taigi along.

"Dad, that's not funny." Guinevere went after him.

Her mother just laughed at them and, holding on to my arm, walked with me to their truck.

"I hope you really like my daughter, Eli, because he's going to put you through the wringer. It's safe to say that after what happened, he trusts no man around our Gwen."

Well, this is just going to be a good ol' time.

"I do—I really like her," I said to her, stopping just short of the car as Guinevere and her father talked about something.

He pulled her into a one-armed hug, and of course she couldn't stay angry, even though she was trying her best to do so.

"I do. Really, ma'am. I'm not sure if she told you, but I would rather just get it out in the open now. It was my fiancée that hers ran off with. Are you going to put me through the wringer, too?"

She smiled. "I guess time will tell. You are here for the whole weekend, after all."

I wasn't sure what I was in for.

Guinevere came back to where I stood. "I'm sorry about him, he's just being…well, being my dad. We are ready to go. Have you ever sat in the back of a pickup truck?"

"It's fine, and no, I haven't."

Whatever he was going to throw at me, I didn't really mind.

Guinevere

"Wow," he whispered as we drove farther and farther from the Cypress airport. My home, like most houses there, was in the forest. The way was lined on both sides with thick, moss-covered Sitka spruce trees. He stared up at them like we had traveled into a whole new world, and in a way, we had. The sun peeked through the tree line above us, and everything glowed. It was a…

"A moment of peace in a life of chaos," he said, his eyes still on the sky above us.

"I was just going to say that. How did you know?"

"You said it once, in an interview." He looked back at me. "It was for the Forbes article on upcoming artists a while back. They asked you how you liked it in New York, and you said it was nice, but you missed Cypress. For you, it was a place of peace in a life of chaos. I didn't understand then, but I think I do now."

"Eli, that interview was almost four years ago."

"It was." He smirked, mostly to himself, taking my hand and not going into it further.

I squeezed his hand, smiling to myself. "I have this image of you up late, researching me."

"That doesn't sound like a stalker at all. It was after our debate at NYU. I saw how all the students were in love with you, and I wanted to know more. Then you showed me your gallery, and I wanted to know what other people thought, too."

"Oh no," I groaned. "I got a few really bad reviews."

"Screw Jeffery Carlyle from the *New York Times*. Only a man with a defective heart could be such a critic of your work," he said.

I couldn't help but laugh. "That's what Mr. D'Amour said about you."

"I wasn't a critic, I was just…" He tried to think of the word.

"A critic?"

"Uneducated. You can hardly blame me for that. Once I knew a paintbrush from a canvas, I was able to realize you really are talented…stop smiling at me like that." He leaned toward me, laughing, and rested his head in my lap. "Honestly, though. When I first saw it, I was moved, and you keep moving me."

"Why can't I see his head?" my dad yelled.

Eli quickly sat back up.

I wanted to jump out of the car. "Dad!"

"Sorry, sir." Eli held me back as I turned to the man whistling in the front seat like he hadn't just killed our moment.

"This was a bad idea," I muttered to myself.

"Why? You don't think I can take it?" he asked when we pulled to a stop. "Don't worry about your dad, Guinevere.

Whatever he throws, I'll do my best. Plus, look at this face. How could anyone hate it?"

Rolling my eyes at him, I stood up.

He jumped out first, reaching up to help me.

"She's been jumping out of things since the day she was born; she doesn't need your help, city boy," my father called out, letting Taigi off his leash.

"It's called being a gentleman, Dad," I said to him, jumping down on my own.

"It's called being a—"

My mother gave him a look, and he didn't finish his sentence…thankfully.

Eli brought our bags out from the car.

I turned back to him. "You can still run. The airport is only twelve miles from here, that would be a breeze for you," I said quickly.

"I'm not running from your father, Guinevere, especially after only a few verbal jabs. By the way, your house is beautiful," he said, stopping to take it in.

Our house was a large log home that sat on the right end of the lake. It was only when you stood at the lake's edge that you could see all the other homes around it. The mountains hung in the background. I took a deep breath, enjoying the warmth.

"Gwen!"

I jumped back when three grown men in plaid shirts and mountain boots ran toward me, lifting me up.

"Guys! Down, now!" I yelled at them as they threw me up.

They laughed, catching me and putting me back on my feet.

Eli's eyebrow lifted up as his gaze shifted to each of them.

I wished I could read his mind. "Eli, this is—"

"Boys, don't mind the city slicker. Come in, we've got supper ready," my father yelled from the door.

I just looked up to the sky. *Kill me now!*

"City Slicker, good luck." They patted him on the shoulder on their way into the house.

"And they are?" Eli pointed to them.

"Okay, crash course, my dad most likely invited them to make you uncomfortable. The boy with the longish brown-blond hair is Jeremy Lawrence, he's 23, and was Stevie's first boyfriend. Never bring her up, because he still has a thing for her. He's now the town mechanic. Malik Washington is the one with the short, curly afro; he's the same age as me and works for the Cypress Police. Last, and most important, is Roy. My dad's been trying to set me up with Roy Griffin since we were kids. He's like the golden boy after my dad's heart, and he teaches photography at the high school," I finished, taking in another breath, and yet he didn't seem one bit concerned. "Did you get all of that?"

"Yep," he said, taking our stuff toward the house.

When I stepped inside, they popped streamers at me. "Welcome home, Gwen!"

Pulling streamers off my head, I laughed. Maybe this would be all right...

Chapter Twenty-One
The Inquisition of Eli
Davenport

Eli

It was cute how worried and nervous she was for me, but there was nothing she could do or say to her father that would make him ease up, nor did I want her to. What her father wanted was for me to prove to him that I was worthy of his daughter. In most cases, for fathers, that's impossible. I would never be worthy, I would just become tolerable. That was fine; tolerable was good. It was just I had no road map to get there, and what made it worse was the last person who had tried was an absolute buffoon of a man. Masoa Poe now had as much faith in me as he did in a snowman lasting in the desert.

"I made all your favorites, Gwen." Her mother led her to the table where she had laid out a whole spread, from baked chicken and salmon to gravy, bread, rice, and pies.

Guinevere looked down the length of the wooden table, and then back to her father. "Thank you, but please tell me you haven't been eating like this. Dad, you had a heart attack. Shouldn't you be eating fruits, vegetables, and nuts?"

She had a point.

"Do I look like a deer to you?"

She frowned.

He shook his head. "Your mother's been keeping me on the health food, okay, sweetheart? This is just to welcome you home. Maybe if you remembered how good home-cooked meals are, you would come home more often."

"Eli's a great cook," she said proudly, taking her seat.

I noticed the boys all quickly sat around her, forcing me to sit across from her and right next to her father at the head of the table. Her mother sat at the other end.

"You cook?" her mother asked me, placing the dishes around.

"Ma'am, my mother wouldn't have it any other way."

She nodded proudly. "Now, if someone else would listen to their mother."

"Who will say grace?" Guinevere changed the subject, quickly raising her hands.

I looked at her and she nodded.

"You don't say grace?" Roy questioned.

"I do." *Not.*

"I'll say it, then." Guinevere clapped her hands together. "Bless this food, and the people who prepared it. Many thanks for the meal and the company, may it fill our stomachs and electrify our souls."

"Not bad." Roy nodded toward her. "I like the 'electrify our souls' bit."

"City Slicker, what does your mother do?" Jeremy asked, grabbing a piece of chicken.

"She's the acting chairwoman of the hospital I work for."

"So, you are both doctors? What type? You look like a dentist," Malik questioned next.

I shook my head at Guinevere, telling her not to jump in. I could see what they were doing: asking all Masoa's questions so he didn't have to.

"Dentists are important to a person's health. I, however, am a neurosurgeon, while my mother's specialty was pediatric surgery." I took a bite of the salmon. "This is incredible, Ma'am."

Guinevere grinned. "What did I say? Home of the—"

"*The* best wild salmon in the country!" I replied, shaking my head as I fought the smile spreading on my lips.

"And you thought I was joking." She nodded proudly while stuffing her face and I couldn't help but laugh out loud; she was cute. She glanced up at me and I kept staring at her.

I was about to say something when her father coughed beside me, reminding us we weren't alone.

"Thank you, Eli. I'm glad you enjoy it," her mother cut in.

Jeremy's eyes narrowed in on me as I ate. "Neurosurgeon, huh? Fancy, but does it count if your mom runs the hospital?"

"I graduated top of my class at Yale Medical. I was offered the choice to stay there, but I wanted to be closer to my family. So of course I went to work for my mother's hospital."

I knew it was coming. I felt it.

Don't ask. Don't.

"And your father?" Roy pressed.

Called it.

Guinevere put her fork down. "Guys, we just got back. Can you save the questions for another time—"

"It's fine. My father was also a neurosurgeon. He died of a heart attack when I was eleven. I was there with my mother and younger brother when it happened." I looked to her father, who had yet to say anything, but whom I could feel watching me. "So, sir, I truly hope you are taking much better care of yourself. The last thing I want is for Guinevere to feel like she was cheated out of time with her father."

Just like I knew it would, the dinner table became silent; it was why I hadn't wanted them to ask—I knew it would just make them feel awkward.

"Okay." Jeremy cracked his neck side to side. "Lightning round. You ready?"

"Do I have a choice?"

"How old are you?" Malik asked, not answering me.

"31."

"Born on?"

"June 23rd."

"Where do you live?"

"Right next door to Guinevere."

They all looked to Masoa, then Guinevere, and back to me.

"He lived there first, and I moved in next door," Guinevere replied. "No, I didn't know."

Roy picked the questions. "Where did you grow up?"

"Townhouse on East 63rd Street in New York."

"This your first time ever leaving the city?"

"No. I've traveled, but mostly to other cities."

"Do you have any kids?"

"No."

"Do you want kids?"

"Eventually."

This time, they looked to Guinevere, who quietly finished off her salmon. Finally, she gave up and glared at them before turning to me. "I'm not a kids person," she replied.

I found that hard to believe. "You love kids. You spent most of your time visiting them in the hospital."

"Oh, I love them, but in expected, limited doses. Plus, I can always just give them back to their parents," she replied.

"She wants her mother to die of a broken heart is what she is really saying," her mother replied, frowning at her.

Guinevere sighed. "If it makes you feel better, I've gone from a hard no to a maybe."

The boys looked at me.

"Are you out of questions?" I asked.

"What's your favorite movie?" Malik asked as seriously as he could.

"Guys, really?" Guinevere frowned.

"I have to agree, that was a weak one." Her mother laughed.

"*Ocean's Eleven.*"

"Me too." Guinevere smiled.

"Wait!" Roy raised his hand. "Which version, 1960 or 2001?"

"2001." I hadn't even known there was an earlier one.

All of them—including Guinevere—groaned.

Her mom shook her head.

"He can't be perfect." Guinevere tried to defend me, but ended up frowning. "Really? Clooney over Sinatra?"

"I really didn't know there was an earlier one," I said to her, causing a few sighs.

Malik grinned. "No one thinks it's a weak question now, huh?"

"Did you know Eli owns a Black 1965 Aston Martin DB5 Vantage Convertible?" Guinevere asked, trying to save me.

All the guys looked to her.

"No way."

"I took a picture." She sang happily and tried to get her cell phone.

"No phones at the dinner table," her mother said.

"It's a 1965 Aston Martin," Malik said to the older woman.

"Mrs. Poe, it's James Bond's car," Jeremy added.

"No phones at my dinner table," she repeated sternly.

"Yes, Ma'am," they both said.

I chuckeled.

For the most part, Guinevere kept them entertained with her stories from the city, everything from randomly dancing on subway platforms to local musicians, the mural she had painted, and even her failed attempt to run. I noticed she spoke with her hands when she told her stories, as if she was trying to paint a picture in the air. Every once in a while, she would shift her hair to the side, shoot me a small smile, and then focus back on the men around her. When she stood up to clear the plates with her mother, so did I, taking them from her.

"It's fine, I got it. Finish your story," I said, following her mother.

"I'll admit it, City Slicker is pretty smooth." Malik whistled.

"Keep talking, Malik. I will get you back, I promise," Guinevere threatened him.

"I'm an officer of the law now, Gwen. I'm not scared of you—"

"Is filling your truck with spiders against the law?"

I looked back as as I put the plates in the sink; she and the rest of them just laughed at his horrified facial expression.

"Aren't we a little old for pranks like that?"

"Said the man who's 'not scared,'" Roy muttered, drinking his water.

"Like giant children, aren't they?" her mother whispered, shaking her head.

"Don't we all kind of revert to giant children when we're around our siblings? As mature as I hope I am, I still enjoy messing with and teasing my little brother," I said as I rinsed the dishes.

"So they don't make you nervous?" Her eyebrow rose.

"Not at all." They were at least talking. My eyes shifted to her father sitting at the head of the table, listening to his daughter.

"I got it, thank you, Eli. You can head back to the table."

"Are you sure?"

"Yes. Besides, once you sit, Guinevere will come over and the boys will go for some fresh air on the lake. Good luck." She winked at me.

I wanted to know if she was in my corner or not, but figured I'd just have to wait and see. Sure enough, when I headed back, Guinevere got up to help her mother.

"It's too warm in here," Jeremy said, right on cue.

"Should we go outside for some fresh air?" I asked him.

All three of them looked me up and down before their gaze moved to Masoa, who stood, turning to his wife. "Sweetheart, we are heading out."

"Really? All right, we will join you all soon," she said as if she was surprised.

Yep, the one I have to really watch out for is her mother. "I'll be fine, ma'am."

Guinevere's eyes shifted to me.

I tried my best to silently let her know not to worry. Grabbing my coat, I followed them out.

Guinevere

"Mom," I said pointedly as I dried the dishes. I knew her; she had something to say. "Just let me have it."

"First, I want to know: is he a fling, or he does he mean more to you?"

"Do you bring flings home to meet your parents?" I asked softly, putting the plate up in the cabinet.

"If he were a fling, I would say have fun. Let your—"

"Mom, if you say inner goddess..."

She smirked. "Sweetheart, no one has an inner goodness, we aren't shooting a Pantene commercial. We all just have sexier versions of ourselves. Besides, life is too short not to have fun, Guinevere."

We are not having that talk. "And if he isn't a fling?"

"And if he isn't a fling, I have nothing to say to you, because you will do what you want. It's who you are. I don't know anything about him yet. I just know that when it comes to men, your track record isn't great."

"I've only dated Sebastian—"

"And how many times have you wanted men you can't have? You used to have a crush on Jeremy, right? But he only had eyes for Stevie. So you just stood there waiting, and he never saw you that way."

"That was different, it was just a little high school crush." It had honestly meant nothing; I never even said anything to anyone.

"Wasn't Eli supposed to marry someone else? He isn't just with you to get over her, is he?"

I frowned, wiping down a cup. "You make it seem like I wasn't also in a relationship."

"True." She nodded, shaking her hands.

I handed her the towel.

"But when your relationship ended, how did you feel?"

"I was upset, of course, and angry and embarrassed."

"And you felt free," she finished.

I stopped, because I had felt that way. For the briefest second right after it happened, I had felt like I could breathe.

"When you truly love someone, when you have found your match and they walk away from you, or you are forced to walk away from them, freedom is nowhere on the list of things you feel, because that feeling comes from being with them, Guinevere."

"So you're saying I didn't truly love Sebastian, fine—"

"I'm saying whether you know it or not, you are falling in love with that man. But is he capable of falling in love with you now, or are you just an escape for him?"

When she said it, I hated how the first thing I thought about was all the times he'd told me he didn't like to have to think about anything around me, how he liked to lose track of time with me. I felt like someone was sitting on my chest.

"What is that proverb you always say?"

"Le ntombazane izinkanyezi emehlweni akhe bayokhanya njengokukhanya ebusuku," she replied in Zulu.

I nodded. "The girl with stars in her eyes will shine like the moonlight... Let me shine, Mom."

She sighed but nodded. "I know you don't want to hear it, but just remember to protect your heart, Guinevere, or it really will break this time."

Eli

Taigi barked, hopping around Masoa's leg. He even howled up at the night sky.

I couldn't blame him, actually. I had never seen this many stars in one place in all of my life. It was like someone had spilled a million tiny diamonds onto a dark sheet. A thin crescent moon sat just to the left of it all.

"So, City Slicker." Malik came over, placing his arm around my neck. "Cypress so far?"

"It's just as beautiful as Guinevere described," I replied as we stopped at the lake, the sky reflected in it.

Taigi ran up to me with a stick between his jaws. It reminded me of the ones he often grabbed when we went running, and I threw it for him. He fetched and dropped it at my feet.

Kneeling next to him, I scratched his neck. "So, we are still on for a run tomorrow, then?"

"Aye, Taigi! You're on the wrong side." Jeremy clapped for him to come over to him.

But Taigi lay down, rolling over for me to scratch his stomach.

"He's been in the city for too long, it's messed with his head," Masoa replied. With one whistle, Taigi was back on his feet and running to his side. "I'll see you boys later. I'll let Gwen know you left."

"See you later, Masoa." They headed off on their own and nodded back toward me with smirks on their faces.

Roy shook his head and added, "Good luck."

The silence was potent as they disappeared, leaving us both at the edge of the water.

"How long have you been seeing my daughter?" he asked, crouched down, flicking a rock into the water. His eyes were so clear the water seemed to reflect in them, and in turn, the sky as well.

"Not very long. We were sort of friends for a time before that."

"Sort of friends. And that means?"

"We fought and teased each other constantly, though I believe I started it by calling her a con artist."

He stood. "You called my daughter a con artist?"

"Yes, I did, right after I found out how much money my mother bought her painting for. I believe she called me Dr. Asshole in return. Sometimes, I swear she's still thinking it in her mind." I smirked.

"Aren't you supposed to be making me like you with your gentleman routine and whatnot?"

"Oh I am, just discreetly. Besides, it's only the first day, you still have to get a few rounds in, sir. Then, and only then, when you're ready to like me, you will." I put my hands into my pockets, staring upward again. I felt like I could look up at the stars forever.

"That story about your father, was it real?"

That was the only thing that angered me, and I turned to him seriously. "If you remember anything about me, sir, please remember this: never will I ever lie on my father's name, nor use my family for my own advantage. There are some lines you just don't cross. Family is mine."

"Is everything okay?" Guinevere came out holding a tray of iced tea.

"Everything is fine," Masoa said.

I nodded, thanking her for the glass.

"Well, Dad, it's been a long day. I'll show Eli his room."

"The one in the basement." His eyes narrowed.

"Of course," she replied, all but pulling my arm as her mother came outside.

"Goodnight," I said to her mother as Guinevere led me back into the house.

"Congrats, you made it through round one."

She led me down the hall. I noticed the floors creaked loudly when we walked. "So this is why he wanted me in the basement?" I wondered if he had somehow made the floorboards creak like that just for this reason.

She flicked on the lights, exposing one wall covered in books adjacent to a giant mirror hanging above a dresser, all over a carpeted white floor. My bag was already beside it, by the door to what I guessed was the bathroom. "Are all of those yours—"

She cut me off, kissing me. Her hands snaked around my neck, and mine behind her. I bit her bottom lip and she opened for me, moaning against my mouth when I cupped her ass. I felt myself harden when her breasts pushed up against me.

"Sorry," she whispered when we broke apart. "I've wanted to do that for a while now."

"Don't ever apologize for kissing me like that," I replied, my hands in her back pockets. We didn't say anything, just stared at each other, her fingers playing with the collar of my shirt.

"I should go before I get you in trouble," she said, though her eyes drifted to my lips.

"You should." But I didn't want her to.

"Goodnight, Eli."

"Goodnight, Guinevere."

Neither of us moved.

"You have to let go of me, Eli."

Releasing her but not moving, I waited for her to leave. She still didn't.

"You're not moving."

"I was honestly hoping you would hold on longer. Goodnight," she said, walking past me.

I grabbed her arm, pulling her back to me, kissing her hard. Hands on the backs of her thighs, I lifted her up and her legs wrapped around me, her fingers gripping my hair.

God, she has no idea how good she tastes.

"Gwen?" Her mother called from the top of the stairs.

Sighing, we broke away and I let her down. She moved to the stairs, trying to fix her clothes. "I'll see you in the morning."

"I'll be here," I replied as she went up, the stairs squeaking with each step. "And Guinevere?"

"Yeah?"

"Next time, I won't let you go," I said.

"Good. I like the way you hold me." She winked.

When she was gone, I stripped, heading straight to the shower.

Jesus, she sets my blood on fire.

CHAPTER TWENTY-TWO
TERROR AND DEAD SHOT

Guinevere

"**S**orry you missed out on a good run this morning?" I asked Eli as we walked up the trail in the woods behind my house.

He had just gotten dressed for a run, wearing the same type of sleeveless hooded navy top and dark, loose-fitting running pants as before.

"It's fine, we both overslept. Besides, I wouldn't have known how to get back anyway," he said, throwing a stick for Taigi, who watched it fly over his head and then made a dash for it.

My parents walked only a few feet ahead of us, hand in hand.

When I was younger, I had thought their public displays of affection were the most embarrassing thing in the world. Now when I watched them, I found myself hoping for a time when I could be like them.

"How long have your parents been married?" he asked, bending down when Taigi came back.

"They got married the day after my mother's eighteenth birthday. They actually ran off together, even after my grandfather asked them to wait."

"Really?" he said, glancing up to my father.

I knew why. He seemed like a real stickler for following rules. "He's a romantic, while my mother, she's more logical, and she said that she knew she wasn't going to be with anyone else, so why wait? It worked."

"So all those books in the basement are his?" He grinned.

"There were a lot of very steamy love—"

"Those are my books, and they aren't steamy, though they are blush worthy, all right. My dad's more into thrillers and mysteries with a dash of romance in them. His favorites are any books that take place around the time of the Second World War." If there was anyone that could go on a book rant better than me, it was my dad.

"Good to know."

"For what?"

"Research. I am still being tested. Lunch this afternoon was proof of that," he replied.

I wanted to hang my head at the thought of it. My father had prepared lunch and made sure to add so many peppers to his famous chili con carne that my eyes watered. I wasn't even sure how Eli ate it. "How much water did you drink after that?"

"I drank all the milk in your fridge, and then a glass of water after that." We laughed. "After going through that, I can make it through anything."

It was then I noticed we had followed my parents right off the path and into the clearing of trees on the flat grassland where Jeremy, Malik, and Roy all stood with lacrosse sticks. The two nets were set up behind them. "Guys—"

"Up here, we don't play no baseball, now do we, boys?" my father asked, grabbing a stick.

"No, sir!" his army yelled.

"Eli, did you know Guinevere played lacrosse?" My mother joined in on the torture, taking the stick Malik handed her.

"Mrs. Poe, Gwen didn't just play lacrosse, she was *The Terror*." Roy stretched the words out. "In fact, when the girls' team was cut her junior year, she played on the boys' team, and they were still scared."

"Poor old Andrew to this day still has a scar under his left eye from that time she socked him." Jeremy put his arm around his shoulder. "Good times."

"Eli, if you would like to be the *ONLY* one sitting out, that's fine. I won't judge you. We get a little rough around here."

My dad threw me my stick, ignoring my glare.

"In fact, that's great. You can be the doctor."

"Dad…is this good for your heart?" I said through my clenched teeth.

"I will be goalie," he stated.

"No, exercise is good for him." Eli smirked. "I'll play. All I have to do is catch the ball with the stick and put it in the goal, right?"

They laughed and my father nodded, throwing him the black one.

He caught it, rolling it in his hands for a moment.

"Eli, they play dirty."

"Hey! So do you!" Malik pointed at me.

"I have no idea what you are talking about." I stretched, raising the stick above my head, and then down to the side. "It's not my fault you all run into the end of my stick."

"See there? It's The Terror rising from the ashes," Roy said, lifting his hands from the ground to the sky.

"All right then, we must pick teams." My mother came forward.

"Whatever the teams, Eli and Gwen can't be on the same side." Jeremy pointed at us both.

"Why?"

"It's a new family rule," my father stated, stepping forward. "Your mother and I will be captains. City Slicker, you're with my wife. Try not to embarrass her too badly. Gwen, you are with me. Malik, you are with the misses, Roy with me, and Jeremy—"

"Doggonit. I know I'm refereeing. There'd better be a round two. I want a turn laying the grass."

We all knew what he meant, but Eli just kept eyeing the stick in his hands. "Laying the grass?" He finally looked up to ask me.

"It means knocking the wind out of somebody so badly that they just lay there like they were part of the grass," Jeremy replied, coming over.

Eli nodded, and then looked to his lacrosse stick. "Do you mind if we switch? My power color is blue."

"Power color? What?" Jeremy laughed.

"Yes, and I'm going to need all the help I can get with The Terror over here," Eli said, switching sticks.

"Hey!" And there I was trying to help him.

"Come over, Gwen," Roy called.

I walked over. "Good luck."

"Thanks. Please watch out for my face, you know it's my moneymaker." He winked.

I shook my head. I was going to say it was actually his hands that were the moneymakers, but it would just sound dirty with my family around. "No, seriously, please don't mess up his face," I said to them when they pulled me into the huddle.

"Guinevere, he is not on your team," my father said to me. "We are on your team, and your teammates want to win, so…?"

"Lay them out." It felt like high school all over again.

"I can't hear you."

"Lay them out!" I said louder.

"Are you just going to hug each other all day over there?" my mother yelled.

"I'm sorry, I didn't know you were in a hurry to lose, sweetheart," my father hollered back.

Sometimes, I could not believe they were my parents.

Jeremy put the ball in the middle of the field.

"I'm guessing you want me to go up front?" I asked them. I saw them nod, as if to say "obviously." When I walked forward, so did Eli. "I can't go easy on you."

"I know, your mother told me."

I nodded.

Jeremy decided this was the time to be funny and begin preaching. "Now let us remember, this is merely a game, and as such let it be played fair, and let it be...a little bloody."

"Jeremy..."

"1. 2. 3."

We both attacked the ball, but he pushed me back with ease, flipping the stick, lifting the ball off the ground and throwing it over to Malik perfectly. They charged both Roy and my father, who stepped out of the goal even more so. Running forward, I tried to reach for it when Malik threw, but Eli jumped over my back leg, spun around Roy so badly Roy went forward, and faced off one-on-one with my dad. When he looked like he was going for it, he passed the ball right back to Malik, catching my dad off guard, and the ball just glided into the net.

"What the hell?" Jeremy said at the sidelines, pulling at his dirty blond hair.

Eli and Malik high-fived, and then Eli looked to my father. "You're right, I played a lot of baseball growing up, but that was only during the spring and summer. My coach didn't want me to get bored, so I played lacrosse in the fall and basketball in the winter. If you'd brought a football, I would have been *screwed*."

"How am I looking now, sweetheart?" My mother, who hadn't done anything, stood smiling brightly at us. When Eli got back to her, she just gave him a high five.

"Guinevere," my father said to me.

"Oh, I know," I said to him, gripping my stick. "Eli, the kid gloves are coming off now."

"I never asked you to put them on in the first place," he replied.

"How can you date someone that cocky?" Roy frowned.

"Well, I'm about to humble him."

When we met in the middle again, he crouched down right across from me, smiling like he'd stolen something, a gleam in his blue-green eyes.

"You know what they called me in high school?" he asked.

"I don't care."

"1. 2. 3."

Our lacrosse sticks smashed against each other's again. This time, I pushed back with everything I had, and he fell back, chasing after the ball as it rolled across the grass. I had just picked it up when he smacked my stick, flipping it and the ball out. He picked it up this time, running back toward the goal. I came up as fast as I could, but Eli was on another level when it came to speed. One moment he was in front of me, and the next he ran straight toward my father, who eyed Malik coming up on his left. This time Eli didn't pass, he took the shot, and because he was slowly trying to elevate my father's and my blood pressure, it went in.

"It was a dead shot, just in case you were wondering," he said, running past me.

Biting my tongue and taking a deep breath, I tried to remember it was just a game.

"Guinevere, you coming?" he called behind me.

"You, Dr. Davenport, are going to get hurt."

Eli

With one swift thrust forward, she checked me so hard I landed on my back, and she fell straight on top of me.

"Oh," I moaned, trying to breathe again.

"Did you just see the point he made?" Malik ran up to us.

"No, I was too busy being murdered," I muttered, dropping the stick and rubbing my chest when she rolled off.

"Whelp, we lost!" Her mother came over to us. "There was nothing we could really do when Masoa, the big cheater, had to jump in."

We had been playing for a little over an hour. I'd scored the first and only two goals of the game, but then her father had come out and decided to epically crush my pride. For a man who'd had a heart attack a month before, he was in damn good shape.

"Anyway, I had Jeremy run back to bring the food I made."

I tried to get up, but my body just wasn't feeling it. "I'm just going to lay here for a moment."

Roy snickered, kneeling down. "And this is why we call it laying the grass."

"Yep, I got that." I groaned again.

"Gwen, you just going to lie there, too?"

She flipped him off, her eyes closed. "Screw you guys for making me play again. I hate lacrosse so much."

"Why did you play in high school?" I looked toward her.

"Her dad was the coach." Roy grinned, standing up and putting a water bottle beside me. "You weren't half bad, Eli."

"Using my name now, I see." I finally sat up.

"Don't get all excited about it." He frowned, walking away.

Guinevere sighed, turning onto her back and lifting her leg up, trying to stretch it. "I get stiff legs."

"I know, give them to me," I said, taking her leg and placing it in my lap.

"Eli—"

"Were you injured while you played?" I asked seriously, pressing on her calves.

Releasing a breath through her nose, she sat up beside me, eyes on her dad, who stood beside her mother, still rubbing in his victory.

"My dad loves lacrosse. He played with his dad, and he played with my brother. So when he passed, I made sure to play, too, no matter what. I got hurt my senior year. Remember Chloe Drake? The woman who was waiting and holding Taigi?"

I nodded.

"She tripped and stepped on my leg."

I winced at the thought of it. "That's Chloe with an extra 97 pounds?"

"Yep, and my leg broke. She felt so bad, and everyone teased her about it. It was practice, and I remember secretly telling her that I was kind of thankful because I didn't have to play anymore."

"But you still played after you healed, didn't you?" She didn't even have to answer, I just knew it. "Are you sure it's not you who is the rock?" I asked, helping her off the ground, because from where I was looking, it looked like she was bearing a lot of weight on her shoulders.

She grinned. "Never in any of the stories I have ever heard from my father did a person beg for the rock to come."

"You lost me." I held her hand, walking back to her family and friends.

"The symbol for rain is the thunderbird, and if you beg hard enough, it sometimes comes. But the rock, no matter how much you beg, will stay in its place, bearing whatever weight is on its shoulders. My father needed some way to make a connection with me after my brother passed. And I came and gave him one. I don't regret it. Every once in a while my legs get stiff, but I have so many memories of him running to me after a game, cheering at the top of his lungs, lifting me up and spinning me around. It's not a burden for me." She smiled, wrapping her hand around my arm. She reached up and kissed the side of my cheek. "You were great, my father just doesn't like to lose."

"Gwen." Masoa held up a water bottle toward her.

She rolled her eyes, knowing he just wanted us to break apart, but went to him anyway.

I couldn't take my eyes off of her as she knocked shoulders with her father and he wrapped his arms around her, telling her something.

It was astonishing how every time I watched her now, it seemed to be in slow motion, my eye wanting to capture every one of her facial expressions, her voice, her movements, to save her in my memory forever. It made me wonder:

How did I get here?

When did I start falling for her so badly?

Is that even what I am doing, falling?

And, most importantly, is she too?

CHAPTER TWENTY-THREE
SIX LITTLE WORDS

Eli

I was sitting on the porch when a beer materialized right beside my face.

"Thank you," I said to Masoa.

He sat down beside me, not saying a word.

It was our last night there before heading back. They had prepared a dinner by the lake, and I had even managed to get the campfire going. Just like on the first night, the sky was coated with stars.

Guinevere played with Taigi, chasing him around the campfire. She had spent the day showing me all of Cypress. It had about one of everything: one movie theater, one grocery store, one mall, and in each one, I noticed how they all welcomed her back, either with a hug, a kiss, or free things. Each of them also thanked her for the money she had loaned them; she had even helped fund a new arts center for the high school.

"You do know I still don't like you, right?" he said to me, opening his can and drawing my attention.

"Yes. Maybe when we come again next time, I'll convince you more," I replied, taking a drink.

"Never going to happen," he muttered.

It took me some time, but I finally just asked him, "Do you mind if I ask you some things?"

"Are they about my daughter?"

"Yes. And you, too."

"Only if you answer mine."

Risky. "All right."

"Ask, then." He waited.

"How do you know when you've fallen in love with someone?"

He was silent for a long time.

"Sorry, I'm not sure who else to ask. My mother, as amazing as she is, doesn't always help."

"Weren't you about to get married?' he asked me.

I sat straighter, my arms on my knees. "Yes, but that doesn't mean I should have been. I set a goal to be married, and I chose a person who I thought best fit what I needed. I never asked myself if I loved her. I thought: this is great, she is what I was looking for. I hurt her and she hurt me in return." I had cared about Hannah. I couldn't lie about that, nor should I have had to, but that was different; I felt different with Guinevere.

"I believe when you start thinking like that, you've already fallen," he muttered.

"How did you know with her mother? Gwen said you ran off together to get married when you were only eighteen." And after all those years, they still held hands while they went on walks.

He snickered, sitting tall and looking at her mother where she was staring into a telescope. "It first hit me when I realized I didn't want her to go home. I wanted my home to be her home. Then I started to think about my life in ten or twenty years, and no matter what, she was there. Once I asked myself those questions, it was clear to me."

I thought back to Guinevere's first night with me. I'd said I didn't want her to be just some one-time screw and asked her to stay with me. That wasn't the reason...I may not have thought her home was mine, but I never once stopped her when she brought her toothbrush, hair dryer, and flat iron into my bathroom. I thought about how I couldn't sleep on her side of my bed, even if she wasn't there...because now it was her side.

"Do you want to know where I see myself in ten years?" I whispered to him when she moved to her mother, staring up at the sky.

"No, but I'm sure you're going to tell me anyway."

I turned to look at him. "I see myself still trying to get you to like me."

"It's going to take more than ten years." He frowned, drinking again. "Eli."

He finally said my name. However, he didn't look pleased.

"She's my baby girl. I would go to hell and back for her, and I can't bear for her to be hurt again."

"I won't hurt her."

"That's the thing. We don't try to hurt the people we care about, we just do. Do you know she didn't tell us how her engagement ended? She just called to say the wedding was off. We had to press Stevie to learn the truth. And again, I felt like I had failed my child. I told her not to go to New York, I begged her not to go, told her the city would chew her up and spit her out. I told her she could be an artist here, and teach at the high school. We had a huge fight about it. The next morning, she and Stevie were in her car, and she didn't talk to me again until after she felt like she could tell me she'd made it. She wrote letters, made sure to call us while we were at work, or when she thought we were busy. If we answered, our phone calls lasted five minutes, if that. All because she didn't want me to think I was right, that she couldn't cut it. So I have no idea what she went through her first year. She wouldn't take money or anything. But the day she was mentioned in the paper as an upcoming artist, she called me and talked for hours."

"She wanted to prove she could do it," I said.

He nodded.

"And you blamed yourself for the void between you both, because it reminded you of your son?"

His head shot toward me, shocked, as if to ask how I knew.

I just nodded, drinking again.

"I can't believe she talked to you about that. She never talks to anyone about it."

"She told me that, too. I was having trouble dealing with my brother's wish to go his own way."

"Damn it." He sighed, standing up. "I guess I'm going to have to get used to you. Make sure to bring her back as often as you can. I still won't like you, but I will adjust."

"Why the sudden change?" I asked, rising as well.

"Because she's in love with you. I thought you were another passing phase, like the other one. But if she was willing to dig up something painful like that just to help you, then there is nothing left to do or say," he replied, preparing to walk back to the fire.

"Can I ask you one more question?"

"Boy, are you a neurosurgeon or a shrink?"

Ignoring him, I asked seriously, "How is your heart? I won't tell her, if it makes you uncomfortable. But honestly, how is your health?"

"Keeping my cholesterol and blood pressure low. You aren't helping the latter with your questions, though. Any more?"

I raised my hands in surrender.

He walked over to his wife.

Guinevere said something to her before running over to me and grabbing on to my arm.

"Hello." I smiled at her.

"Come on." She dragged me off back toward the house, and neither her mother nor father looked back; they just held each other, looking up at the stars. It almost looked like they were dancing.

Taking the lantern from her and taking hold of her hand, I was led farther and farther down the path.

"Where are we going?"

"Shh, you'll ruin it," she whispered.

We walked a little more until we came to the same clearing as before. She let out one low whistle, and it echoed in the trees above us. One firefly came shining right in front of us, then a dozen more, and then the whole clearing glowed in the darkness. They were everywhere, like Christmas lights.

"I wanted to show you this before we left. When I was a kid, I thought I could train them or something, to make their lights blink with whatever song I whistled. It didn't work, obviously, but they did come up when I whistled." Letting go of my hand, she tried to catch one. She held her hands closed for a second, then opened her fingers slowly, but when she did, there was no firefly. "How is it possible that I can't catch a firefly in a *field* of fireflies after all these years?" She laughed at herself.

Putting the lantern down, I came up behind her, wrapping my arms around her to pull her closer to me. When I felt her body, I rested my head beside hers, lifting our hands together.

"Let's catch them together," I said softly into her ear.

She leaned into me. "Okay."

"You have to be really still and wait for them."

She held her palms open on top of my mine, and we stood there. Her breathing matched mine, her heartbeat felt like mine. And then the firefly, most likely mistaking us for another tree in the forest, came and sat right in her palm, followed by several more.

I wanted to say it then, out loud to the world, but all I could manage was to say it to myself.

I'm in love with you, Guinevere.

Guinevere

By the time we got back to the house, running from the downpour that had suddenly, almost magically poured over everything in Cypress, I felt like I couldn't breathe. I went into my room and, still dripping wet, fell back on my bed. My heart felt like it was trying to claw its way out of my chest. I lay there for a moment, staring up at my teal ceiling, my old Orlando Bloom poster still hanging there. When I looked at it, I felt nothing like I had all those years before. The person I was giddy for was one flight of stairs away.

I want to see him. I'd just seen him and I wanted to see him again. My brain wasn't thinking rationally. I opened the door, and my mom was already walking by. She stopped, turning to me.

"Goodnight," I said to her.

"Go." She nodded her head at me. "If your father asks, I'll take of care of it. Go."

"Mom—"

"Well, if you don't want to—"

"Thank you," I whispered, walking past her and down the hall.

Taking a breath at the top, I walked downstairs as softly as possibly, stepping on the outside parts of the staircase so it wouldn't squeak. When my foot hit the carpet, I saw him sitting at the edge of the bed, shirtless, a towel over his head as he stared at a teardrop necklace he dangled by its chain in front of him. Due to the continuing rain, only a bit of light entered the room through the window above the bed.

"It's pretty," I whispered.

He froze for a moment, picking his head up to look at me. His hair was still dripping wet, like all of me at that point.

"Who's it for?"

"You," he muttered, not moving, his gaze glued to me. "I bought it while in town today. I've been trying to think of when to give it to you. The rain killed my moment."

"Is now a good time?"

He stood, coming over to me, and I turned around. He brushed my hair to the side, bringing the necklace in front of me and clasping it around my neck. I faced him, and he centered it in the middle of my chest.

Never looking away from him, I pulled off my shirt, dropping it beside my feet.

"Do not tempt me like this, because I will fail," he said with his hand on my bra strap.

Walking around him and standing in front of his bed, I unclasped it, letting it fall to the ground. "There is nothing wrong with fai—" His lips were on mine before I could finish, his hands on the sides of my face, his tongue in my mouth when I wrapped my arms around his neck. His kiss went from my lips to my chin, and down my neck. His hand cupped my breast, squeezing tightly, and then pulling on my nipple hard, while the other traveled up my skirt to the round of my ass, pulling me to him. Kissing back up my neck and jaw until he was at my ear, he whispered, "I'm not letting you go, Guinevere."

"I wouldn't have come down here if I wanted you to," I reminded him.

"So what do you want?"

"You. You, in every way possible. So why do you still have your jeans on?" I unbuttoned them, pushing them down and reaching inside, grabbing hold of him. "Would you like me to demonstrate?" I didn't give him room to debate it before kissing the tip of him, then licking over and over again before taking him into my mouth.

"Guin...Guinevere," he moaned, grabbing on to my hair.

I took him as deeply as I could into my mouth, my teeth light on his skin before my tongue licked around him. I could feel him throbbing, and I sucked harder and faster, him thrusting forward, fucking my mouth. When I took my mouth off of him, I held on with my hands, stroking slowly as my tongue licked his tip and my lips kissed the side.

"And you say I taste good," I said before taking him back as deep as I could into my throat. I didn't want to stop until I made him feel the same way I had.

However, he stopped me, pulling back his erection to stand high and proud. He took my other hand off his stomach, pulling me up to my feet. He ran his thumb over my bottom lip.

"If you think I'm going to let you control me this easily tonight, Ms. Poe, then you are sexy, but also mistaken. So get on your hands and knees."

I couldn't stop myself from being excited and did what he asked of me. I could feel his body behind me as he stripped me out of my skirt and underwear. He hovered over me, the heat of him pressed up against my ass, along with his hand, rubbing soft circles.

"You push me too far, Guinevere," he whispered into my ear, kissing the side of my face. "I was going to take a cold shower—a custom I am now used to because of you, stroking myself because I can't be inside you..." He kissed my shoulder and gripped my breast. "Then you appear, dripping wet, and strip for me." He pulled my nipple, rubbing himself against my ass. "And I think to myself, I won't *fuck* her tonight. Instead, I will make love to her slowly, softly, and passionately."

"But then I took you into my mouth—"

When I spoke, I felt his hand slap my ass so hard I gripped the bed and bit down on my bottom lip to keep from moaning in bliss.

"Then I felt your teeth on me, your tongue, enjoying me like I was vanilla ice cream."

"Aren't you?"

SLAP.

"Ahh!" I moaned, my body starting to shake.

"I told your father I wouldn't hurt you, your father who is somewhere in this house. But you like your sex with a side of pain, so what can I do? You've made a liar out of me, Guinevere."

SLAP.

I dropped my head, gripping the sheets so tightly.

SLAP.

My mouth watered.

SLAP.

My ass shook, and he purposely pressed himself against me. I could feel how wet I was for him as he rubbed himself back and forth. I bucked against him, hungry for more.

SLAP.

"Eli..."

SLAP.

I wasn't sure if he was hitting me harder, or if I was just becoming more sensitive—maybe both. All I knew was, I liked it. I liked it too damn much, and the fact that both my parents were home and I was trembling at the hands of Eli was too much for me to bear.

SLAP.

"Harder," I whispered.

SLAP.

"Harder."

SLAP.

"Yes."

SLAP.

ELI! I screamed in my mind as I came. I couldn't even manage to stay on all fours any more, the front of me collapsing onto the pillows, my ass in the air, too sore to come down.

"The first of the many orgasms you will have tonight." He kissed it, rubbing circles on it before his tongue traveled between my thighs. I could barely breathe as he licked and sucked on me, my mind going hazy. Whatever fatigue I had felt before vanished when he held on to my thighs. Sitting up onto him I gripped his head below, rubbing myself against his mouth.

He didn't slow down, determined to make me lose my mind, and I could see myself in the mirror on the wall, not hiding anything from view. I saw the way my breasts bounced as I arched back and rode on his tongue. The longer I looked, the wider the grin became on my face, and when I looked down at him his eyes were closed, his grip tight on my thighs. I loved the fact that he enjoyed it this much, wanting more of me...everything of me.

Gripping my own nipple, I couldn't stop myself, and I wanted to scream his name to anyone who could hear me.

"Two," he grinned, wiping the corner of his mouth when I all but collapsed onto the bed next to him.

"Eli…" I wasn't even sure where I was going with that. My mind was nothing but silly putty at that point.

On top of me, he kissed my lips lightly and moved, laying soft kisses on my neck. I held on to him, almost hugging him as he let me breathe, kissing my chest.

"Eli," I called again, stronger, and he stopped, looking up to me. The only thing on my mind as his blue-green eyes stared back at me was, *I'm in love with you, Eli.* I wished more than anything I could say it to him, but saying, "Make love to me," was the best I could do.

He brushed my hair back from my face and, kissing my forehead, smiled down at me. "As you wish." He shifted between my legs and slowly slid into me, his hands reaching up to take mine. His head, his lips, his eyes all hovered above mine, and he thrust into me.

It was like neither of us would ever be able to look away.

"You are beautiful," he said to me.

I tried to speak, but he kissed me softly.

"You…" he moaned out, and I held him, trying to rock into each slow and powerful thrust forward. "You, Guinevere Aurora Poe, are the most beautiful woman in the world to me. Let me say it. You should hear it."

I couldn't have spoken even if I'd wanted to. Instead, I wrapped my legs and arms around him, and he hugged me in return, his forehead on top of my mine, no gaps between either of our bodies, and we both found release.

Chapter Twenty-Four
Tick, Tick, BOOM

Guinevere

"Home sweet home," I said to Taigi, opening the apartment door for us. Taigi was not as excited as me. He just walked over to his bed and curled up into a ball. "Well then."

"He could just be tired," Eli said, putting the bags down at the door before walking into my kitchen. "Your fridge is empty. Guinevere."

"But I have a cellphone and a list of great takeout places."

"After having your mother's cooking for the weekend, takeout just feels like a disappointment," he replied, grabbing water for himself. "Did you call her to let her know we got back?"

"Shoot," I said, pulling out my phone.

He shook his head, walking over to my window and resting against the wall with a pillow at his back.

"When do you get to go back to work?" I asked him as I dialed.

"I can go back Friday." He pulled out his phone.

We had left Cypress early that morning. All the guys had come and even called Eli by his first name, which was a start. My dad hugged me for so long I thought we were going to miss our flight. My mother...well, she just gave me a look like she could read everything that had happened the night before with Eli. I had stayed with him until the sun came

270

up before sneaking back to my bedroom. You would think being a grown woman, I wouldn't have to sneak anywhere, but I was not ready, nor would I ever be, to have that battle with my parents.

For the first time in forever, I didn't panic on the flight. I just thought about the night before or held on to Eli, and everything felt all right. I wasn't scared. Sore, yes, but not scared.

"Hey Mom, it's me. I just wanted to let you know we got back safely. I'll try and call a little later. Love you, bye." I left the message, hanging up. Right after I did, my agent, Tara, called.

"Hello, Tara?"

"Hey, Gwen, is this a bad time? I wasn't sure when you came back from your parents," she said.

I grabbed a glass of water for myself. "That's fine. What's up?"

"Well, I have a new project for you. I think it would be great, but you should know something."

"What is it?" I asked, putting my glass on the counter.

"Well, it's from Sebastian—"

"Tara, I'm not interested."

"Your contract isn't up, and of all the things they sent over, this is the best one for your career."

Damn me for not cutting ties when I had a chance, I thought, putting my hand on my forehead.

"Fine, what is it?"

"Sebastian is starting a new magazine, called *The Real,* and is partnering with *National Geographic* to do it."

"And they want me, too?"

"They want you to be the main photographer for it. You would travel around the world, shooting people from all walks of life. The rich, the poor, everyone, and it will be featured in *The Real*. Everything would be paid for, of course, and you would get a team…"

My eyes shifted to Eli, who sat comfortably next to Taigi, petting his fur. "Find another project, Tara," I said.

"Gwen, this is amazing, you would be opening yourself up to so many opportunities —"

"Tara," I said as softly and as sternly as I possibly could. "Find another project for me to do to finish up my contract, all right? I will talk to you later. Thanks." I hung up before she could say anything else.

"Is everything okay?" Eli straightened some.

"Everything is fine. Did you find anything to eat?" He looked like he didn't believe me, but looked through his phone anyway.

"What are you in the mood for? Thai? Chinese?"

"How about we get a hamburger and fries? The more I think about it, the better it sounds," I said, walking over to him and offering my hand to help him off the ground.

He took it, standing up. "That works. How do you have so much energy after—"

"After last night?" I grinned, holding the door open for him. "I have no idea, but I'm sure it will hit me later. For now, I want to eat. The cereal and toast we had this morning was nowhere near enough. Bye, Taigi."

I closed and locked the door. He took my hand, leading us to the elevator. We both stopped when we saw Toby there, slouched with a half-bottle of whiskey in his hands. He looked up at the numbers above us.

"This…isn't…my…floor…" He hiccupped, slipping backward.

Eli ran to catch him.

The bottle slipped from his hand, falling to the ground.

"Toby," Eli called to him.

"Dr. Davenport?" He laughed, patting his shoulder and trying to stand straight. When he came back up, he had the neck of the broken bottle in his hand. "You are a son of a bitch, you know that?" The elevator doors closed again. Eli shook his head when I tried to come closer and I pressed the button for Toby's floor.

"You doctors can't do shit." He laughed again, and when Eli tried to hold him steady, he pushed him away. "All you did was make my daughter feel worse! And then you come in all proud and mighty like you are some fucking god, and stop trying to save her! Time of death, 8:43 PM. You know, that is all I hear now! Every goddamn day, that's all I hear. Time of death, 8:43 PM. What gives you the right, huh? What gives you the right to say my daughter's dead!"

"Toby—"

"And you!" He cut him off, turning to me.

The moment he did, Eli stood right in front of me.

"You and your stupid, goddamn fucking painting! You weren't helping anyone! Every time I look at it, I want to set it on fire. Why did you have to go draw it? You should have put an X over everyone's face—"

The doors opened again, and he collapsed, shaking.

"Call an ambulance. He most likely has alcohol poisoning." Eli was on his hands and knees.

I was already on the phone as Eli turned Toby's body to the side to help him breathe, keeping his head elevated at the level of his knees. The fact that we lived so close to the hospital had never come as more of a relief than it did in that moment when the ambulance pulled up. I waited for them outside and held the door open as they, alongside Eli, helped Toby from the elevator onto a gurney.

"I'm going to go with them to the hospital, go ahead—"

"I'm coming too. I'll be there soon. Go."

Nodding, he kissed the side of my head before heading into the ambulance with them. When I saw them racing down the street, I finally allowed myself to take a deep breath and calm down.

Every time I look at it, I want to set it on fire. Why did you have to go draw it? His voice screamed in my mind as I walked down the street, gripping on to my bag. I hadn't thought of how he would feel looking at a painting of his family when everyone in it was dead but him. It most likely didn't bring him any of the same joy I hoped my work brought Meryl, Logan, and Eli.

Even though it had only been three days, it felt like forever since I had last entered the hospital. Maybe it was vanity, or maybe I just needed to remind myself that it was there, that I looked to my mural. It was somewhat old news now. Anyone who worked there would get used to it, and new people probably didn't come to see my painting. A few kids sat in front of it while their parents were on the phone. They stuck their fingers up the painting of the grandfather's nose.

At least they're smiling, I thought, walking to the nurses station. "Can you let me know when I can see a Mr. Toby Wesley, please?"

"Gwen?"

Turning, I saw Ian come up to me, handing the chart to the nurse and smiling.

"Welcome. I thought you and Eli went on a getaway?"

"We came back today. Do you remember Toby Wesley? Molly's father. He lives in our building, and we ran into him. He was really messed up. The ambulance should have just brought him here," I said to him.

He frowned. "Eli came in with them?"

I nodded.

"We have a better chance of finding out at the ER. Follow me." He pointed in that direction and I followed, vaguely remembering the highway crash that had led me there the first time. This time, thankfully, it was much tamer when we got there.

After walking us to the nurses station near the door of the area, Ian turned to the nearest nurse. "Has a Toby Wesley been checked in?"

"We have a record of him. He's being prepped for emergency surgery." He nodded, about to walk off, then stopped. "Dr. Davenport?"

"Just got an update that he is assisting."

Ian frowned. "Call the chairwoman and let her know. I'll go try and pull him out now—"

"We've got a doctor coming in now." A nurse hung up the phone, rushing toward the door.

"Who?" Ian said, already grabbing gloves.

"They said it was Dr. Michaels," the nurse said.

"Hannah?" He went toward the door as the paramedics brought in a woman who couldn't have been Hannah. I took a step back as they wheeled her in. My heart started to race, and blood pumped to my ears.

"What happened?" Ian asked, looking into her eyes.

"She was out at lunch with a few other people from the clinic and fainted. She came to a little bit before demanding to be brought here."

My eyes were glued to her stomach. Her clearly pregnant stomach.

It's Sebastian's. It's Sebastian's.

"She said the baby's father was a doctor here."

I wanted to collapse, but it made better sense to run...to run far, far away from all of this.

Eli

Stepping out of the OR two hours later than I would have hoped, I stretched and pulled off my cap to find my mother and Ian both waiting for me. Ignoring them, I went to the sink to wash my hands. "I know what you guys are going to say. No, I didn't officially come back yet. But I brought him in, and I wasn't going to just drop him off and go on my way again," I told them, but neither spoke as I turned around. "Mom, it's fine. I only stood watch; I didn't operate in any way, though we are going to have to put him on the donor list."

"Sweetheart, we aren't here about that," my mother whispered, pushing off the wall, her arms folded. "Just listen to me—"

"Is it Guinevere? Is she all right? She said she was coming here, and I haven't—"

"It's not Gwen, Eli," Ian stated as I was already halfway out the door.

"If it's not Guinevere and it's not Logan or my mother, why do you all look like someone died?" I snapped at them.

"Hannah came in—"

"If this is about Hannah, Mom, I—"

"Listen to me, Eli!" she yelled.

I went still. "Hannah came in, bleeding...she's pregnant. She has cervical insufficiency and her water broke. We are trying to slow down her labor, but there is only so much we can do, you know that."

"You guys can't possibly think it's mine. She was having an affair, you know that, right?" They couldn't be serious. "Shit, did Guinevere hear any of this? She might have gotten—"

"Hannah had a non-invasive prenatal DNA test, twice, from a toothbrush you left at her place, and both times you came out as the father. 99.97% positive," Ian kept spitting out the nonsense.

My brain couldn't wrap around it at all, and I felt nothing but panic.

"Eli, I checked her charts. She is going to give birth, and you are going to be the father of a tiny, premature baby, so you need to go—"

"Mother." I stopped her, shaking my head. "What I need to do is make sure Mr. Wesley doesn't drink himself to death so I can put him on the donor list. Then I need to call Logan, well, because that little brat isn't answering his phone, lost it or something. Then I need to unpack, because 24 hours ago we were in Cypress, Alaska. And 24 hours ago, being a father was nowhere on my list of accomplishments. So I don't know what Hannah told you, or why you are—"

"Eli, I know this is hard for you. I understand you are confused and upset, but right now it can't be about you. It needs to be about Hannah, and your baby."

"What baby?" I yelled. "Hannah was here for months. She told me she missed me. She got mad at me for going on dates. But never did she ever tell me about a baby. So either the baby isn't mine, or she doesn't want me in her life."

Ian said nothing, his arms crossed. I realized I preferred him making jokes.

"Was Guinevere here when this all happened?"

He didn't answer.

"Ian. Was Guinevere here?"

He nodded. "Hannah came in when she was looking for you in the ER."

Of course. Of fucking course! Heading out of the room, I pulled out my phone and dialed. It felt like the phone rang forever before I got her voicemail.

"Pick up, Guinevere. Pick up," I said, dialing again, and this time I went straight to her voicemail. *Fuck.* This was insane. Nothing made sense. I thought back to all the times I'd seen Hannah up to this point. She hadn't looked any different to me. She should have at least been early in her second trimester when I'd seen her last. She should have been showing.

"Dr. Davenport."

I looked up to find that I was in the maternity ward, and an intern in pink came up to me.

"Dr. Michaels is in room 617. Dr. Milroy said she may need a C-section, but she is still holding off. Please let us know if you need anything." He nodded to me and walked around, heading back down the hall.

I didn't want to see her, but I needed to hear her say it. I needed her to explain. When I slid open the door for 617, I spotted Hannah laying back, her hand on her head.

She looked to me, and then back to the ceiling.

After walking up to her, I took a seat beside her bed.

"It is yours," she said. "I have proof. I showed it to your mother. The baby is yours. I don't need money, or—"

"Why didn't you say anything?" I tried my best to speak calmly while staring at her stomach. "You were here for how long? You could have said something Hannah!"

She snickered and her jaw cracked to the side. "Why? So you'd tell me you don't love me anymore? That I should get rid of it so you could run off into the sunset with some other woman? Sorry but no. I was going to hide and wait and avoid you until I gave birth, and then I was going to show her to you. I was going to put her in your face so you couldn't walk away, not without completely rejecting us. I know you. Eli Davenport, reject his family? Never. This is our chance, Eli.

We can have a second chance. Me, you, and our daughter. Just think, this is what would have happened if—"

"If you hadn't run off with another man? If we had gotten married? But you did and we didn't. So there is no second chance and using a baby as a way to make me stay with you is low, Hannah. There are a lot of things I could call you, but I never thought manipulative was one of them—"

"What can I do!" she yelled at me, her blue eyes angrily trying to brush away tears. "I made a mistake. A mistake I will regret every day of my life. I wake up and I'm so angry at myself. I love you, Eli. This is a good thing. We were a good thing! I'm sure we can get that back."

"Hannah—"

"So because of her, that woman, you're going to abandon us? Have you even seen our daughter?"

"*That woman* is my girlfriend—"

"And I'm the mother of your child."

"Wow," I whispered in disgust. Talking to her was useless and honestly scared me a little. Had I really been so blinded by her before that I hadn't realized the type of person she was? She only cared about herself. She wanted everything and she wanted it on her terms.

Once again, I found myself staring at Hannah, wondering, *How the hell did this happen?*

"I won't abandon her," I said after taking a deep breath. "No matter who her mother is, I'd never abandon my own daughter. But you Hannah...I could do with not seeing you ever again."

With that, I left the room, but not before hearing a sob from behind me. Running my hands through my hair, I tried to breathe. I didn't want to hurt her. I didn't want to be harsh, but she didn't seem to understand.

This is a mess. FUCK! Less than twenty-four hours before I had been certain my life was back on track, and then this happened. *And Guinevere...*

I reached for my phone in my pocket when I heard someone come up beside me.

"Dr. Davenport, congratulations. Do you want to see your daughter?" A nurse smiled happily at me.

Gripping on to the phone tightly, I put it back into my pocket and nodded without saying a word.

Guinevere

I knocked on the door.

Nathaniel opened it, his hair slicked back as always and his reading glasses low on his nose.

"Gwen?"

"Stevie told me to visit the Hamptons, so surprise, here I am! Nice house. It's very...white."

Stevie came up, dressed in a light green floral dress, her red hair up in a ponytail.

"Stevie! You look nice. So, I was in town and I thought I'd come and see you. I'm sorry, I was going to call, but I dropped my phone in my toilet. This place really is nice."

Nathaniel looked between us both and just headed back inside.

"I'm sorry, were you guys in the middle of something? I can go and come back. I bought a car." I pointed to the white Audi convertible in her driveway with Taigi sitting in the passenger seat.

"Gwen, are you all right?"

"Not at all, I think they cheated me on it, really. Did you know you could buy cars right off the lot? It was a little too expensive, but I was in a hurry. At first, I was going to take the bus here, but I would have had to walk another hour just to get to your house from the station. Then I was going to take a taxi, but I knew that would have looked bad if you all had company. So I said, 'What the hell, I'm a millionaire! I should splurge right?' So I went to the dealership and bought myself a brand new Audi and drove here. It's nice, right?" I pointed back at it and Taigi barked. "Taigi loves it."

She walked up to me and placed her hands on my face. "You sound like you've lost your mind and it's scaring me, Gwen. What happened? Are your parents okay? Is everything okay?"

I bit my lip, trying to stop myself from breaking down, but it didn't work. Nothing worked, and all I could do was hug her.

"Okay, cry first. We can talk later."

Chapter Twenty-Five
Love Me Enough To...

Guinevere

Later didn't come for two days. Every time I tried to talk about it, my eyes would start to burn and I would break down again. Stevie and I sat on the beach, Taigi's head on my lap as the sun rose over the horizon. She handed me the chocolate bar, and I broke myself off another piece.

"He called me," she whispered. "Eli. He called last night, wanting to know if I had spoken to you. He sounded like he was—"

"Please don't," I begged, brushing Taigi's fur. "Each time I think of him, I think of her, pregnant. If I stayed in his life then I would be jealous, and upset, and...forced to see her as long as he wanted to be with me. I just see myself getting hurt, and hurting him in return."

On top of the fact that I wasn't even sure if I wanted kids, let alone being step-anything to anyone.

"So you are never going to speak to him again? It's not his fault, Gwen."

"I know. I know it's not his fault. All of this was before me, but it doesn't change the fact that he's going to be a father, or is one already. I don't see any room for me. There is no room for me in his life. It's neither of our fault, but I can't; I don't want to spend my life waiting on the side-lines, hoping one day it will be just us." I tried to laugh, but my voice cracked. "Remember how I said Nathaniel wasn't the right guy for you? Thank you for telling me to shove it, because I would hate it if I had messed up your life as much as I have mine."

"You didn't mess up your life." She took my hand. "Things just happen, and life is just life. And you were right about Nathaniel back then, he was a tool. He cheated on me."

"No, he didn't." If he had, I was going to kill him.

She nodded, spinning the ring on her finger. "It was a few weeks after I dropped out. I met the girl and punched her right in the face, but I couldn't face you. I didn't drop out because of Nathaniel, I dropped out because I couldn't keep up, and there you were, excelling at the speed of light. I felt like my world was crumbling, and I couldn't face you or my parents, so I broke up with Nathaniel and worked at a bar that year we didn't speak. I could have called you at any time, but I just wanted to be on my own. Nathaniel and I had just gotten back together when we became friends again. I never told you because it seemed dumb in hindsight, and I knew you would be upset you hadn't come earlier."

"I'm a pretty bad friend. I'm so sorry I wasn't there, Stevie, and here I am coming to you now, crying all over your shoulder."

She shrugged. "You came because you trusted me, and I'm happy. I feel bad that I didn't trust you enough back then."

I pulled her into a hug, and we both fell onto the sand, laughing.

"Promise me no matter what, you will tell me if anything happens, all right? And if Nathaniel ever—"

"I got it, I got it. Go, you have your own love life to sort out."

That was the problem. I had a life, but I no longer had a love life.

Eli

I was a father.

My daughter's name was Sophia May Davenport.

She weighed 3lbs, 4.3oz.

And she was beautiful.

She was even able to breathe on her own, but would not leave the NICU for a while, and she couldn't come out of her incubator yet. Even so, she was still beautiful. I had spent the last 48 hours next to her. She would need a few more tests, but my mother believed she would make it. Right then, Hannah was in with her, sitting in her wheelchair, while I stood outside, signing papers.

"You look like you've had a rough couple of days."

Hearing her voice made me freeze. I quickly prayed that when I turned around she would be there, and thanked God that she was when I did.

She held up a cup of what smelled like coffee for me.

Ignoring it, I pulled her into my arms…only she didn't hug me back. She just stood there.

"Guinevere," I said, breaking free. "I know this is messy and confusing, but I will work it out, I promise you—"

"Eli, it's okay," she whispered, placing the cup in my hand. "Don't worry about me, I'm going to be fine. The only person that should be on your mind is your daughter. Congratulations. I really hope she gets much stronger."

I hated this, how she smiled and it was so obviously fake, how it felt like she had closed the door on me. She had become cold.

"Guinevere, don't." I could feel it coming. "I know I can figure this out. Don't shut me out. Give me a chance. Give us a chance—"

"Eli, we were just a fling."

She all but stabbed me with her words, smiling still. "We were two lonely people who found comfort in each other, and now it's time to get back to reality. You've been a great friend to me—"

"Stop it." I couldn't listen anymore.

"Eli—"

"Stop saying my name like that, like I never mattered to you. You are lying to my face right now; it's so clear I feel insulted that you think I wouldn't notice."

"*National Geographic* is starting a new magazine called *The Real.* I'm going to be leaving for India, and then South Korea, and Russia. I'm going to take pictures all over the world, Eli, and you're going to be an amazing father. "

"You are running." She was running as far as possible from me, and it hurt in ways I couldn't begin to describe.

"I'm going to—"

"To take pictures, I heard you, but don't go. You love me, so don't go, Guinevere."

For the first time, the fake mask she had been hiding under started to crack, and she couldn't force that smile any more. "I never said I loved you, Eli. So let's just do this—"

"Simply? Easily? Does any of this look simple or easy? Guinevere, you told me with your hands, your eyes, your body, that you were in love with me, and now you are running to India without giving me a chance."

She shook her head, brushing hair behind her ear. "It was just sex, Eli—"

"You said it. You said it, right before you fell asleep in my arms that night. You must have thought you were only thinking it, but you said it with your own two lips, six words: I'm in love with you, Eli. So don't tell me it was just sex. Don't smile and say we were a fling." I cupped her cheek, forcing her to look at me. "It wasn't, we aren't. With every fiber of my being, I know that what is between us is more than that, because I'm in love with you, too, Guinevere. So love me enough to say the words. Please."

When she looked back to me, her eyes filled with tears she wouldn't let fall. "Love me enough to let me go, Eli."

My hand dropped from her face and I felt my eyes burn. I couldn't. I wouldn't let us end that way, and yet she was going to leave. She didn't deny she loved me, and she was still just going to leave me anyway. "Okay," I whispered, and I hoped it hurt her to hear as much as it hurt me to say.

She nodded, walking away.

"Guinevere," I called.

She stopped, but didn't turn back to me.

"Eat a lot in India, and laugh even more in South Korea, and remember to keep warm in Russia. Wherever you go after that, be safe, stay healthy, and when you are ready to return home…come back to me. I will be here. In a year, in five, or ten, or twenty years, I'll be right here, waiting for you to come back to me."

Her body partially turned.

And partially I hoped.

But she just kept walking away.

"Are you—"

"No," I said to Ian, handing him the cup of coffee she'd given me as her parting present. "I'm not all right."

Chapter Twenty-Six
The Hero and the Heroine

Guinevere

I felt sick. With each step I took across the airport, my heart ached, but I kept walking, pulling my suitcase behind me as I went.

This was right.

This would be great for my career.

It's what I'd always wanted.

Why does it feel like I'm trying to convince myself? It's the truth! I love what I do and now I get to take photos all over the world. Places I have always dreamed of were just one plane ride away and yet I wanted to—

"Gwen?"

Turning around, Bash smiled brightly, a plane ticket in his hand, his jacket casually laid over his arm. I couldn't do this.

"Bash—"

"I know. You hate me right now, and you should, but we fell in love through your art once, and I'm not going to deny that I hope it happens again because you are the—"

"Bash. I forgive you." I smiled, facing him. "And I don't hate you. Hating you makes me tired. But you need to understand I don't feel the same. There isn't any art in the world that can change that. I'm not going to rebuild us, so please let me go."

Before he could reply, I felt a shiver go up my spine at the voice behind me.

"Guinevere."

I didn't turn around, gripping on to the handle of my suitcase.

"Guinevere."

He called again, his voice closer.

I glanced up to Bash, and the look on his face made me want to laugh, yet for some stupid reason, my eyes began to water.

"How did you even get here?" Bash questioned.

Eli simply ignored him. "Guinevere...I'll wait," he said calmly.

Taking a deep breath, I partially turned back to him. He stood there in blue scrubs, his dark hair a mess, his eyes only on me. When I faced him completely, the corners of his mouth turned up slowly until he had a full blown grin on his face and his smile made me smile, I couldn't help it.

"Don't look at me like that." It made me feel better and hurt all at the same time.

"Sorry, I can't help it," he replied, taking a step closer to me. "Yesterday you asked me to love you enough to let you go and I did, because I never want to stop you from doing what you want. I thought I could bear it. Actually I'm a little embarrassed because I even gave you that stupid speech about being happy, but I'm a lot more selfish than I thought. When I woke up this morning I realized I didn't want you to be happy without me because I'm not happy without you. I get why you're scared, but trust in the fact that I love you in ways I can't even describe though I wish I could, because then I'd know why I can't think straight when we are in the same room. Don't run from me Guinevere. Love me enough to stay."

He didn't just take my breath away, he was the air in my lungs and I had no words, just tears. Cupping the sides of my face, he brushed them away with a smile. The more I looked at him, the more I loved him. Like a movie, everything—all the pain we had gone through just to get there—played in my mind, and I realized maybe it wasn't just love between us, but fate.

"Okay," I finally managed to say, letting go of my suitcase.

"Thank you," he whispered over my lips, and I knew the moment his lips were on mine…it had to be fate.

It had to be him.

Eli

Neither of us had said a word since leaving the airport, and it wasn't as easy as taking her hand and running off. She had to pick up Taigi and postpone—not cancel—her trip. She promised to call Sebastian in the morning and I would have been lying if I'd said I was fine. Part of me felt like I was only delaying the unavoidable.

"I'll get some wine," I told her when we stepped inside my flat. She didn't reply, just took a seat on the couch as Taigi curled into a ball at the base of it. Leaning over, she stroked his fur softly. Grabbing two glasses and two bottles, I moved back over to her, sitting right beside her.

"Are you trying to get me drunk?" she said softly, the corner of her lips turning up.

"Yes," I admitted, and she finally glanced at me. The look in her brown eyes was different from what it had been at the airport, proving maybe she had just said yes because she was caught up in the moment. "We have our best conversations when we are in the process of getting drunk."

Uncorking one of the bottles, I filled her glass and then mine before leaning back into the couch behind me.

Again, silence.

It was killing me. She wasn't the silent type; she was a rambler and I liked that about her, so I guessed it was up to me.

"What are you afraid of?" I asked as I drank.

"You can't be serious," she replied, still not drinking, just staring at the glass.

"But I am. I want to hear it. Everything going through your mind. Even the things you think I'll judge you for thinking. The one thing I love about us, Guinevere, is that we talk, we laugh, we tease each other, we laugh more, and we drink. Before being my girlfriend, you were my friend; I love that."

She drank, not a little bit, but her whole damn glass, the wine even slipping out the corner of her mouth. When she was done, she inhaled deeply and wiped her mouth.

"We're going to hate each other," she confessed as I refilled her glass. "Not in the beginning. We'll try to be understanding, but eventually I'm going to get jealous. I'm going to see you and your daughter and feel like the odd man out. Which is horrible, Eli. She's your kid. I'll know that, but I'll still be hurt. You'll feel guilty and then annoyed because I'm not going to be happy or I'll start avoiding you because of it. Slowly we will wear each other down until... until we're fighting all the time, fighting because we love each other and don't want to let go, but realistically know we should. I can see it so clearly, me not seeing you because of work and then when I do you have to be with your daughter. Besides, I still have things I want to do with my career too... I'm selfish, Eli. I don't like that I am, but I don't want to share you with Hannah or your daughter or anyone. I feel like they are standing between us, like they are the thing between us... I want to spend some time getting to know you and being with you. Those are the things I'm thinking about."

I finished my first glass and started to refill, my mind racing to the point that I was starting to get a headache.

"In your books, how would the hero and heroine work this out?" I questioned.

Her mood lightened up and she even giggled. "The heroine would have gotten on the plane and we'd have to wait for book two to see them struggle to fix everything later."

I had missed hearing her sound cheerful. "Who do you think would play me in the book to movie version if there was one?"

"Tom Hiddleston," she said without even a moment of hesitation.

"We look nothing alike Guinevere."

"I know!" She grinned, reaching for the bottle. "But he's hot and I'd happily play myself, thank you very much."

I rolled my eyes. "Yeah good luck with that."

"A girl can dream."

"If you are going to dream about a man fucking you in the shower and on the bed, in your parents' basement, it needs to me."

Her eyebrow rose and she looked ready to challenge me. "And if I don't?"

"The moment I feel you hot and bothered beside me, I'll happily remind you one thrust at a time."

Her eyes glazed over and she swallowed slowly before looking away.

Grinning to myself, I kicked her foot on the coffee table. "We aren't a movie, or one of your romantic book couples. We're real people who have to deal with real shit day in and day out. Just because you find the love of your life doesn't mean nothing else comes up. My daughter, Sophia, she's important me, and I can't even explain it, but I'm happy she's alive no matter who her mother is. I love her…but I also love you and I don't want to choose. I'm selfish like that. I want you both."

"Eli—"

Reaching over to her, I took her glass and set it on the coffee table next to mine. Opening my arms for her, she hugged me, burying her face into my neck.

"Later you should rebook your flight to India. I don't want to ever hold you back either. But when you go, remember you're got a boyfriend waiting at home. We'll email each other back and forth; who knows? I might even have enough time to visit, when Hannah is with Sophia. We are going to share custody and Hannah knows that is the extent of our relationship. We're going to work Guinevere, and we aren't going to hate each other; we're going to miss each other to the point that nothing else matters."

"Eli," she whispered, sitting up between my thighs, her eyes searching mine as I brushed my thumb over her lips.

"I told your father that in ten years I'd still be with you. I meant it."

When her lips were on mine, I felt my body finally relax. We weren't running away from each other, but toward one another. Yes, there had been and would be bumps in the road, yes, we'd fight, and yes, I was sure starting a long distance relationship wasn't going to be nearly as romantic or fulfilling as I'd hoped, but it was something…something that closed the space between us.

"Ahh…" She moaned into my mouth as one of my hands cupped her breast and her ass, thankful she had worn a skirt that day.

We weren't ending…we had only just gotten started.

EPILOGUE

From: Guinevere Poe <Guinevere.P@poeartistry.com>
Subject: I Have A Question For You…
Date: September 8 at 2:18 AM
To: Eli Davenport <E.Davenport@nph.com>

Dear Dr. Asshole,

Have you ever been sneezed on by an elephant? Well I have…twice…by the same elephant. His name is Anugtaha, which I have been told means one who has grace, and the keeper here joked he may be allergic to me. I have a feeling you are smiling at the irony in that. But do not be alarmed, Anugtaha and I will be the best of friends before I leave here, as you know I become more loveable the more time you spend with me. ☺

I hope you're doing okay. I called, but the time difference and everything is still throwing me off. I won't lie, I'm still nervous about being so far away from you. I'm not sure if I'm running or following my dreams. Yes, I'm having a good time, but all day as I was traveling around I would see things or want to go places and the very first person that came to mind was you. It's so strange to me how just a few months ago I didn't even know you existed and now I can't function the same without seeing you.

I'm going to stop before I get too sappy.

Keep being *kinda* cool,
The Con Artist
P.S. I love you…

From: Eli Davenport <E.Davenport@pnyph.com>
Subject: I Have An Answer For You…
Date: September 9 at 3:48 PM
To: Guinevere Poe <Guinevere.P@poeartistry.com>

Dear Con Artist,

No, I have never been sneezed on by an elephant, but please relay this message to Anugtaha for me: don't look into her eyes my friend, it's how she gets you. One moment she's a normal annoying human being, and the next you can't think of anyone more beautiful. If she stares at you and smiles, well then you're a goner and there is no hope, just accept it.

As for you Guinevere, I don't care what the time difference is, the only reason why I would miss your call is because of work. The rest of the time I'm waiting to hear from you anyway. You are running, but that doesn't matter because I'm standing at the end of the road waiting. Just enjoy everything in front of you right now. You may only get to see those things once. Yes, I miss you and yes if I could pick between you being there and you lying next to me, of course I'd pick next to me. I'm almost as jumpy as Taigi; every time the door opens our heads shoot up like we expect you to walk through the door.

I also won't get too sappy.
Stay healthy, smile a lot, be safe,
Your boyfriend
P.S. No way I'm calling myself Dr. Asshole. :p
P.P.S. I love you more than the sun loves the sky.

From: Guinevere Poe <Guinevere.P@poeartistry.com>
Subject: I'm Not Sure If You Are A Devil Or A Saint
Date: October 12ᵗʰ at 3:00 AM
To: Eli Davenport <E.Davenport@pnyph.com>

Dear Boyfriend,

Calling your girlfriend at midnight to have phone sex was....is...urgh! I don't know whether to yell at you for making me miss you more, for making me want to kiss you and make love to you and fuck you, or thank you for saying everything you said. See, it's morning here and my mind is still reeling.

I don't know what to type. My mind is blank. When I can think of words again I'll call,

Your very frustrated girlfriend

P.S. I don't know if I ever told you this, but your phone voice is sinful.

P.P.S. I love you more than the British love their tea.

From: Eli Davenport <E.Davenport@pnyph.com>
Subject: I'm Whatever You Want Me To Be
Date: October 12th at 1:00 PM
To: Guinevere Poe <Guinevere.P@poeartistry.com>

Dear Girlfriend,

I'm glad it was as good for you as it was for me. Yes, there will be Facetime, I need to see your face as you get off on my voice. And don't lie, your mind isn't blank, it's just filled with all the things you want me to do to you. After all, what did you call me last night between moans?

If you only knew how hard I was for you,

Your Sexy Pussy Fucker

P.S. I'm forever going to use that name against you.

P.P.S. You've told me nothing about Seoul or South Korea, our night together really has you dazed. Don't forget you have a job you need to finish so you can do more than just Facetime.

P.P.P.S. I love you more than Peter Pan loves Neverland.

From: Guinevere Poe <Guinevere.P@poeartistry.com>
Subject: Please note…
Date: October 12th at 3:17 AM
To: Eli Davenport <E.Davenport@pnyph.com>

Dear Sexy Pussy Fucker,

Please note that I was not in the correct frame of mind and should not be held accountable for anything I said, especially when you're talking about tying me to a bedpost and…

Anyway, sorry I forgot, Seoul is beautiful and the food is **AMAZING**. Tell Ian I will never forgive him for not introducing Buldak into my life earlier.

Love,

Your Cherry On Top

P.S. I was not the only one giving out names.

P.P.S. You haven't told me much about what has been going on back home. How is Sophia?

P.P.P.S. I love you more than a dominatrix loves her whips.

From: Eli Davenport <E.Davenport@pnyph.com>
Subject: What I'm Thankful For
Date: November 25th at 7:13 AM
To: Guinevere Poe <Guinevere.P@poeartistry.com>

Dear Cherry On Top,

I'm thankful that I met you. I'm thankful that not only did I fall for you, but you fell for me too. I'm thankful that you're completely different from me because you make me see the world in a whole new way. I'm thankful you're alive because it makes me feel alive too.

Sophia is growing by the day. My mother says she has my father's eyes. I never realized I was missing so much until you both were in front of me. Sometimes I get your messages while she's over and for the rest of the day nothing can bring me down. I feel blessed that you both are in my life... so blessed in fact that part of me feels guilty for those who have lost so much. Toby has gotten better, but not much. He's lost his company, but luckily he's got a good amount of wealth built up. He's moved out of the city and now lives in the Hamptons where he spends most of his time fishing. When I visit we don't talk much, just sit outside in the cold. I understood he was hurting, but it never really hit me until I realized how badly I love you and Sophia. If I lost either of you I don't know how I would be even able to fish.

Anyway, be safe. All right...really.

Eli

P.S. I love you more than fish love water.

From: Guinevere Poe <Guinevere.P@poeartistry.com>
Subject: I'm Thankful For...
Date: November 25th at 9:19 PM
To: Eli Davenport <E.Davenport@pnyph.com>

You. Eli.

When I thought my life was over, when I couldn't laugh or sleep or even focus on the people around me, you helped to bring me back.

I'm thankful your brother punched knives, forcing us to go to the hospital. I'm thankful for all of our fights and drunken rants.

If I could go back, I wouldn't change anything. You were and are my second chance.

I only hope that one day Toby gets that second chance at love too.

If you're safe, I'm safe.

Your Guinevere

P.S. I love you more than Cinderella loved Prince Charming.

From: Eli Davenport <E.Davenport@pnyph.com>
Subject: Merry Christmas
Date: December 25th at 9:47 PM
To: Guinevere Poe <Guinevere.P@poeartistry.com>

My Guinevere,

I miss you.

Your Eli.

P.S. I love you more than Romeo loved Juliet.

Eli

Almost a week had gone by and we hadn't had much time to talk. She was busy getting ready to move to another country for the month and I was swamped between work and Sophia. Even so, I still missed her. It was one thing to say, "Let's have a long distance relationship," and another to actually be in one. Thanksgiving, Christmas, and now New Year's...the holidays were hard enough to get through by yourself, let alone apart from the person you wanted to spend them with.

"Urgh, Eli what is wrong with you?" I groaned, lying back on my couch. Hannah had Sophia for New Year's Eve and most of the next morning before we would trade off. It wasn't the life I wanted for my daughter, to be bounced between parents, but I honestly didn't know what else to do.

The last few months have been insane.

Grabbing my phone again, I refreshed my inbox.

Nothing.

When had I become this person? The type of guy who waited by the phone? It was annoying me and even still I was tempted to hit the refresh button again.

"Five."

"Four."

"Three."

"Two."

"One."

I counted down, hearing the cheers roar outside the window.

Happy New Year.

For the third time I hit refresh and the moment I saw the notification, I sat back up against the couch.

From: Guinevere Poe <Guinevere.P@poeartistry.com>
Subject: Happy New Year
Date: January 1ˢᵗ at 12:01 AM
To: Eli Davenport <E.Davenport@pnyph.com>
Being away from each other like this is hard…too hard, Eli.

"That's it? She has to be fucking kidding me." I muttered, tossing the phone onto the other side of the couch and getting up. Taigi glanced up at me, barked once, and then turned his head away as if he couldn't even be bothered. "Don't start with me."

Pulling off my shirt, I threw it on the couch before heading to the bathroom. Whatever freak out Guinevere was having, I'd deal with it in the morning. I was far too tired to even—

BARK

BARK

"Taigi!" I hollered as I pulled off my pants. He whimpered, then went silent.

BARK

BARK

BARK

BARK

What in the hell?

"Taigi what is—" I started to say as I headed into the living room. Then I saw her. My Guinevere, dressed in a dark, knee-length red dress and gold sparking heels that were not on her feet but beside them. Next to that was a winter jacket. Her brown hair was a mess, some parts of it blown out from what I could only guess had been the wind, other parts curled tightly. She was even sweating a little bit, her chest still rising and falling.

"I... Gu..." I couldn't put what was on my mind into words because I wasn't sure if I was dreaming or not.

"I'm late," she said, taking a deep breath, a frown on on her beautiful lips. "I wanted to make it here before the count down. But this city is like a maze—"

With each word I walked closer and closer to her, until I was right in front of her. My hands cupped the sides of her half-frozen face.

"You're here," I whispered, amazed.

"I'm late, but I'm he—"

I kissed her. I couldn't not kiss her. Her body pressed up against mine and her arms wrapped around my neck. *God I missed this.* All of it, the taste of her, the sounds she made as I grabbed her ass, my hands traveling down until I reached her hips and lifted her up, her legs wrapping around me tightly.

"You're here," I repeated softly.

She grinned. "I'm here. I'm also homeless because I sold my apartment hoping that my Dr. Asshole, Boyfriend, Sexy Pussy Fucker, Eli would take pity on me and let me stay with him."

"I don't understand." I still wasn't a hundred percent sure this was real. She was in my apartment, in my arms, and she wanted to stay.

"Didn't you get my email? I don't want to be apart any more. I want to be here with you. So do you mind, Dr. Asshole, Boyfriend, Sexy Pussy Fucker, Eli?" She smiled so wide I couldn't help but smile back.

"I'll have to think about it... Your snoring is kind of a deal breaker..."

She made a face at me before trying to pull away, but I only held her tighter. I didn't want to let go or look away.

"Guinevere."

"Yea?"

"Don't panic when I say this but...I'm going to marry you."

She didn't say anything and I knew she understood what I meant. There was no doubt in my mind that she was the one I was meant to be with all along.

I loved her more than I loved myself.

Discover More by J.J. McAvoy

Single Title Romances
BLACK RAINBOW
THAT THING BETWEEN ELI AND GWEN
SUGAR BABY BEAUTIFUL

The Ruthless People Series
RUTHLESS PEOPLE
THE UNTOUCHABLES
AMERICAN SAVAGES
DECLAN + CORALINE (prequel novella)
A BLOODY KINGDOM – Summer, 2016

Child Star Series
CHILD STAR: PART 1
CHILD STAR: PART 2
CHILD STAR: PART 3
CHILD STAR – full novel